WINNER OF THE 2018 MICHAEL GIFKINS PRIZE

'*Attraction* peels back the landscape to reveal deeper truths.
The writer is right inside her material—a road trip that
delivers a political and sexual coming-of-age narrative.
The book is a slow-burning fuse that brims with intensely
felt experience. Porter is an exciting new talent.'
LLOYD JONES

'*Attraction* abounds with sharp imagery,
intergenerational relationships, and the natural,
historic and domestic environments of modern
New Zealand. Ruby Porter is a gifted new writer.'
PATRICIA GRACE

'A provocative and stylish first novel
from a major new talent.'
PAULA MORRIS

Ruby Porter is a tutor of creative writing at the University of Auckland. She has been published in *Geometry Journal*, *Aotearotica*, *Spinoff* and *Wireless*, and a selection of her poetry is available on NZEPC. *Attraction* is her first novel.

RUBY PORTER
ATTRACTION

TEXT PUBLISHING MELBOURNE AUSTRALIA

textpublishing.com.au

The Text Publishing Company
Swann House
22 William Street
Melbourne Victoria 3000
Australia

Published by The Text Publishing Company, 2019

Book design by Imogen Stubbs
Cover art by Ann Marie Coolick
Typeset in Adobe Garamond Pro by J&M Typesetting

Printed and bound in Australia by Griffin Press, part of Ovato, an accredited ISO/NZS 14001:2004 Environmental Management System printer

ISBN: 9781925773552 (paperback)
ISBN: 9781925774368 (ebook)

A catalogue record for this book is available from the National Library of Australia

For my three mums

i

Don't write this down.

That's what Pita always said: his class was about the kōrero. I was learning to speak.

—Kikokiko means flesh, he said. —Kikorangi is the blue for things which are physical, things which can be destroyed.

He used his jeans as an example.

—Kahurangi, he said, —is the blue for things which can't be destroyed, like the sky, and the sea.

But he's wrong. We are destroying them, turning the kahu to kiko, the sacred into flesh.

+

—Let's go, Ilana says, only hours too late.

The cars dart between steel lanes and crowd at the lights, a school of fish, cramped and slippery. We're stuck at the end of Ponsonby Road, because she missed the turn-off onto Hopetoun. She says I didn't warn her in time. I say she reacted too slowly. But really, I don't say anything.

There's a man splashing water from a Pump bottle onto the windscreen of the car ahead. Ilana keeps inching closer. From the back he looks like Pita, but when he turns around he's much younger. Then he stares right at me, as if he knows what I was thinking. And he doesn't wash our windscreen.

+

There's a Mobil where a tree is said to have grown, where Ponsonby and Karangahape Roads intersect. Te Rimu Tahi, that's what this area was once called. Wikipedia tells me, *No European saw the tree, so its exact location is unidentifiable.*

As if to say only Europeans have eyes.

+

My mum buys her lotto tickets from that Mobil. She rings ten minutes after I leave to remind me to pick one up. —Somewhere lucky. Maybe Matamata, or Thornton. Get it where you feel the pull.

I say, —Okay, Helen, and hang up.

I've always called her that, because I have two mums. She met Chris not long after I was born, and Chris moved in when I was eighteen months old. They were together for ten years. My dad was never really on the scene.

My earliest memories don't come in images, but in thoughts. Realising it was my third birthday. Wondering what to call my mums. Recognising Helen walking down the road, while in a car with Chris. I haven't retained the picture of her, or the road, just that knowing. Maybe it shocked me that her life existed outside

2

of our house. Maybe it shocked me that her life existed outside of mine.

I say, —What's your first memory? No matter how vague.

—It's not vague, Ilana says. —Falling into the bath. I don't remember the feeling, but I remember the view of the ceiling.

Through the soft light of water.

—And I remember Mum, pulling me out. That was the scariest part, her being that frightened. You know, cos I was a kid.

+

Ilana is the kind of person who's waiting for her parents to die, just so she can get the tattoo. She has a lot already: snakes and jaguar heads and stylised women, even a stick-and-poke rose. Once, she would've had a lot of piercings—now, she has the indents of holes, slowly growing over. She likes to give off the impression of a dark childhood, one she can't talk about, but I think it was a hackneyed kind of dark. Cheating dad, probably, arguments where expensive vases were thrown. Water soaking into the Persian rug. She had one serious girlfriend at high school, the artist of the rose, who must have broken her heart—because she never mentions her, except when she's drunk, and then only as *that BPD bitch*.

+

I hop in the backseat when we pick up Ashi in Papatoetoe. I don't mind. I feel safe here. Bo, my huntaway cross, is next to me. His little golden eyebrows are like apostrophes on black fur. With him, I don't have to speak.

—You look good, Ilana says. She didn't say that to me.

3

Ashi's hair falls straight, a kind of reddy-brown at the moment.
—It keeps coming out this colour, she says, —no matter what I try
to dye it. I was going for magenta.

Her arms are shaved. She started in Year Ten and now she
says she can't stop. Her face is perfectly symmetrical, except for her
nose, which seems to veer a little in the direction she's looking, as
if it always leads, and she always follows.

It takes her two trips to grab everything. Suitcases bursting,
zips sliding backwards. Loose towels and extra pairs of shoes. A
black plastic bag from Liquorland. You can hear bottles clink
together as she walks. Now the boot is brimming, haphazard, and
I have to resist the urge to repack it myself.

I should go say hi to her mum, but I don't. She'd hug me and
force cashew barfi down my throat. She'd want to show me every
room in their house, even though I've seen it all twice. They were
renting centrally until they bought out here last year.

I was nervous when I introduced Ilana to Ashi. Ashi is my oldest
friend and I guess Ilana is my newest.

It was at an activist party a couple of months ago, Auckland
Action Against Poverty T-shirts and Rihanna on the speakers. Free
West Papua flag on the wall. Wooden pallets in the place of tables.
A Karangahape Road flat, above the laundromat, open late. Helen
used to point there and say, —It was a doll hospital, back in the day.

That night I was on edge above china ghosts. I had a bulky
canvas bag and a navy parka, even though it was November. I'm
afraid of getting cold. I put beanies in my pockets, just in case.
And I carry my things with me at parties, too scared to put them
down, to lose them amongst people I don't know. But I must've
looked heavy and encumbered as I tried to squeeze myself into
conversations.

Ilana was in her uniform of dark jeans and dark T-shirt, no bra. Ashi wore a tattoo choker, ribbed crop top, rugby socks pulled high. She wears a lot of bright colours, peach and mustard and cadmium red. —Colours white people can't pull off, she said.

Ilana loved that.

They sat outside the whole night, smoking durries and talking furiously.

All I could think to add was something Helen had said. *Do you know that, downstairs, they were still finding eyeballs in the floorboards decades later?*

+

If you look at a map, I imagine the roads make an equilateral triangle. A defiant arrow, forever pointing east. It's supposed to take seven hours each leg: Auckland to Whāngārā, Whāngārā to Levin, Levin to Auckland. It always took more than seven hours with Helen.

She's a teacher, so we shared the same holidays, and four times a year we'd be off, alone on the roads with the trucks and their headlights, the Southern Motorway a tangle amongst the Bombay Hills. The electric blue of early morning.

We were always gone before dawn—last time we left at three-thirty.

That was over ten years ago now. We still visit my grandma in Levin, but we've stopped going to Whāngārā together. These days we only etch lines north and south, back and forth.

+

Not far out of Auckland, land is being excavated. Tractors move at half-speed as though in some kind of trance, some kind of harmony. I must've been staring, because Ilana makes eye contact in the rear-view mirror and laughs. —Probably digging for a body, she says.

When I think of dirt I think of the black stuff in Helen's garden, the bags of soil from Plant Barn that I had to lug to the backyard, until I got arthritis. I think of her dark fingernails after a day outside and the sound of the hose left on at night. But this earth is the colour of newspaper kept too long. It's ugly: not just the anaemic clay, the whole site. There's no other way to describe it than a gash in the landscape, gaping, yet to be sutured.

I guess all roads are a kind of scar.

ii

Everywhere yellow cress sprouts from the gravel. The side of a building, low and squat, says it remembers our World War I heroes. Poppies as round as plates hover beside the words in sickly bright acrylic.

We turn off the motorway too early. I tell Ilana this, but she says, —Ashi has GPS.

This road takes us through Mangatawhiri. I get a glimpse of the river: if you followed it north, you'd come to dams, supplying Auckland taps. I filled bottles at home. In Whāngārā, we will only have rain water.

—This is where the Waikato Land Wars started, I say. —Governor Grey ordered troops to march through this stream. It was the aukati separating Kīngitanga lands from the North.

Ilana's reflection goes a bit steely. Her lips visibly thin.

—War doesn't just begin when a white man declares it, she says.

I want to redeem myself, but all I have are numbers, memorised. A thousand Māori dead, the confiscation of three million acres.

—Pita taught me about it, I say, —that's all. Some of his tūpuna fought here.

Her face softens, fleshes out. —It wasn't an attack on you, eh, she says.

Flat hills encircle us, occasionally dipping below the horizon or turning into a slim purple border. Monterey pines dominate. An old brick building has a newer, gaudy facade. Now a cafe called the Castle, it stares out at a disused petrol station, pale and minimalist in comparison.

I came this way with Nick once. His dad bought a farm outside of Mangatārata, the midlife crisis of a Pākehā banker. A whole week there has filtered down into a day's worth of memories: waking up before the sun, tracing and retracing the boundary line, his father's overcooked green beans, the silence of men.

But the drive is still crisp in my mind. Winter's hardness was just beginning to show. The branches of the poplars seemed to curl inwards, as if for warmth. The snow was crunchy-dirty, only white from a distance. There were three dead sheep—Nick pointed them out. Every time I turned the heater on, he put the window down. He was always too hot and I was always too cold.

+

Summer has its own kind of hardness. The land looks burnt, dried up. As if ochre has got into the palette and mixed with the other colours, at least around the edges. Brownish yellow and brownish green and brownish grey, rust red. Terra Pozzuoli, one of my tubes called it. I used to put a touch in for most skin colours. It's the same red they paint maraes.

Often within a hundred metres of a marae, there's a church.

+

Ilana's car is a 1998 Nissan Pulsar and the backseat headrests are missing, but I still fall asleep, slouched against the door. At five foot eleven, I'm used to slouching. I was relegated to the back row of class photos, jammed next to the boys. Sometimes I feel like my life has been a lesson in occupying less space.

My neck is sore when I wake and I dread a crack, that uneasy percussion when the body rights itself. None comes.

—Your mouth was open, Ilana says.

—She made me take photos, Ashi says. —But I deleted them straight away.

She checks her make-up in the rear-view mirror, twisting this way, then that, for a sight of her jawline.

I look out the window and don't know where we are. We could be coming up to the farm, or we could've already passed it. Nick and I helped mark where the fence posts would go. It took the three of us all week. His dad wanted to put up *a proper one*, not *some wire bullshit*. The standard rural fence, with the spindly wooden sticks: that was his favourite topic. He wanted one six-feet high, or eight, if the local builders didn't rip him off *just for being an Aucklander*. We were invited, I guess, to keep costs down.

I watch for an oversized fence, over-new.

+

Ngātea was drained with canals and stopbanks, turned from bog to orchards to industrial service town. There's a special on for cow feed. We stop so I can walk Bo. He strains at the lead when I tie him up outside the bathroom. My period is due, overdue. I'm scared it will come in the wops, no toilet for miles. I keep

9

imagining staining the seat.

Back at the car, lit cigarettes hang from both their windows. They're tailies, which means they're Ilana's. Ashi's taking her time, savouring it, the same pace in, the same pace out. Ilana never takes her time with anything. She inhales sharply, the flame racing to her fingertips. They've swapped seats. Ashi has her creepers on, and I wonder how she can feel the pedals through all that sole.

I got my learner's when I was fifteen and I am still on it at twenty-three. With two mums, one of them should've taught me. No one else was offering. I have a big extended family and not much to do with them. My grandma had two boys and two girls. Helen was the oldest, though she had me late, and I'm the youngest cousin. Her brother Lloyd, the one that's still alive, lives on the Gold Coast. He's onto his second wife and his third business, selling automated pullets for broiler chickens. Ones that overfeed them so they reach slaughter weight faster. And my aunt Francine lives on a dairy farm in Taranaki. She names each bobby calf before she shoots them, she's that kind of tender. Her daughters, Eden and Pearl, studied at Otago.

We haven't seen any of them in years.

+

The tarmac is spotted with roadkill, cystic acne of the highway, picked at by birds.

—I like when it's still 3D, Ilana says.

She alerts us to the good ones, innards pink as jelly, all along the way.

New Zealand flags fly from front yards. There's an American flag by a flashy house planted on a hill. In the smaller, poorer towns, you'll only see He Whakaputanga, or, more often, Tino

Rangatiratanga. I fail to recognise a modern Kīngitanga flag, manu and stars, marking the reign of Dame Te Atairangikaahu. The first and last Māori queen. But Ilana points it out, and I pretend I saw it too.

I don't remember her death, but I do remember her burial. I was in Levin at the time and we watched it on TV. It's one of those faint memories, like seeing something happen in a dimly lit room. Taupiri Mountain, usually so colourful with flowers and spinners and taonga, was that day black with mourners. And I remember the karanga, which sounded only part of this world, part of the next, as if following Te Ata away.

She was buried in an unmarked grave, as a sign of equality with her tūpuna. But there is a purple rose named for her, grown by her husband outside his home.

+

My grandma is still in her own house even though she's terminally ill. She says she's always managed and that's not about to change.

Cancer isn't cells that stop living, it's cells that refuse to die.

+

There's a real ugliness to parts of the countryside. Large sheets of plastic weighed down by tyres. Barns twice the size of houses. Occasionally there's a pile of clay or gravel, taller than me, behind woven wire fences. Everything looks worn out, or half finished, expired. Graffiti has crept into the forgotten places. All the industrial buildings are pre-nineties, and, sometimes, the only way you can tell they're still in use is by looking for fumes.

Ilana points to the RSA mural in Paeroa. A volcano erupts, a tank is fired. The explosion barely breaks the surface of the sea. It's like most murals: rounded lines, too-strong highlights, too-weak shadows. Under the clear stretch of sky stand three soldiers, a navy officer and a nurse. One soldier is probably meant to be Māori, but he looks African American. Behind them float spectral figures, blending right into the blue. To honour the fallen, I guess, but the ghosts look almost comical.

—There's work for you yet, she jokes. —Who says painting is dead, eh?

+

I began at Elam School of Fine Arts five years ago, swallowed each day by Grafton Gully. Back then I was a figurative painter. I stretched Rothko-scale canvases and made obsessive marks I called faces, pressing so hard I indented the linen and messed up all my brushes. When I'd finished, they sagged off their frames, loosened and heavy with oils. I had to keep a heater on in the studio the whole time just to get them dry.

Often, I painted Nick. Some were paintings that glared from my studio floor, the way he did when we were fighting. Some were paintings that made me forgive him, made me melt like butter on a bench. I always thought I could figure him out through painting, but I always went in circles.

He loved them. He told his friends he was dating an artist. I gave him a cropped portrait of his face, broad and dimpled with a dominant brow, titanium white mixed in both hair and skin. *A flat-warming gift*, I called it, and it was on his lounge wall the next day.

Painting taught me how to look closely. I study people the way others study menus, petrol prices, the phone in their hand. Ilana's neck is muscled, with a mole just a little off centre, millimetres to the right. Her hair stops short at the nape. Even her twitches are self-assured.

Ashi's movements are gentler, less assertive. She wears earrings that dangle and occasionally catch. Her right hand keeps darting to her lobes to adjust them, or to check they're still there.

+

Karangahake Gorge grows up from the ground around us as we drive. The river is rocky and fast, the trees, unmoving. Near the entrance, there's a house with a Volkswagen bus rusting out front, and a placard reading *Save Karangahake*. The one next to it: *For Sale*. The car park is full today and people are crossing over the iron bridge. Signs say surveillance cameras are operating. The concrete remains of the Victoria Battery stand stark and imposing. Once they would have housed cyanide tanks on their shoulders. Now they're only a reminder of the gold mined, and the gold left to mine.

—Is this the gorge you were talking about? Ashi asks.

—No, I say, —this isn't the one.

She wants to shoot portraits under the arches, but I say, — Maybe on the way back.

+

I met Pita at an opening at Fuzzy Vibes in March last year. He was in a button-down shirt and suit pants. I was in a black lace dress, one size too big. Everyone else wore faded T-shirts, cuffed jeans.

We were bent over the plywood table, trying to read the size-eight font of an artist's book, staples down its spine. It probably looked like a first date.

—I don't make art, he told me.

—Neither, I said, —not anymore.

I had finished uni five months earlier.

—I teach Māori, he went on. —Irene's one of my students. That's her photos over there.

—I've been wanting to learn.

There were seven of us when we started lessons. Most I knew from Elam, people like Soph and Lauren.

—How is it that I've come to know so many artists? Pita would say. He thought we all painted.

His apartment was near the top of Queen Street. It had blackout curtains, a fridge that made ice. He would brew us coffee and arrange brie and crackers on a plate, still in their packets. An open bag of sour snakes to the side. I'd eat one or two, just to be polite. His lounge suite was new and leather, but there was an armchair by the window, threadbare. He always sat in that. On the opposite wall was a framed quote, tacky and cursive. *Because he himself was tested through what he suffered, he is able to help those who are being tested.* It took me a while to realise it was Christian. It took me a while to realise he was Christian, too.

+

There's a Hell's Pizza in Bethlehem. We get Lust and Purgatory. Lust has five types of meat on it, but I can have Purgatory. I'm not that hungry, so I only eat one slice, saving the best mouthful for last. Neither of them notice.

Ilana eats the part with the most bacon first. Then she folds

14

the slice in half and bites it like a sandwich. She leaves the crusts, chewed bare, in the box. Ashi is a neat eater, wiping her lips as she goes, even though there's no food there, not once.

They switch places again. Ilana says she's the more confident driver, by which she means faster.

—I joined a Christian modelling group when I was nine, Ashi says. —I was scouted. Hannah's sister was in it, remember her?

She turns around in her seat.

—We'd do a session of modelling then a session of prayer.

—Modelling for God, I joke.

—Posing for Jesus.

Ilana takes her hands off the wheel, stretching them out as if she's on a cross.

—I could get into it, though. I mean, we would dissect the passages. It was rational. There was one about finding coins in a fish's mouth. It's one of Jesus' miracles, I think. He told his disciple that if he caught this fish, they'd both have the money they needed to get inside the temple.

—Sounds super rational, Ilana says.

—No, that's my point. We decided it was saying that if you follow Jesus, it will pay off. It wasn't taking it literally, that's all. I didn't believe in it.

Ilana puts her arm around Ashi's shoulder. I wish she wouldn't do that while driving. Then she says something about them sounding onto it, for kids.

If I had told that story, Ilana would've just laughed.

But I'm not really listening. I've turned to the land again, framed by glass and metal and the backs of heads.

+

In second year, I found my palettes more interesting than my canvases. They weren't really palettes. The wooden ones you have to clean before the paint dries. I could never be bothered, so I'd clingwrap any flat surface I found: books I didn't like, old DVDs. I stopped throwing the clingwrap away and started pinning it to every inch of allocated wall. They were plastic skins, flesh coloured and puckering like cellulite. At the end of semester I handed them in instead and got my first A+. And Nick stopped referring to me as an artist.

+

Ashi and I went to the same primary, same intermediate and same high school. And then we went to Elam together. When she found out that no one actually *made* art anymore she changed to medicine. That was when Nick started saying, —Your friend Ashi, she's so smart.

He never said that about me.

Ilana didn't go to uni. She's older than us, twenty-six. She might have done a semester, years ago, but she doesn't talk about it. She thinks it's a waste of money and I pretend I agree.

+

Train tracks stay loyal to the side of the road. Only once do I see a train. Its engine is emblazoned KiwiRail but the carriages are branded Maersk Sealand or Salmarine, with a London flag.

On these straight stretches Ilana often pushes 120 kilometres per hour. She says she has trust issues, but she trusts everyone on the road with a tonne of metal. She trusts herself.

I know what I would be like behind a wheel. Not to be trusted.

+

Leading up to the ASB stadium at Mount Maunganui is a series of billboards: Coke telling me to *Open Happiness*. One's for an investment-management company. *Reel in Top Returns*, it says, above a picture of a father and son fishing. There's a mound of dirt, at least ten-feet tall, sprouting new tussock and a sign which reads *Individual Land for Sale*. I know it's a turn of phrase, an advertising trick, but I imagine plunging my hands into that soil, and I imagine paying for it.

+

My favourite part of the drive is through Pikowai, with the sea on our left, and on our right, the sandstone cliff face, white and lined, like the growth rings of a tree. In some places, roots break through the surface and dangle towards the asphalt. I wind my window down and stick my arm out to the breeze. I like that feeling, as if it'll just snap off.

The east coast has a different look about it. Norfolk pine and cabbage trees cut their silhouettes into the sky.

Matatā is coloured with orange and purple cannas. Kids sit on the edge of the playground. Christmas trees have been lugged outside and left there. One still wears its decorations, tinsel and plastic clashing against dead branches.

Ilana and Ashi are hungry again. We stop in Whakatāne for a bakery. There's a Hannahs shoe store that stocks Clarks, Union Jacks in each corner of its window. *The British Invasion Has Started*, it announces, only two hundred years too late. They eat mock-cream donuts out front, their hands white and powdery.

On the road which takes us south, there's a sign for a cemetery and crematorium.

+

The first funeral I went to was my uncle Stuart's, when I was four. He was the youngest of the siblings. Closeted, depressed, romantic, he loved Milton as much as he loved heroin. I don't remember a lot of that day, except that Helen wouldn't move from her chair for a very long time. It must have been a small Levin church, but it's grown to the proportions of a school hall in my mind. Someone gave me a helium balloon, and I watched it bolt for the ceiling, impossibly far away.

+

Do you know every time you remember something you're only remembering the last time you thought of it?

I read that in an article online called *Why It Hurts*.

+

The Ōhope church tells me to *Have a Heart*. Most of the signage is real estate. The *Entry Level Do-Up*, the *Contemporary Townhouse*, the *Trendy Ōhope Beachside Living*, the *Lock-Up and Leave*. Ashi reads them out as we drive past. I cringe at the way she says Ōhope, with big round-mouthed Os. I know Ilana will have noticed, but she doesn't correct her, like she would if it was me.

I thought Ilana was Māori, when we met, because of how she

18

pronounced Te Reo. She is three tones darker than your average Pākehā. I didn't know it came from a bottle until the first time she stayed over, and rubbed orange off against my sheets.

+

Pita said, —Don't worry about pronunciation, it comes later.

And our mouths opened. We were going around the table saying rakau and moving blocks of colour.

+

There's a fruit store selling corn and avocadoes, five for five dollars. It advertises watermelons with hand-painted posters saying *Danger! Watermelons*. I don't get the joke, but Ilana doesn't stop laughing and buys two.

Not far past Te Kooti Road is an entrance to a long driveway, planks of wood erect. *Ko kāwanatanga he taihara.*

—The government is illegal, I say, for Ashi's sake, mainly.

Ilana pulls over, and leaves a watermelon on their letterbox.

+

My home in Auckland floats amongst a sea of white and beige. Our lurching jacaranda jostles against the freshly pruned bushes on either side. If those houses are plastic surgery patients, botoxed to the nines, then ours is a mother in an Irish poem, sinking deeper into her spot.

I still live with Helen. She bought that place when I was two, before the property boom. People movers turned into SUVs, sharks gliding along the street, hunting for the last available park.

+

The Waioeka Gorge eats you whole. I always have the sense of being digested when I emerge at the other end. Once, I went through on a bus. The woman next to me wore a cross, and kept wanting to talk, even though I put my headphones on. The others set their eyes on the seat in front of them. If you looked out the window, everything fell away.

It's what I'm hoping will happen in Whāngārā. That everything will fall away.

+

I feel carsick about fifteen minutes in. I try to suppress it—Ashi will be disappointed if we have to swap seats. And Ilana will be annoyed. She might think I'm pretending, just to sit next to her. I try to concentrate on the new Grimes album. Her voice is saccharine and sultry. It's the only music all three of us like. On a tight corner, Grimes screams and my stomach careens over the edge. I throw up. Luckily none gets on the upholstery. It's all over me instead.

—At least it's pretty liquidy, Ashi offers.

I'm down by the river stringing my singlet in both hands, fresh T-shirt on. She's still stroking my hair though I've stopped vomiting. Ilana walks Bo upstream, topless.

—No chunks, I mean.

—Yeah, I say.

+

I don't remember if the woman with the cross asked me whether

I believed in God, or something else, like if I went to church. But she was shocked when I said no.

—What are we without religion? she asked, as if I would have an answer. —Religion is what gives you a soul, she went on. —Without God, we are nothing more than animals.

I get this feeling, when I'm on a bus taking corners like these, that I wouldn't mind dying. As long as I'm with lots of people. There's a real comfort in knowing you're not alone when it happens.

+

We get stuck behind a blue Mazda that goes at least ten kilometres under the speed limit, even on the straights. Sometimes, out of nowhere, it speeds up. But then its brake lights come on and it slows just as fast. We get dangerously close.

+

My grandma still has her licence. Helen's always hiding her keys, but Grandma always finds them. When she drives, she's either hugging the centreline or mounting the curb. She doesn't believe in road rules. She believes in other cars giving way and making room for an *elderly lady*.

I remember a man from down the street giving me sympathetic looks when he said he'd seen her headed home from the shops. I realised later that he thought my grandma was an alcoholic, swerving across lanes at two in the afternoon.

Sometimes I think driving will kill her faster than cancer.

+

Two-thirds of the way through the gorge there's a house painted green. The people who live there sell drinks from a small truck. I know it as the Living Water Bush Cafe, though that might just be Helen's name for it. She does that: gives her own names to things. *My Kitchen Rules* becomes *My Cooking Rules, One Hundred Years of Solitude* becomes *A Thousand Years of Silence*. Until I was eight, I thought North Head was called Ashi's Hill, because Helen took us there together to slide down on cardboard boxes.

I have no idea where she'd have gotten Living Water from. The only sign reads *COFFEE* in childish capitals. Helen would always get one to take away, triple shot, because they never made it strong enough. I think she pitied them. She couldn't fathom anyone living inside this valley by choice. —Such an isolated existence, she'd say under her breath, even though we were back in the car.

On this trip, we don't stop. Ashi doesn't even slow down.

+

I watched something once about water having a memory. It's a largely unfounded theory, used to prop up homeopathy, but there was a video online of a recent experiment backing it up. They dropped different flowers into glasses, then put the water molecules under a microscope. Every drop had its own face. Some resembled frost—others, paint mixed with turps, bleeding. The hydrogen bonds had all changed. It was like looking through a kaleidoscope, or up into galaxies.

I don't know how reliable that study was. Still, I like to think of it at times. I think about how we're mostly just water, fifty per cent, at least. And I think of what we drink. I think of the seas and the rivers. I think of all this memory, washing over us and passing through.

At first I kept the pain a secret, but I couldn't hide it from Helen. She took me to see natural healers. They asked me about my sleeping habits and my love life. They gave me strong herbs and diluted Pulsatilla. One of them told me I had a parasite that would eventually make me blind.

My GP diagnosed the arthritis. It had taken two years. By then, it felt as if all of my bones had melded together, fossilised in my eighteen-year-old body. I couldn't even make a fist. Nick still tried to hold my hand, and got angry when I clutched his too loosely in public.

I was put on methotrexate and prednisone. The prednisone puffed up my cheeks and kept me awake at night. And the methotrexate dried me from the inside out. I'm still on it today.

+

If you shut your eyes to the road, this gorge looks prehistoric. You can pretend the men with the ships and the guns and the money haven't reached it yet.

Ashi slams on the brakes and the possum runs from the tarseal.

—You should have run it over, I say.

—I thought you think all life is sacred?

—Not possums.

For once, Ilana agrees with me.

—Why do you guys villainise them? Ashi says.

Because they're somewhere they shouldn't be, tipping the balance, destroying the bush.

On some hills, entire forests have been felled. The dead trunks form a carpet of soft grey fur.

This is how we know we are coming out the other side.

+

An Edwardian church shares a plot with a ready-made house and a rusting tractor. The attached cemetery is surrounded by white pickets. I've been noticing the fences of cemeteries this drive. A few had brick walls, a couple were wire. Some had none: they just appeared at the side of the road, unannounced. I tried to get photos. Each time, I wanted to tell Ilana or Ashi to stop, slow down, but I didn't want to say why.

This one, though, I do capture. It is separated into small sections, planks of wood nailed horizontally. They fit only two graves each. The barriers look like the type horses jump over, a morbid obstacle course. I imagine someone training their mare, stamping on all the flowers.

+

By third year, collecting became my practice. Hoarding, Nick called it. Tampons, which I left out to swell in the Auckland humidity. All of the letters real-estate agents sent to our house. Brazilian wax kits that came in shapes like *Landing Strip, Bermuda Triangle, Heart Breaker* and *Thunder Struck*. Books in my bookshelf that I didn't want to read. Books in my bookshelf that I said I'd read, but hadn't. Clocks that didn't work. Dashboard Jesuses. George Bush memorabilia. Pill containers and blister packs. I called my work anti-capitalist, a comment on consumer culture. But that was a bit weak—I bought most of it at Look Sharp on the days of my crits.

The first thing Ilana ever said to me was, —I hate artists.

We were at an art-school party in Kingsland. Everyone was drinking red wine from boxes and wearing Nike Frees.

—It's okay, she said, —I can say it. I only ever date girls from Elam.

She and Sophie had been together for a year, but that was in first year, before Soph and I became friends. We still are: I invited her on this trip. I invited that whole crowd. Soph never responded. A couple clicked *Maybe*, but that was it.

I didn't want to tell Ilana I don't smoke cigarettes, so when she offered me one, I took it, lit it, and coughed. She told me everyone in her family dies of lung cancer. Durry dancing on her bottom lip. She said straight people were dull, that the New Zealand Army was an occupational force. That all of her prose was basically poetry, and all of her poetry, basically prose.

—I can't believe you're fucking her now, George said the next day.

But Laurie said congratulations, as though it was an achievement. That was how I saw it. I would spend nights, zooming out and in again, holding her face in the palm of my mouse, wanting every pixel of her. I would walk past her work—Mermaids on Karangahape Road—and poke my head in, even when I knew she wasn't there.

+

—Granny's back, Ilana says.

The blue Mazda has caught up and is tailing us closely. I get a call from a private number, but ignore it. The concrete skeleton of the Waipoa freezing works rests out in a paddock. The rows of corn and grapevines look too neat, too linear for this landscape. Everything around us is gently curving, in and out of sight. I lean back and close my eyes and feel the late afternoon in each corner of my face.

Road signs tell me this is temporary.

+

We enter Gisborne. Its hills lie around, naked, great thighs enclosing us. Here, I can see how the land ripples and bulges.

Not like Auckland. Auckland hides beneath its concrete shapewear. The coverall wraps of city struggle to stretch themselves over its curves. Only occasionally do you get a glimpse of what lies beneath: a strip of bush, a field that always floods, a very steep road. Only occasionally do you remember her belly full of fire.

+

I say it's going to be hot, and we're probably not going to want much during the day. We're already getting a lot of fruit.

—I'm not a fucking bird, Ilana says, as she puts a couple of bags of Eta chips in the trolley. Chicken flavour, salt and vinegar.

Pak'nSaves are stressful. Too many people, too much Arial Condensed Bold. The yellow signs—really just white, A3, 100gsm paper—all pucker with printer ink. *Twisties for ninety-nine cents. Home Brand white bread, five for four dollars. Coke Range 1.5 Litres, $1.49.* Cardboard boxes tower around us. A kid is screaming in front of the Arnott's selection.

Ilana grabs a loaf of Vogel's, Hellmann's Mayonnaise. She

would never admit it, but she has expensive tastes. She grew up in Kohimarama but now she just calls it *out east*.

—We'll need ice cream, eh, she says.

—What's your favourite flavour?

Ashi is looking at me but I can't think what to say. I can't even remember what flavours I like. We get Jelly Tip.

A woman barges into me while I'm choosing tampons, then tells me to be more careful.

There's a faint smell of linoleum and Dettol and that fresh muffin scent they pump straight into the air conditioner. The floors and ceilings echo muted greys and high-pitched reflections. The lighting is giving me a headache. For a second, I feel like I might throw up again, then it passes.

The confectionary aisle doesn't tempt me, neither does the bakery, but I don't want to go past dairy.

And Ashi and Ilana keep piling the food in. Penne and spaghetti, pizza bases, garlic bread, basmati rice, tins of chilli beans and chickpeas and tomatoes in pulp. I try to explain that there's probably the basics at the bach. But Ashi turns to me and says, —Don't worry, Ilana and I will pay for the meat.

Bacon, chicken nuggets, pork and fennel sausages.

I don't make any more suggestions.

+

I come from a long line of butchers. My great-grandad Conrad had his shop right here on Gisborne's main road.

Now, palms line it like soldiers at attention. There's a colonial boat hoisted on a pole. I think it's supposed to be a replica of the *Endeavour*. Pita said that, to Māori, the ship had looked like its own island: above, white kapua, clouds, blown taut. Cook and his

27

men killed nine tangata whenua that day, down on Poverty Bay. Pita grew up not far from here, Ūawa, and he read about these parts in Witi Ihimaera's *Māori Boy*. When I told him of this trip the first thing he said was, —You should read it, e kare. Whāngārā's mentioned in there. You make sure I give it to you before you go.

He said this often, but he never had the book on him. I stopped asking. I figured he'd changed his mind. He texted me a few weeks ago to say he'd bought one for me, a Christmas present. *Ahakoa he iti he pounamu. Though it's small, it is pounamu.* I didn't have anything for him so I put off meeting up. I didn't get around to it. But last week I found, nestled amongst the snails in my letterbox, the book, still wrapped in its Whitcoulls paper bag.

+

Every time I return to Gisborne another family shop has closed, replaced with some chain. Bendon, Bunnings, Paper Plus, Rebel Sport. There's a Stihl Shop on the corner of Carnarvon Street, telling me to love my land.

But it's not mine, is it.

+

Helen grew up in Kaitī. Her old house is a street back from the main road. I ask Ilana if we can drive past it. She scoffs. —Are you going to show me baby pictures next?

I get these kind of urges all along the way. I point out the things I can, the generic things. Like the dairy where they blend berries into your ice cream right in front of you. Like the place at Tatapouri where you can feed the stingrays, go cage diving with sharks. —Let's do that, Ilana says, like I knew she would.

But I don't mention how, one summer, I bought so many ice creams they knew me by name. I don't mention that I cut my foot open on the rocks at Tatapouri during low tide and had to have two stitches. I still have a faint scar. I don't mention the time I ran away, angry I was being made to miss Lucy's eighth birthday party (wave pools and hot chips) and made it as far as the paddocks we're passing now.

We have peeled away from the sea. This is where the trees come close, huddle in and reach around. They tunnel the car. Driving along these roads feels like tracing the lines of a palm, worn and outspread. I am overwhelmed by something, something stronger than memory, something bone-deep. It warms me and it pains me. I don't mention that, either.

+

Pā Road veers right straight after the bridge. It's narrow and you're supposed to toot coming up to each corner. Helen told me to tell them. I don't. No one does it, except her.

Wood and wire fences encase the sections and dot Pukehapopo Hill. Waiomoko River coils beside us like a snake. Cement tanks stud each lawn. They look dip-dyed, their lower halves coloured with mould. Boats beached, some usable, some not. Metal-barred gates, low and wide, cut into the grass in fading semicircles.

You'd never know this earth is unforgiving. Everywhere, plants have been willed to life. Harakeke shares a ditch with cannas. There are big lily pads of leaves, waxy as Mackintosh's lollies or fresh crayons. Dill flowers strain for the sky on thin necks. The wispy green of wild fennel, liquorice in the air, if you lean out far enough.

I tell them about the house down the way, where they filmed

Whale Rider, its soft yellow weatherboards, loosening with time. I tell them about our garage, locked for so many years no one knows where the key is. I tell them about the trees and how much they've grown. It was Wayne, my grandad, who planted them.

The telephone lines loop long and low, but they skip our bach. We didn't get connected, not number 373. That's what the letterbox says anyway. All of the bills and the rates are addressed to 371.

—It's not right, Helen always said, —there's something not right with it.

She's obsessed with house numbers, what they total. She adds up all the digits until she has a single one. Forty-eight becomes twelve becomes three. Numbers adding up to nine are the best, according to Helen. Eights are good too, and sixes mean change. But she would never go near a four. Four is an omen to her, a sign of falling boulders. *Fours invite it in*, she says, but she never says what. When pushed, she'll say, *a part of yourself*, or, *something that should stay buried*.

iii

The bach is a puzzle of corrugated iron and repurposed wood. If
you squint, you can see it's on a lean. It's small too, only four
rooms, including the bathroom. But the porch is wide and flat
and faces the sea. A metal wind chime, hung by Helen, sings every
time a breeze blows up the shore. And the sound of waves is a
constant. It follows you through every doorway, in every corner of
the garden, wherever you are. I tell them, —You'll notice it most
when you wake up.

   To be woken up by waves. Sometimes, in Auckland, I crave it.

   When I open the door, nothing is as I remember. The imitation-
marble lino in the kitchen has been supplanted by slate tiles.
There's carpet in both the bedrooms and new suede couches that
I'm scared to spill drinks on. The fridge is chrome and silent,
nothing like the old one. The cutlery is matching, heavy to hold,
and the seventies plastic tablecloth has morphed into beige linen.
Helen's shell collection that used to clutter every spare shelf has
been gutted. All that remains are the intact ones, the model shells,
occasionally punctuating a careful arrangement of coffee table

books and glazed earthenware.

The photo frame that used to house a picture of me, aged two, sitting on my grandad's lap, now holds my cousin as he holds up a dead shark. There was another, when I was eight and smiling, in my orca T-shirt and below the birch tree, light splintered across my face. My legs stuck out in front of me as if they're unattached to my body, still unaware of how much space I take up. But that has gone too. The whole photo wall in the lounge has changed: once a thing of pins and corkboard, now faces peer out of individual windows. Everything falls parallel. The only picture of me that remains was taken at my grandma's. I'm seventeen, inside and in shadow. My crooked mouth and crooked gaze are only softened by a dark sweep of cheekbone. I look even more distant behind the glass.

—There you are, Ashi says, —in the left corner, see?

Ilana pinches the fat below my shoulder as she walks past. — Can we smoke inside?

I say, —Sure, but I open all the windows.

The electricity switch is on a board squeezed next to the kitchen cupboard. I start two rubbish bags beside it, tip and recycling. I'm really particular about getting the groceries unpacked before any go off. Too particular: I tell Ilana the tomatoes shouldn't go in the fridge, they're on a vine. She doesn't unpack any more after that.

+

I remember one of our first dates, if you could call it a date, last July. We ghosted a party in Kingsland and ambled back to mine. It was the time of the Queensland fruit-fly scare. I lived within Zone A. During the day, you could sometimes see men in white suits, looking like beekeepers or workers in a nuclear plant. Walk a few roads one way and you'd pass a yellow sign, apocalyptic:

You are exiting a Controlled Area under section 131 of the
Biosecurity Act 1993.
Do not move any whole fresh fruit or vegetables beyond this
point.
Contact 0800 80 99 66.

—Should I ring it? Ilana asked.

—No one's going to pick up, I said. —It's two a.m. This is New Zealand.

She kept skipping ahead and kicking gates and stealing mail from the flashiest houses, the ones with the manicured lawns and freshest, palest paint jobs. The letters were from real-estate agents, just covert advertising in unmarked envelopes. That got to her. She stopped in front of a face-lifted villa on Williamson Avenue and broke the stalks of a fistful of lavender.

—For you, she said.

It was sarcastic, I knew that, but I thought it was kind of romantic. I put the flowers in a pitcher by my bed, after she'd left, of course, and kept them there until they lost their smell.

I searched for something to press them with. There was an old lined journal that I used to write in, a draft of a birthday card to Nick on its first pages. We weren't even in a relationship at the time. *You have such a way of speaking, never saying too much.*

It's funny how we justify things to ourselves.

When I checked on the flowers, a week later, they had left an inky stain on the pages and some of the words had transferred to their petals. Not whole words, just fragments. Little stutters of unrequited love, spelt backwards.

—They're beautiful, Ashi said.

But I couldn't look at them without seeing that letter, so I chucked them out. It was probably the last artwork I made.

I still call myself an artist, and click *Attending* to openings, though I very rarely go. A guy from my year, Finn, landed a solo show at Blue Oyster. I remember Laurie lowering her voice to say *it's because he's Māori*. That didn't make me feel better. But meeting Ilana did. She's a musician who sold her guitar to cover bond.

Even so, I feel guilty around Helen. I remember saying to her just before Christmas, —Where has the year gone?

She stayed silent for a long time, then said, —I think you should start paying board.

+

I return to the photo wall, and look for Helen. She appears once, in her twenties, slightly younger or older than I am now. Her hair is tangled. She's sitting on Bastion Point—it's a photo from the protests. My grandad makes it up there twice, but one is black-and-white and really small. His white beard creeps against dark skin, thick cheeks. It looks like candy floss, left outside to crystallise. I can't see my uncle Stuart anywhere. Instead, there are a lot of photos of my cousins from Australia. I count Lloyd's daughter Jane, and Jane's wide mouth, eleven times. Her English boyfriend, seven. Lloyd and his second wife, Jules, replace all the pictures of his first. Fifteen years ago, Jules was pretty enough to read the TV news. Now she's ten per cent plastic, bright red acrylics always pinching into the fabric of Lloyd's shirts. Their skin is like crepe paper from too much time spent on boats. He grimaces when he smiles.

—You didn't say, Ilana says, —that there's no reception.

—It was better last time I came, I lie. —If you were with Vodafone, you could get it right in the kitchen.

I take them down the beach to point out the spot where the cell towers will find you. If you look to the bach, the marae is on your right, and the island on your left. The whale, Paikea's whale. —It doesn't really look like a whale, Ilana says. But she takes a photo of it anyway.

Ashi smooths her eyebrows, thumb and forefinger like the legs of synchronised swimmers: slow, simultaneous. Then she takes a selfie, waves stroking the sand behind her. I don't know who they send these Snapchats to—I only see their yellow screens. And something invisible radiates up off the beach.

I sit amongst the club rush and call Helen.

—How's the bach? she says when she picks up. She always says, —I know when it's you ringing. I don't need to hear your voice.

—Good, I say. —Well, it's looking good.

—Lloyd and Jules said they really tidied it up last time they were over.

—Yeah, they did.

—It probably needed it.

—It's so weird now.

—What do you mean?

—It's like they're around me all of a sudden. I don't even remember a time when we were here with them all.

—Yes you do, remember when you were ten?

—No.

—Well, there was then. And when you were four, too.

She's probably right, but I won't acknowledge it.

—Mum said there've been rips lately. She said Francine noticed them when she was there in December. She said to tell you.

—Okay.

—You be careful.

—Okay, I say, —I'll be careful.

—You're not a strong swimmer.

Helen paid for classes for five years and I still can't swim to save myself.

—I know I'm not, I say.

Not like Helen. She's a natural, floating like a saint.

—Don't go out as far as your friends.

—I know, okay.

She believes she can breathe underwater, too.

—I just worry about you, that's all.

I'm not sure what to say next. Neither of us hangs up for a while. I can feel her there, at the other end of a telephone line, five hundred kilometres away. I can feel the signal bouncing up and down the east coast. It carries our silence.

Even the alive are ghosts.

+

There are some things you can't paint over. There are some things you can't wipe clean, no matter how much bleach you use.

Grandad Wayne lingers in everything here at Whāngārā. He built the house, he built the deck, he built the shed, he built the blood-stained gutting table. But the place I feel him the most is in the garden. Once it was just a field of lupins. But he weeded and he weeded them. He dragged seaweed up off the beach and soaked it in barrels. He dug canals down the length of the property. He made it so that life could grow in this dirt-that-is-really-sand.

Helen told me he scooped up a pōhutukawa seedling from a gutter on Wellesley Street. She said they were looking for Stuart.

She said Grandad thought it was a sign that he would be alright. And he was, that time.

I don't know if the seedling made it. It would be strange that, if it outlived both of them. There are a lot of pōhutukawa now, amongst the Norfolk pine, the kauri, the apples and the Moreton Bay fig. Oleanders and agapanthus and camellias cram in around their feet. There's only a patch of sea left visible, suspended between the bushes.

One day, this will all be under water.

iv

At Whāngārā, you feel as if you're on the edge of the world. The night seems to bend over and the stars just fall.

I walk along the beach, cracking sand like a crème brûlée. Bo chases the waves because there are no birds around, and barks at something in the distance. When I go inside, Ashi offers me roast potatoes. She cooked them on the same tray as the chicken. There's a faint buzz that could be the oven or could be the light bulb.

+

Helen would spend her first evening in the garden, calling me every ten minutes to show me some flower she'd found. *It must've seeded by itself!* she'd say, or come in with a praying mantis on her hand. Slow sway side to side. At dusk, she'd cook fish in butter, or steaks, rare. I never liked steak. She didn't let them rest long enough and the blood scared me, mashed potatoes turned pink.

+

—I put your stuff in our room, Ilana says.

I like the way she calls it *our room*.

She's given up on jeans. Men's cut-offs sit high on her waist, fastened with a shoelace.

I say, —Whose shorts?

—Brendan's, she says. He's her new flatmate, new because she's always moving.

—Don't you have any? I joke.

—No.

Ilana hates owning stuff. Stuff ties you to people, to places, to situations. You can't just leave if you have to pack first.

When I helped her with her last move she left half her clothes still hanging. —Not taking them? I asked.

—Nah, she said.

—Can I have this?

It was a long black jumper, faux-leather patches on the elbows. Most of the brown had worn off, white plastic below.

—Go hard, she said, without looking up.

Ilana hates stuff because she needs an escape plan. She lives her life with a hole cut into it. Most of us have them, but we try to stopper them, fill them up. Ilana would rather hers be gaping, a permanent way out, an end-row seat, an exit sign flashing green.

+

She pushes her thigh against me, hard, so it almost hurts. The air is drier here and we don't sweat as much when we fuck. I reach beneath the elastic of her briefs, graze my fingers up and down her pubes. It's been five days since she last worked and her skin prickles all over. I'm looking forward to the regrowth, to the softness that will come.

+

Ilana quit Mermaids when they wouldn't give her leave. She'd been looking for a reason to for a while. Her other job at the King's Arms is part-time, so she'd stuck around for the extra money.

—It's not as much as you'd think, she'd say. —Some nights I only take home a hundred.

I went to watch her once. She was always telling me to, I was always making excuses. My card declined on the door. I was stuck trying to remember her stripper name.

—It's a boy's, I said to the bouncer. He looked back at me, blank. —Dark hair, pixie cut, gap toothed.

—Oh, Alex.

She came outside and kissed me rough in the fluorescent foyer. She paid my door charge, too.

The inside was suffocated with mismatched damask patterns. They reminded me of the wallpapers at my grandma's house in Levin, turned black, and shiny. A music video was playing on four screens, shots of bikinis on Bondi Beach, but it was out of sync with the stereo. That was Sugababes' 'Push the Button'. A skinny girl was mouthing every word as she rubbed the pole up and down with a flannel, trying to make it seem like part of her routine.

I sat in a padded velvet booth by myself. I thought Ilana would stay with me longer, but that would've ruined the illusion for the customers. It was a Wednesday night, so there weren't many, but one tried to sit next to me. He asked why I was there. I said, —To see my girlfriend.

It was the only time I've called her that and it still didn't work.

—I bet you're missing dick, he said.

I moved to the swivel chairs in the centre. The surface of the stage was like water, reflecting everything. A band of colour

40

surrounded it, bubblegum blue blending into pink: a slushy of two sickly flavours, one on top of the other. The lighting there was hard and opaque. It shot down from mushroom lights, spotlights, disco balls. The kind of lighting schools would hire for Year Ten socials.

The skinny girl was naked except for a garter where she collected her cash. I couldn't stop looking at her ribs. She seemed pissed off I hadn't bought any dollars at the counter. But she was sweet as anything to the men. After a round she would shed her cash onto a pile in the middle of the stage.

My favourite moment in strip clubs is when you see the act drop. The song came to an end—Drake, by then. Her movements went from slow and undulating to fast and straight. She dove to bundle her money in the clothes she'd taken off. She had to search under the stools on my side to find her undies.

I expected Ilana to be next. A different girl, tall and in only a men's shirt, came out instead. But then they turned on the showers: just a big glass box, lit magenta, in the corner. There was Ilana, with the skinny girl and her nice ribs. They were soaping each other up. Ilana moved as if she was boneless. Her hair wouldn't sit flat, even when wet. I stayed through their whole performance, but I didn't want to. Karangahape Road tugging at my feet. I could hear the sounds outside: cars whizzing by, someone throwing up. It felt both closer and further away. I tried to focus on the tiles behind Ilana. We made eye contact just once. Then she grabbed the skinny girl by the wrists and held them above her head, the way she does with me.

+

I don't come. I never have, during sex, not with anyone. But Ilana gets me the closest, takes me right up to the brink. And I am an expert faker. Sometimes, I even fool myself.

It's not as if Ilana comes every time either. About half, maybe, if I believe her.

—My antidepressants, she says.

I wish I had thought of that.

We keep the lamp on for a while. Ilana wouldn't say it, but I think she likes to fall asleep in the light. It's always me who turns it off.

Here, I am the killer of cockroaches, too. I get up every time one emerges on the creamy walls. The Raid runs out on the seventh roach. We'll have to go back to Gisborne in the morning.

I've heard that if you flush a cockroach down the toilet, it'll climb back up the drains. But for now I just wrap them in tissue and do it anyway. Then I think about undead cockroaches when I pee. And I think about my period, which still hasn't come.

+

I used to skip them with the pill because Nick's bathroom had no bin, and because once, when I didn't, he woke with a start. He said he dreamed the bed was full of blood.

I remember that time because I had thrown my tampon out the window. I tried to aim for the bush. I couldn't bring myself to flush it. A lecturer had told me about how her garden exploded into sanitary pads. —The last tenant must have been flushing them for years, she said. She used it to explain Freud's return of the repressed.

+

I can't remember much of my dream except that there were possums everywhere. Somehow we'd brought them in the car with

42

us and they were now scattering, breeding throughout Whāngārā, their fur knotted with blood.

+

We fall asleep on separate sides of the bed, but our bodies always meet somewhere in the middle. I wake wrapped in Ilana's limbs. It's not something I'm used to. Sometimes I would touch Nick as we slept, but mostly we kept a film of air firmly between us.

Not *us*. She takes up all the air and I like it. The weight of her body sloping into the mattress. The heat we generate (mostly hers).

But this morning, it's too hot. I get up before she's conscious.

+

Waking early is something I learnt from Chris. She won't sleep later than six-thirty. —Following in my footsteps, she said. — Thank god you chose the right ones.

Chris squandered most of her twenties working at petrol stations. Her parents paid her rent and she spent what little money she earned on a weed-and-ketamine habit. Helen met her when she was six-months clean. She's the most sober person I know, she won't even take painkillers. Black coffee is her only drug.

Chris must've been with us, on that holiday here when I was ten, because I remember her on Christmas Day. Her crumpled red crown, the kind you get in crackers, was growing dark patches from her salty hair, the way mould grows on our ceiling at home. She'd made her glazed carrots, the ones she does with fennel seeds, but no one really touched them.

I don't have any other memories of her from that holiday. She probably spent a lot of time in the tent she shared with Helen.

+

Ashi and I bonded over not having dads. Her mum was a single parent.

Helen and Chris used to complain about never having money—Helen was a primary-school teacher and Chris was a law student. I learnt early about defaulted mortgage payments and declined cards in supermarkets. Helen was nervous each time I had friends over, because their houses were cleaner and carpeted and insulated. I thought Ashi's mum must've been the same. Scared of our central-city friends, the way some kids didn't know how to bottle it, wiping dust with their forefinger, *where's your second bathroom?* And their parents who always insisted on coming inside, who would open your cupboard doors when they thought you weren't looking.

But I was wrong. Ashi lived in a tiny flat with low ceilings and blistering wallpaper near the bottom of Franklin Road. She and her brothers shared a room. When I was eleven and finally went over, Ashi's mum said she'd been telling her to invite me round for years. She'd cooked a week's worth of bhaji and laid out Monopoly on the sitting room floor.

I learnt that it was Ashi who had been embarrassed. And I learnt a different meaning for poor.

Ashi's not poor now. She tutors kids looking to get into medicine. She's been on two trips in the same number of years, Melbourne and Vietnam. I still haven't been overseas.

She's outside, the light playing with the lines of her body, changing them.

44

—Can you sunblock Britain? she asks me.

Vitiligo creeps over her shoulders. She used to wear sleeves and high necks, waterproof concealer when we went swimming. She struggled to find one to match. But then she decided it wasn't worth it, she would keep them visible, the patches, where the cells turned on themselves and the pigment fell away. We sat up one night with my grandad's atlas, naming them. We found the UK, Finland, Libya, Peru and Kazakhstan, Canada draped like an epaulette.

+

Campsites sprawl along the bays between Whāngārā and Gisborne. If Helen was here she'd say, Pouawa, or Okitu, or Wainui. But they all look the same to me. Vans parked, tarpaulins on a lean, tents pitched between trees. Flags flying. The most common is Tino Rangitiratanga, though occasionally there's a New Zealand flag. It looks almost reactionary in comparison. The Union Jack, that tattoo of colonisation, always crisp on the skin of trembling fabric. There's a flag for Double Brown, a flag for Pepsi, too.

+

Ashi chooses a can that reads *One Shot: MultiPurpose Insect Killer*. It never takes one shot with cockroaches.

Ilana is waiting in the car. She'd said, —It's just bug spray, we don't all need to rush in.

I can see her through the glass doors, smoking out her window. I hang back, buying a lotto ticket for Helen because I forgot to yesterday. In the distance, Ashi shows her the Raid, and they both laugh, probably about me. There's an ad on the noticeboard, a

45

family of four looking for a place to rent. *A garage will do*, it says. Ilana shares the rest of her cigarette then Ashi stamps it out.

+

—What would you do if you had a million dollars?

Ilana throws me an over-the-shoulder look. She's at the wheel. I'm in the backseat again. It's a pattern that's formed, solidified.

—Buy a house, probably.

I know this will make her scowl. I know her cheeks will huddle up around her eyes and her lips will rise away from her teeth, so small and serrated they look as if her adults never came through. I look everywhere but the rear-view mirror.

She turns to Ashi. In profile, her eyes still haven't relaxed, but her mouth has gone all soft and inviting.

—Probably pay off my student loan.

—After that?

Ashi takes her cap and squeezes the peak between her hands before putting it back on. It's a red knock-off Trump one, *Make America Great Again*. I wish I could wear it, but on me it might not look ironic.

—Probably holiday forever, barely come home.

She looks at Ilana as if checking it's the right answer. —What about you?

—Same, trips overseas. And durries, food, booze. And rent.

—See, that's stupid, I say, —you'd burn through it and have nothing left.

It feels as though I just intruded on someone else's conversation.

—Oh, should I be investing it? Start complaining about rates and voting National?

46

Nick refused to tell me how he voted. I didn't think he supported John Key, but I can be like Helen, at times, good at believing what I want to.

I met him when he was living next door in Ponsonby with his then-girlfriend, Rhiannon. Her hair was dyed ashy blonde—you could tell by the colour it was unnatural—but I didn't once see regrowth. She wore grey-marle everything. Nude stilettos chipped into the concrete at eight each morning when she left for work. An office job in Parnell, HR or PR, Nick didn't really say.

I was seventeen at the time, had never been kissed. He was ten years older. It was a Wednesday in June when he came over to complain about my too-loud Joy Division and we had sex on the couch. That became our norm: Wednesday afternoons. It was the day he wrote copy from home for his real-estate firm (he always assured me that he wasn't an agent) and Helen had her PTA meetings. Four till five, our golden hour. I would run from the bus so I had time to change out of my uniform and stuff it beneath my bed. I'd put it back on later, so Helen wouldn't suspect anything. Once he asked if I could wear the skirt while he fucked me. After that, I didn't bother to change.

When I think of Nick, I see his face, every detail intact. But back then I forgot it weekly. There was a time when I knew that I had a crush on someone just by forgetting their face. It was like feeling for them in the dark. I could clutch onto a single feature: Nick's eyebrow swept out of place, the dry bit at the corner of his lips, the soft part of a chin. But I couldn't hold them there long enough to stitch him together. I would grasp at the fragments as they turned loose and fuzzy. I spent a year not knowing his face, only his body.

Right now, I have Ilana's face stuck in my head like a song. But then again, I learnt her lines in Facebook photos, her bones in binary.

+

Waves come in sevens. I read that in a Cosmopolitan sealed section. It said, take a leaf from the ocean and make your seventh thrust the strongest. I don't know if it works for fingering. I haven't tried.

+

I go as far out to sea as Ashi—Ilana is streets ahead. I'm the tallest, so I can touch the sand here, on tiptoes, and pretend I'm swimming. Ilana calls back to us, but I'm not going any deeper. When the breakers come, I try to relax and let them lift me.

Bo is running after stray seagulls, a dot in the distance. There are kids in a driftwood hut. Someone is riding a horse. A sinew of opaque foam stretches along the shore.

+

I was late to speak, nearly two. Helen told me the bach was full to the brim: family, strangers. She sat with me on her lap, everyone talking around her, talking over her.

—No one did a thing, she said, —to include me in the conversation.

So she took me down to the beach.

—All you could hear were waves, she said.

They're all I can hear right now.

Then, she said, I said it. My first word. A small finger pointed

48

to where I swim right now. *Sea.* Nothing else, just sea.

+

Moments keep returning to me from that Christmas when I was ten, with dubious jump cuts and shifting scripts. Helen and Grandma fighting over the Seabed and Foreshore Bill, TV blaring.

—What if they stop us from using the beach? Grandma said, as she drew on a cigarette. This was before she quit.

Even back then, I knew the beach she meant, and I knew who *they* were.

Lloyd said it was absurd, of course the beach was everyone's.

Helen said no one would be allowed to say these things if her dad was still alive. Then she turned silent and she stayed that way.

The Seabed and Foreshore Bill was the biggest raupatu, the biggest theft, these islands have ever seen.

+

I've never felt comfortable with our bach at Whāngārā. Helen said it was better when Grandad Wayne was alive. There's a Māori family with our last name in Tokomaru Bay, just north of here. I think everyone thought that's where he came from. I don't think anyone thought he was white. And I didn't want to. I would look at the photos taken of him in summer: wide nose, thick eyebrows, skin dark as bark. I would ask about his father, the alcoholic, his mother, unhappy. I might have really believed it.

But it's not true. A photo of Conrad, Wayne's dad, hangs on a wall in Levin. He's wearing his army uniform, he looks handsome and proud. Of course, it's taken before he reached Gallipoli. Before he watched his friend get blown to pieces, before the alcoholism.

He looks like the ghost of my grandad as a young man. Wide nose, thick eyebrows, pale skin.

I have never felt comfortable with our bach at Whāngārā, but I still come back here.

+

The sun eases itself down into the water, extending long limbs of light all the way to the shore.

—Hey, a man yells.

My first impulse is to hold my breath and duck, hide beneath the water like a child.

—Hey, he yells again and I turn around. He's come right to the sea's edge and his shoes are getting wet. He's going to tell me I shouldn't be here. He's going to tell me this is tapu land.

—You know this part's a marine reserve?

—Oh, I say.

—Te Tapuwae o Rongokako. We set it up with DOC.

—Oh.

—I saw you walking here above the strandline. You can't do that. That part's private land.

I gawk at him like a beached fish. My mouth opens and closes but no words form.

—Sorry, Ilana says. —Thanks for letting us know.

+

We start drinking as soon as we get inside. We let our VBs froth onto the new suede couches.

—Does the name Ashi mean anything? Ilana asks, and swigs her beer.

50

She keeps getting closer to Ashi on the couch. I'm on the other one because there's no room for me on theirs. Ilana sits like a guy, as if her knees have lodestones in them, north facing north, repelling wide apart.

—Smile, it means smile.

And they do, legs touching.

—Mine doesn't mean anything, I say. They both turn to me as though they'd forgotten I was there.

+

When I was obsessed with Ilana, in the early stages, I searched her name to find out what it meant. I was looking for an internet sign, some cosmic coding, divine engineering, that would prove we were right together. The first thing that came up was *She Knows*. I thought it was perfect. I thought it was Ilana to a T. But it was just the name of the website—it turns out Ilana only means tree.

+

She used to leave a lot of hickeys and bite imprints. I got the feeling she was marking me. We fucked other people, or she did, but her mouth never left my skin. In a way, I was hers. Whenever I tried to do the same back she'd always say, —I have work on Wednesday.

+

Ashi's period has come now but mine still hasn't. Even with her, I won't sync. When she was at Elam the whole year bled in unison, every four weeks.

—Maybe you're pregnant? Ilana jokes. Perfunctory smirk, a

51

crack of knuckles.

Then she reminds me I'm cooking. I say I forgot, but I hadn't.

I fry chickpeas in spices from the cupboard: coriander, cumin, cinnamon. The sumac is old. It falls out in clumps into the pan, dark purple dust balls. I don't think anyone else saw.

—Did we get feta? I call from the fridge.

—You said it was too expensive, remember?

But we have milk, and I can make ricotta, if they can wait an hour. —Is it really necessary? Ilana asks. But Ashi says it sounds great.

I wait until the milk is bubbling, as if there's something living under the surface. Take it off the flame and add lemon juice. After ten minutes, it congeals, small lumps forming, pale floating growths, malignant, multiplying. I line a colander with paper towels and let it drain. A sickly bile runs into the steel bowl below.

After an hour, the curds are still loose. I spoon it on anyway. Ashi says it's delicious, but Ilana leaves half the ricotta on her plate.

+

Her body shudders as she falls asleep. I think she is deficient in magnesium. I lie still and listen. If you're not used to it, the waves at night will sound like rain. You'll go to your window and check, once, twice, or stand beneath the sky holding your hand out, waiting to feel something.

+

I dream that Stuart and Grandad are alive still. Or maybe I dream that I'm alive back then. They're not actually here with me. They're out checking the craypots. Helen sings as she pulls weeds from under the house.

—They were growing right up through the floorboards, she tells me.

+

Whāngārā is a place where those who are hapū live and those who are Pākehā holiday. My grandad bought this section as a ninety-nine-year lease, back in the fifties. My grandma says everyone was happy with the sale. She says, —It was advertised in the paper.

—It's fine, she says. —Leave it.

But no one acts as though it's a lease. They're all here, the dead, scattered into this dirt-that-is-really-sand.

+

Stuart left one day on a plane and returned two years later in the luggage compartment, already cremated.

I don't know a lot about how he died. It's not because my family stopped talking about it—though they did—but because no one really knows. His body was found in his Bristol flat when he was two weeks late with the rent, not a scratch on him.

+

Ilana's shins are always covered in bruises. It comes with the job. Sometimes I kiss them, but she prefers when I press my thumb in, feel her tenderness. I haven't done that in a while.

Now, her pinks are turning to purples, to blues and greens. Some are almost yellow. She's on the mend. I don't have hickeys anymore—the last of them faded a month ago.

She's saying that we need more garlic bread, apparently, and Gordon's and Kronenbourg, because she's decided she can't stand VB. A new pouch for Ashi, Park Drive 30g, and Winnie Blues (tailies, of course) from Gisborne. I say I don't want to come, and Ilana doesn't argue, just takes the card from my outstretched hand. She knows the PIN. In a week or so, I'll be sitting in front of my laptop, scrutinising every last transaction.

+

Helen said staying here with Lloyd meant Moët on the porch, roquefort on fresh sourdough, four-ply toilet paper. She says drinking red wine was scary if she was near them, their clothing, their thick new towels. She says Lloyd used to say, —Don't worry, it's on me.

Then, a fortnight later, he'd send everyone an estimate of what it came to, their share, a bank account number.

+

I ring her from the beach, read her the lines of her lotto ticket. She says she feels good about this one. Helen's the kind of person who texts in codes from the inside of junk-food packaging: Magnum sticks, bottle caps. She's the kind of person who believes scam emails. But mostly, she trusts in Lotto.

She tells me she's been to the doctor, and the mole on her arm is nothing (I say I told her so). She tells me about the latest in the family email thread, *Issues with Mum's Will*. She tells me she's been out in the garden all morning. She would usually be in Levin for most of January, but she's been asked to nanny some kids from her class. Their parents are having marital issues and said they need to be in the Northern Hemisphere right now. Money under the table.

I have two Facebook messages and five notifications—none of them look interesting. There are three missed calls. Unknown number. I clear them from my phone logs.

+

At some point Helen stopped coming to Whāngārā. She said, —It doesn't feel like mine.

It didn't feel like hers with all of Lloyd and Francine's friends around, stopping by, staying for *just one night* or *just one more*. It didn't feel like hers without Stuart, without Wayne. It didn't feel like hers when she put on weight after the break-up with Chris and stopped swimming, too self-conscious to be seen in togs. It didn't feel like her land, like land she should have any sort of ownership over, no deed in her mother's drawer.

+

Last night there were cars clogging the marae carpark and Ilana said, —Let's go see.

But I said no. I prefer to go when it's empty.

The road is rough and hot on my feet. Chickens roam, proud and glossy. There's a rooster I've never heard before.

I pass one property, fallen out of use, where young burdock has seeded in tire tracks. Two parallel lines of weeds. When they mature, they'll sprout purple burrs, so sticky they sometimes catch birds, sometimes kill them. Things grow back, but not always in the right way.

Grass as high as porches. Ragwort as high as houses. Some look new, or newish, prefab homes just planted on the spot. A couple have stilts—for the view, I guess—with satellite dishes, and plastic frames holding glass. Most don't. Most are weatherboard and colourful, pink, yellow, flaking. There are gaps below and above a door, windows that never fully shut. One roof is a patch-work quilt, a hundred nailed pieces of tin. Only a few sheets aren't entirely rust, grey around their edges, iron-oxide heart growing.

The entrance to the church is an archway, the names of men engraved on its flanks. 1939–1945. The dead have been separated into two columns. All the Māori names are in the list on the left, the longer one.

+

Stuart moved to England soon after I was born. He was depressed in New Zealand. At his lowest, he'd asked Helen to go with him to a Christian prayer group.

—Exploring his options, she said.

—A tourist experience, she said.

—You'll try anything once, she said, —when you're desperate.

That was where she met my dad. They slept together only one time. She said she was down about Stuart, and Andrew was just there. He left hers by ten. But then, Helen says, he must've driven straight back, because he was at her door fifteen minutes later, rattling the glass as if it was going to break. He'd lost his cross.

Sometimes it's his cross, sometimes it's his wedding band. Helen has two versions of every story.

+

Most say Paikea came from Hawaiki. Others say that's a different Paikea, that this Paikea, Whāngārā's Paikea, was here all along.

56

One summer, two years ago, I wanted to come in February, before uni started. But my cousin Jane and her boyfriend were over. They were taking a break between jobs. That's what Grandma called it, *in between jobs*. They booked the bach for a whole two months, then only stayed a week. I heard, afterwards, that her boyfriend said, —We couldn't last any longer. Whāngārā, Gisborne, it has no culture.

He was talking about theatres and five-star restaurants.

+

Marae turn inwards. If you stand in front of them, they stare back at you. But I imagine they look inside themselves, too, with a hundred pāua eyes.

There are two wharenui. The tekoteko of the larger, newer marae, Whitireia, is Paikea, riding his whale.

The cemetery in the distance glints with colour. Bo keeps running towards it and I keep calling him back. I am clutching an envelope, one twenty-dollar note within. A kind of koha.

The door of the wharekai reads *whakatuwheratia*. Open. It isn't. The plaque goes on, *He tohu maharatanga ki a tatou tamariki i hinga i nga pakanga o te ao*. Something about preserving, for the children, the memory of what was lost in the world's wars. Then there's a part I can't translate. Ilana would be able to—she never explains how. If I ask, all I get is, *I grew up around it*, or, *I took a paper when I tried uni, once*. Then a laugh. It annoys me because I feel like I try harder, but to me, it comes slower.

The paper in my hand is limp, the seal has lost its stick. On the outside I've simply written *Ngati Konohi*. I've forgotten the

57

tōhutō on the a in Ngāti.

I thumb its fraying edges, and decide to keep the money for myself.

+

Pita's mouth, which could never quite wrap itself fully around Proper English, fell into place like water over stone when he was taught Te Reo.

Now he teaches on contract: primary schools and businesses angling to meet a bicultural quota. And there's one-on-one tutoring, or beginner groups like ours. But he hardly ever lets us pay.

In August, his sister died. Protein had been building up in her kidneys for months—the doctors blamed antibiotics. Pita was distraught. I think he lost some of those contracts. Our lessons became less regular, and when we did go round, the air in his apartment was stale. Dishes piled up in his sink and the curtains stayed pulled. He adopted a uniform of trackpants and sweat-shirts. He'd always apologise and we'd tell him not to, until a quiet would descend and he would say something like, —More than anything, I'm just mokemoke now. My sis. My sis.

+

I retrace my steps. The dry white grass, the kind that blends with pebbles at the side of roads, has been wisped into the patchy curl of a bald spot. Back of an old man's head. My feet look like something that surfaced from the deep, exoskeletal, blue-white bones twitching through thin skin.

I'm slow to get out of the way of a car, silver and low and missing number plates.

In the middle of our lawn lies something that wasn't there before. Plant matter is my initial thought, wide leaves, maybe branches. But it's a head: orange roughy, or a fish just as big. Skeleton to match. And, a metre away, a lump, unidentifiable. I don't know whether it's animal or not. In one place, there's a fold like lips, but it looks as porous as mesh, as rubbery as a shoe inner. The fabric could be skin or the skin could be fabric—either way it's a kind of leather. When I turn it over with a stick, I can see it has two holes for eyes, and pus-yellow balls fallen right inside the skull.

It's another thing entirely. It's an eel.

The remains are so dried and decomposed that they hardly smell anymore. I decide to bag them up, going first for the spine arching right out of the grass, scared Bo might choke on the long spiky ribs, broken off in places, snapped back. I gag. It's not as sharp as I imagined when I pick it up.

The patterns on the orange skin are like a snake's. They cover inside and out, the hard dark curve of cheek, the pale throat. The remnants of flippers, like parched harakeke, ridged by fibrous threads, extended. Its mouth is permanently open, as if surprised by death. Its one tooth is huge.

+

I check the poster on the wall of the bathroom: *New Zealand Seafood, A Healthy Future*. The decapitated head is actually that of a snapper. I scrub my hands, even though they only touched plastic. Then I undress and shower, imagining what it would've felt like to squish the rotten eyeballs of the eel between my fingers.

Below the sink, I find La Mer Moisturising Soft Cream. It must belong to Jules. It is rich and white and unctuous. I rub it all

59

over myself in front of the mirror. My legs, my neck, my breasts, my vulva. Trying to use every last bit. It takes a long time to dry.

By now, my period is six days late. My stomach looks bloated.

+

I don't tell Ilana or Ashi about what I found. I've shoved it to the bottom of our rubbish bag.

The woman from next door arrives soon after they do. She's in her seventies now, a widow, like my grandma, living alone.

—I got quite a few today, she says, —so I brought you guys this.

In her hand is a crayfish, blood orange and skeletal. I'm glad she's already killed it.

—Thanks, I say. I can't remember her name. There used to be a photo of me and her grandson, holding out our sandy hands for the camera. I haven't seen it in so long I wonder if I've made it up.

Ilana steps in, takes the cray off her. —How long would you boil it for?

—Oh, ten minutes, tops. Wait for the shell to turn orange. Get the water from the sea.

—Thanks so much, I say again. Ilana says, —Ko wai tōu ingoa?

—Nellie.

—Kia ora, Nellie, she says.

—Kia ora. You guys have a good one.

Nellie heads back, a slight limp making her whole body slant towards the earth. I wonder how she caught them. I imagine her hobbling over the rocks where my grandad used to set his pots.

We stay out in the garden, fingernails scratching our names into the budding green passionfruit. I almost write mine and

Ilana's, but stop myself. I explain how, when they ripen, the letters will show up white against the crinkled black skins. I've never stayed late enough to watch it happen, I just know it does.

V

There's something painted about the hills here, as if they're not quite real. But get close enough and they reveal their lines to you: wrinkles, creases, the staves of music. Cows dot the ridges like a child's attempt at drawing crotchets, black and squat.

Tidelines crisscross the sand like threads, suturing land and sea. Bo rounds up all the gulls and oystercatchers. A staffy tags along. I collect shells. Only the damaged ones, cracked and beaten and malformed. Ashi has wandered in the other direction, looking to call some guy, keep some snap streak alive. Ilana strides with her shoulders back and her face turned towards the sun. Sometimes I lag behind so I can walk in her footprints. There's no need to talk. At a certain point the beach turns to rock and we have to go back. That's what I think but Ilana wants to climb over, like she always does. And I say, —The tide is coming in.

Like I always do, and it almost always is.

+

Nick made me cry down on this shore. He got angry that people would see: the kids building the castle, the man tugging his boat to the water.

—If you don't shut up they'll think I've hit you.

I had told him how Helen thought I was like Stuart. She meant it as a compliment, small warning thrown in. But Nick took it as an insult. He said, —You have to watch amounting to nothing. It'll happen faster than you realise.

+

I study the way Ilana swims, not really swimming at all. The ocean's body turns to meet hers instead. The whole horizon tilts a little on its axis. I think, she is always the swimmer and I am always the sea.

We bring the beach back up with us. We leave it everywhere. When I taste her I get grit on my tongue. There's so much in my underwear that I think I must be ovulating sand.

+

Ilana wants to sunbathe naked. —I can't have tan lines for work, she says.

—Didn't you quit?

I feel played, somehow.

—Nah, I left when they said I couldn't, that's all.

—Isn't that quitting?

—Mermaids isn't the only strip club, eh? I might need money when I get back.

I don't understand why she needs so much money. Her rent is cheap.

—Then do it on our lawn, I say.

—Why do you care so much about what other people think?

But she doesn't go down to the beach. She lays a towel between the kauri and the gutting table, and sunblocks only her tattoos. First, the thigh-gracing jaguar, teeth bared, then the snake, eating itself round her bicep. She spends longest on her ribs: one of those stylised flappers, the twenties curls, bloody dagger behind her back. Finally, I notice, she even dabs at the rose. Then she sits there, beer in one hand, ciggie in the other. Defiantly naked.

Ilana had heart surgery when she was born. She still has the scar—those ones never go away. It's more white than pink now, gently puckered and scarcely raised. It looks as if string got stuck beneath her skin and is worming its way out.

I always wonder what the customers make of it. This shiny little strand of hypertrophic tissue, which says she was once lying on a table with her chest cut open, and now she's lying on this stage for you.

Maybe they don't even notice. Maybe they simply watch her dance.

+

Whāngārā is a place dictated by rhythms. A place beating, breathing, crashing in them. Just because you can't see something, doesn't mean it's not there. A horse in the distance, quick patter of hooves. A car driving along Pa Road. The rip, steadily sweeping everything away.

You have to listen carefully. It's imperceptible, at first, silent against the waves. But then I hear it: the rain. So light it refuses to settle. Water hovers in the air like a mist. Taps the roof gently, as if it's a shoulder.

At home, rain means pots down the hallway and in the kitchen, the tink against metal. I'm surprised there are no leaks here. Lloyd must've seen to that.

+

Ilana comes in but doesn't bother to dry off. Ashi lends her a T-shirt that says *I Woke Up Like This* over Botticelli's *The Birth of Venus*. They've started swapping clothes—Ashi's in a black sweatshirt of Ilana's. I'm not jealous. I don't like sharing mine. But I stare and I stare at that T-shirt, Ilana's breasts making damp spots as though they're leaking milk. The woman in the painting, holding up the blanket to cover Venus, looks as if she's pissed herself. Opposite her, a patch of sea, fish-scaled with foam, turns very, very dark.

+

Waves are an endless buffering. They shudder and crash and make the unseen seen: the pull of a moon, a current underwater. Splintering into spray, drops and pixels on the screen of Ashi's laptop. *The Blue Planet*, David Attenborough, my choice.

Its tongue weighs as much as an elephant. Its heart is the size of a car. Some of its blood vessels are so wide that you can swim down them.

I miss the width of the whale's tail, Ashi and Ilana are laughing too loud. It's something about the cray but I didn't hear the joke. Ashi stabs at it with a fork, Ilana pulls flesh out with her fingers. The shell is stranded, legs up in the air. We're all pretty high. Cam, Nick's old flatmate, sold me half an ounce. He groped my arse when we said goodbye, too. I could feel it there all day, the imprint of his hand.

+

Nick hated that I smoked weed. He told me it was why I'd never be successful. He used to say, —Look at Cam. Twenty-eight and still at uni.

+

The smoke gets right inside my chest and makes everything warm, even people. Ilana strokes my thigh and tells me I'm cute with red eyes. We've managed to fit onto one couch with her in the middle. My arms are crossed in front of me. Now, the crayfish is merely a husk. Its feet join above its body like a hollowed-out ribcage. There's a time-lapse shot of a tide on a shore, bars of sand rising up as if of their own accord. Ilana lights Ashi's bong for her though I know she can do it herself.

+

All of Ilana's blaze spots were ones she'd been to with Soph, but she never mentioned that. She'd just bring her up at them, more than anywhere else. —Soph didn't get my jokes, she'd say, or, — She was a mouth-breather.

It wasn't something I'd noticed.

We were at North Head, or Maungauika, as Ilana calls it, as I should, and she said, —What if it went off when we were here?

—The gun? They don't keep it loaded.

—No, the volcano, she says, —the one we're walking on.

In. We were walking in it. Ilana had lead me down to the bunkers. Our feet trod where men once slept. It was inexplicably cold for November.

—Have you heard who built these? I said.

She was smoking most of the joint. She knew I wouldn't follow her, not all the way in.

—Prisoners, prisoners built them.

—That's fucked, she said. Then, after another toke, —You know all the most useless things, don't you?

I forced a laugh. The batteries cracked the landscape into soft and hard. Their lines jutted out, brutal angles blurred, just a little, by the encroaching grass and Old Man's Beard.

—Soph fucked like a straight girl.

They must've had sex there, up against the concrete maybe. I couldn't stop picturing it. I didn't know how a straight girl was supposed to fuck, but I was scared that one day Ilana would say the same thing about me.

+

The fins of orcas stick out of the water like knife points. They force themselves between a grey whale and her tiring calf, launching on top of it, again and again, trying to drown it. One takes a bite. The blood stains the water and the mother has to continue north alone.

They've eaten nothing more than its lower jaw and its tongue.

—Bleak, says Ashi.

Eighteen months later, there's a skeleton of a calf on the sea floor, bone bare. The ocean doesn't waste a thing.

As far away from the sun as it's possible to be on this planet.

I've felt like that, at times.

Ilana doesn't want to watch the next episode. She says

Attenborough is overrated, the sea is boring. She puts on a documentary series about a murderous real-estate heir. In the first scene, they find his neighbour in the bay, floating in rubbish bags. I go to my room to read.

Pita has folded down the corner of a page, marking a passage. Paikea was called Kahutiaterangi back in Hawaiki, back in the original Whāngārā. His half-brother, Ruatapu, wanted him dead, but Kahutiaterangi escaped. He didn't settle until he found a new Whāngārā, a place just a bit closer to the sun than the rest of the world. As close to the sun as it's possible to be on this planet.

He didn't settle until he found this beach.

Then he changed his name, so Ruatapu couldn't find him. Paikea means humpback whale. He's a direct ancestor of Ngāti Konohi. He's a direct ancestor for the whole of Ngāti Porou.

+

Pita is Ngāti Porou—Ngāti Raukawa and Tainui, too. His parents were beaten at school when they spoke Te Reo. So they protected him: he wasn't taught. He learnt at seventeen, from a Ngāti Whātua kuia, at a marae north of Auckland. It took four years of immersion. The Western dialect is different to the Eastern, and when he goes home to Ūawa, like for his sister's tangi, he still trips up. Tupuna instead of tipuna, kai te haere instead of e haere ana.

+

Snippets of Ashi and Ilana's conversation reach me, uninvited, like someone knocking on your door. Ilana complaining that more of her pay isn't under the table, how everyone she knows has degrees. I hear Ashi say, —Yeah, they're pointless.

Ashi is the kind of person who prefers red wine one night and white the next. She's always making her mind up to be a vegetarian, then deciding against it. I wasn't surprised when she quit Elam. But as soon as she went into medicine, she gave it her all.

—Not your degree, Ilana says. —We'll still need doctors after the revolution, eh.

It takes Ashi two hands to count the guys who are probably (definitely) in love with her. She is like a bucket of water in a house fire. Everyone around her falls to flames, on their knees with love, but somehow she never catches.

—You must be a bit queer, Ilana says with certainty. —All the best people are.

I lie with the pillow over my head to block them out. But when you're lonely, walls are at their thinnest.

+

Ashi and I weren't always best friends. Know anyone that long and they're bound to hurt you, at some point.

We sat together every day in Year Thirteen English, until she said to me, —You know Nick isn't going to leave his girlfriend.

I must've been talking about him again.

I told her blue hair didn't suit her, and changed seats. She hung out with the plastics and their puffer jackets after that. I saw them wandering up to Karangahape Road in one big, loud group every day at the last bell. I sat alone in English, my head in a beaten copy of *Owls Do Cry*, until two weeks later, when they kicked her from their group because she wouldn't wag Photography for a smoke.

She may have come back to me, but still, I was heartbroken. Ashi can be mean sometimes, too.

+

Every time you remember something you're only remembering the last time you thought of it.

+

Ilana bought NOS from the dairy on Karangahape Road and she comes in to tell me that they've decided to use it tonight.

Ashi was what parents called *the responsible type*. When we filled our dean's desk with packing beads on the final day of high school, she just stood back and watched, looking over her shoulder. She didn't smoke until nineteen, didn't touch weed until twenty-one. I've offered her other drugs before: crappy MDMA, which turned out to be flour, mushrooms I found in council bark on the side of the Northern Motorway. She always said no.

—You don't have to do this, I say to her, when I follow Ilana back into the lounge.

But she lies, —It's something I've really wanted to try.

I don't actually like NOS. Everyone laughs and I have to pretend to.

Ilana stretches the balloons, squeaky plastic membranes, powdery. They slap back into shape. It's almost a wet sound. I feel nervous about cracking my whippet, about the coldness that spreads from the metal to your fingers, about the hiss, the dry scream of the oxide, until I realise Ilana is cracking all of them. Then I feel angry at her for assuming I can't do my own.

The liquid gas, compressed, shoots into the balloons and swells inside them. She pinches their necks and passes them around.

Moving fast, unscrewing the cracker, slipping the whippets out to the floor, frosted and pale, as though dipped in talc. On to the next.

Ilana explains to Ashi how to inhale: hyperventilate into the balloon as if it is a bag. Slow, deep, again.

NOS displaces the oxygen from your lungs, dissolves into the bloodstream, hits the brain within seconds. Ilana collapses on top of Ashi. Both their bodies judder with laughter, rocking in slow motion.

The sound pulses in my ears. Not them laughing—I can't hear that. The alien sound. That's how it's always described. But I think it's like a helicopter, somewhere near my face, blades swooping round and round. The walls are approaching. Thudding like a heartbeat. I'm in my own pocket of air, my own silent womb, except the silence is deafening. It becomes so loud that it is the only thing that exists. There's no light left, no colours. It keeps getting deeper, this black. I'm drifting in it, surfing backwards, pulled into its frequency and trapped between the waves. They shorten around me, press me to my seat. I'm waiting for the moment when they let go. When it comes, the room has shrunk.

Tears on their fuzzy faces. Far away and all too near.

My head is still swimming. My limbs are heavy. I can't just feel myself panicking, I can see it too. As if from up high, the lamp above our heads, that strange block of light. That's all I am. Something else, leering down, if leering wasn't an active verb.

They're sober, sitting straight, a little uneasy. I know that I have to say something, let the tension like blood. It'll trickle out but you can't get rid of it. Everything must go somewhere.

—Enjoying it?

Ilana.

—You okay?

Ashi.

Say something. Just say something.

—Are you sure she's done this before?

Ilana to Ashi.

I get up and go to bed. When Ilana comes in, hours later, she smells of gin.

—The toilet's broken, she says. —It doesn't flush properly.

—I'll check it tomorrow, I say, and pretend to be asleep.

+

I am talking but not in English. I am dancing but my feet are still. I am swimming but the water is boiling.

When Ilana pulls me out, my skin has turned bright orange.

She tells me I'll be alright if I follow her, if I just keep moving. But I can't see where she's gone.

vi

On the road to Gisborne in the morning, all the colour of the land has drained, bit by bit, into the sea. It's like a photo left too long in sunlight. Every green looks bleached, every yellow, burnt. A kind of summer skin, with blisters of red in the road signs, purple in the hydrangeas.

But the sea is bluer than any blue. I imagine diving into it. Ashi is driving us to town. Ilana has stayed behind, where the waves will reach her.

We need to find a plumber. It's not the toilet that's broken, it's the pipes. They're overflowing. You can flush, but you have to try a few times. And it makes sewage bubble up from a grate outside, below our bedroom window.

—The rain's stopped, I say, and Ashi nods, smiles.

It cleared up minutes after we left.

+

The Citizens Advice Bureau is in a grey-and-white flat-roofed building, like 1960s beachside apartments, plonked right in the heart of Gisborne. The upstairs is lined by balconies with frosted glass banisters and the downstairs is shared with Remax Real Estate. By the door is a yellow sandwich board (*Free! Friendly! Confidential!*) and a standing flag reading *Information for New Immigrants.*

—Can we use your directory, please?

There's a pause before the *please.* It's tacked on and obvious, sticking out like a wonky tooth.

—What?

The woman behind the counter is well past retirement age. Her freckles have coagulated at points on her face, large brown spots petering into little ones.

—A phone book, I say, —do you have a phone book?

—Yes, she says, with one slow, deep nod.

—Can we use it? I say.

She looks at me for long seconds before turning and going into a back room.

All around posters battle each other in font size and colour. Their advice rings out, then quickly absorbs into the grey carpets.

Looking for work?

Think Globally, Cycle Locally.

Travelling Far?

Men's Issues: Talk about them mate to mate.

A CPAG poster has been blu-tacked, unofficially, below the rest. *305,000 Kiwi kids live in poverty. That's 29%.*

Hanging by sellotape is just a printout. *WE ARE UNABLE TO PROVIDE FOOD VOUCHERS ON REQUEST.*

The woman returns with a man, not a phone book. The lines on his forehead are concentric, tidemarks in the sand.

—What were you after? he asks.

—A directory, I say, —we need a plumber. We got the answering machine with every number we found online.

—I can help with that, he says, reaching below the desk. —What exactly is the issue?

—Every time we flush, sewage comes out a grate.

The lines on his forehead converge.

—Where are you staying?

—At Whāngārā, I say.

—Oh, Whongārā, he says. He pronounces it like my grandma. —Do you have a tank?

—There's a rainwater one, Ashi says.

—Not a septic tank?

—Yeah, I say, —we do.

—It sounds like that's your issue, he says. —Hang on.

He flicks through the *White Pages* himself, then picks a number and dials.

—I can speak, I say. One finger raised, lips parted: the only response I get.

—Yes, hi Barry. Norm here. Yes, yes I did.

He has a low, wind-up laugh, like tyres spinning on gravel.

—Yes thank Susan for me, he says.

Another round.

—Yes but Barry, I'm ringing you because I have two pretty girls here. Yes, lucky me, I know. Yes, they are. Yeah look, Barry, they need your help. It sounds like their septic tank needs emptying. They're all the way out at Whongārā.

The scratch of his beard is audible.

—Yes, I'd hope so too. Well, look, thanks Barry, thanks Barry, I'll check.

Norm looks up. —How long are you lovely ladies there for?

—Another week, I say.

—Well look, Barry's actually still on his Christmas holiday, but he can come in a day or two, just for you. Write your name and address down here.

He picks up the yellow notepad.

—Is your grandad Wayne? He asks.

—Was, I say.

—Oh yes, yes sorry about that. I know him, I mean, I knew. I knew your grandad. Your great-grandad too, as a boy.

I want to ask him how he knew them, but he's already back laughing into the receiver.

—No, not yours Barry! I wasn't born in the bloody nineteenth century.

Scratch, scratch. Spin, spin.

+

We drive through the back roads of Kaitī. London Street, Glasgow Cresent, Queens Drive, Cambridge Terrace—that's where Helen grew up. The houses are mainly state ones, boxy windows, blue weatherboards. They have huge driveways of mismatched concrete, each addition like pentimenti, visible. Occasionally there's a flat-faced villa, paint shedding to bare wood, a flimsy verandah.

Helen says she remembers the cattle trucks and their smell: cow shit and fear. She remembers losing her new scarf, which Grandma had knitted all winter, on the hill. And she remembers a woman on Oxford Street, who she saw every day on her way to school, pulling dandelions and clovers from the edge of her lawn, toes searching the topsoil. —She scared the hell out of me. I never wanted to be like that.

Helen always says this when she's down on her knees, poking

a butter knife between the bricks in the path that leads up to our front steps. She refuses to use the sprays. They're just chemicals, that's what she says. She does all the weeding by hand.

+

There's a marae and a church at the base of Kaitī Hill, and signage about a replanting program. Ashi winds Ilana's Nissan to the top. Once, it would've overlooked a rock, Toka-a-Taiau, marking the boundary between Ngāti Porou and Tūranganui. But it was blown up in 1912 to expand Gisborne's harbour. Kahawai and snapper left soon after.

—Are you okay? she says. —After last night?

We stare down over Poverty Bay and Young Nick's Head. Cook had offered a reward to the first person to spot a coast. That's how a headland was named after a twelve-year-old. That's how Aotearoa was *discovered*. But tangata whenua were never lost.

—You shouldn't feel embarrassed, she says. People only say that when you've done something embarrassing. —Ilana said she's seen that before.

Ashi continues, —You know, someone have a bad trip on NOS.

—Can you leave it? I say.

One of the walls of the Cook Observatory is just corrugated iron, covered-up graffiti, unmatched paint. There's rust on the window grate and the brick overhang is whittled, like a bitten fingernail.

A notice says it is the world's easternmost observatory. It's closed for not meeting current earthquake standards.

There are two Cook statues, a fake Cook and a real Cook. The newer one is the real Cook and it's down by the river. No one

77

knows who the older one up here is: his uniform isn't British Navy and his face is all wrong. Ashi takes a photo.

I've driven to Kaitī Hill a few times with Helen but only once did Grandma come along. She wanted a photo in front of the pōhutukawa that Princess Diana planted. But the midday sun threw down a light she didn't like. She realised when we got them developed—we were still using film.

Off from the road, near the bottom, an obelisk stands encased by hollow metal bars, but they're low and we climb right over.

To our boys who in the Great War died or were found willing to die for the Empire.

The memorial was paid for by the freezing works where my great-grandad Conrad had his first job.

—I wish I'd met him, she says.

—You mean my grandad.

—Yeah, the political one.

Wayne was a recurring character in Helen's stories. Ashi's heard a lot about him. He was imprisoned as a pacifist during the war. He volunteered in a Youth Justice Residence in Palmerston North, where he loved all the boys, and hated all the staff. He threw an egg at Muldoon once, and it nearly landed.

+

I often asked Helen about her ancestors, when I was a kid. Hand-me-down stories, from Wayne to her to me. Stretched to fit. She spoke of grandfathers at different removes each time. *Great great great*, Helen would count out on her fingers, or, *great great great great*.

78

There was the leader of the butchers' union in London, a Marxist who didn't like to share. He had two houses, two wives and two bankruptcies. One of his sons was the butcher for London Zoo. He fed carcasses to the lion and, eventually, they became so close he could walk it on a leash around Trafalgar Square.

But don't trust me on that. Grandma says she's never heard any of this.

+

I have four missed calls. My only email is from Change.org telling me I got Laurie to sign some petition. I say to Ashi that I'm ringing my mum and she just asks which one.

Helen says, —I wish Lloyd would stop. Hasn't he got enough?

He thinks he should get the bach, because he has the money to renovate. By which he means flatten it and build something two-storeyed.

—He said we could have half of Levin each, and Mum's savings. He said it makes sense for us financially, we can sell Levin, it's money that could help with our own mortgages.

—But it doesn't make sense, I say, —even financially.

—Francine's really considering it. Her husband's nearly sixty-five. He wants to retire soon. How's she supposed to manage that farm herself?

—The bach'll be abandoned, the amount they're over.

—I'm worried they'll forget it's a lease.

—Yeah, I say, —that too.

—You've been missing out on the new *MasterChef.*

She tells me about all the contestants who are twenty-three and younger.

MasterChef is Helen's new favourite. It used to be *Lost and Found*. Always, at the episode's end, when the mother was reunited with her son, the brother with his half-sister, she would cry. Or, at least, make hiccuping sounds, like a dog does just before it throws up. I hated *Lost and Found*.

—Your family is who raised you, I would say, —your family's who's there.

I don't get the obsession with blood.

+

Most of my sharpest memories from childhood, the ones that can really cut, come from behind doors or in backseats. I learnt a lot that way. I learnt that Chris didn't think Helen listened enough, and that Helen thought Chris was too hard.

—You're hard and what's worse is you see it as a good thing.

Helen didn't like Chris' *homophobic parents* and Chris didn't want to spend *every bloody holiday* with my grandma.

Sometimes, when we went to Levin, Chris drove through to Wellington and picked us up on the way back, a week later. She lives there now, in Petone. She took a job as a public defender working on Lambton Quay. But it wasn't the sole reason she left, a whole life in cardboard boxes crowding the boot of her old station wagon.

+

It takes only seconds. Pa Road is empty, a grey line that cradles the hill, clings to the wildflowers. And then it isn't: a silver car, the same one I saw yesterday. It doesn't shoot round the corner, it just appears, huge and fast. Ashi yelps and tries to swerve out of the way. Brakes. Our tyres lose their grip and the back of the Nissan swings into the ditch. The front mounts the road, horizontal. The other car doesn't slow down. It hurtles past, millimetres between us. I don't get a look at the driver—their window's too dark. And it's raining again.

Ilana says it never stopped.

vii

—I still don't see it.

Ilana's talking about the island, the whale that froze, turned itself to rock.

—I see him, I say.

I'm talking about Bo, skidding around its edge. He's been cut off from the beach by a lane of water. And he's no swimmer: he keeps looking across at me, starting in my direction then heading back. The tide is coming in, fast. The rain is a constant.

—Bo, come here! Bo, come here!

Come. Here.

The cold surges into my feet, the way light surges into your eyes when you walk outside on a bright day. For an instant, it's all I feel.

When I'm knee-deep, he follows suit, slipping into the sea where two currents meet. They push him and they pull him, knocking him right under.

Those sinking moments. They stretch on and on. I fix on the spot but I can't seem to wade towards it. And all I can think is, why didn't I teach him to swim properly? Why didn't I keep an eye on him? Then he pops up again, more skittish, more determined, more reckless, too.

He's swept to my right, this side of the divide. I scold him and I praise him because I don't know which is best.

+

I graduated high school around the time Nick and Rhiannon broke up. I thought he had done it to be with me. I cried that Christmas because we didn't talk daily, only fucked weekly, and he still wasn't my boyfriend.

When I told him I was going to study fine arts, he was impressed. He had heard finance. He didn't know what to say when I corrected him, except, —That's something.

I repeated his words over and over again, but couldn't remember where he'd put the emphasis. *That's* something. That's *something.*

+

Pain doesn't race, it ambles. Since this morning it's made its way from my hands and feet, up my arms, my legs, into each rung of my skeleton. My body is becoming stone.

Hemp seed oil, glucosamine, folic acid, turmeric: that's every day. Whole dandelion, devils claw, Siberian ginseng, paracetamol, ibuprofen, prickly ash and liquorice. They're for the bad days. If they don't work, I'll go back on prednisone.

What's worse than the pain is the fear. That this flare-up might last, might do real damage. I might be a cripple by thirty, walking stick in hand. One doctor told me I would probably never work full-time, maybe not at all. He took his glasses off just to say it.

+

It's Ilana's night to cook, so Ashi and I make pizza. The base goes a little soggy and she cut the onion too thick. I have only one slice.

Ashi's hair spills down each time she leans in for a piece, and each time she tucks it behind her ears. Her lips are so full they look swollen.

+

All through school boys liked her best. She had her first boyfriend at twelve, I had mine at eighteen. She had dates to both our balls. I went alone.

It meant a lot to me when Nick said, once, that I was prettier than her.

+

Ilana's never called me beautiful, but she has called me pretty. It was one of our earliest nights together. She showed me *Tangerine* and we smoked weed through her shisha pipe. I didn't get very high—it wasn't enough. But every time I stood up the tobacco gave me a head rush and I had to sit down again. I was still getting accustomed to her body: I'd been used to Nick's bones, right under the skin. When I burrowed into Ilana, I softened. Her warm flesh held mine. I kept pressing my fingers into her thighs through denim and feeling them bounce back like rising dough.

I spent three weeks learning her body. It was August and we

hung out most nights she wasn't working. I remember her saying,
—It always rains when we're together.

Tonight, she smells of smoke and I smell of sunblock. When I scratch her back, skin gets under my fingernails.
—You're peeling, I say.
She pushes me off.
—Your hipbones, she says, —they're digging in.

+

In November Ilana said, —If you're going to flat, you need to chuck some stuff.
She asked me when I last painted.
—About a year ago.
—Then what are you doing keeping these?
My oils were stored in a Gladware container. Acrylics in a plastic bag. There was a shelf of brushes and mediums, and a roll behind my bed of unstretched linen.
—They're expensive.
I didn't want to tell her that I might paint again. We threw them in the bin, along with some old clear files of research.
My room felt so empty that I slept on the couch for three nights.
—If you're a real artist you won't need them, she said.
Like how she doesn't need her guitar to be a musician, I suppose.

+

Something thuds against the roof. We both jolt.

85

—Must be a cat, Ilana says, but I think it was a possum.

—Where's Bo? I haven't seen Bo.

—He's under the bed, Ilana says. —Look.

Legs and tail scrunched up in a warm bundle.

She heads back to the lounge as soon as Ashi finishes her shower.

I read *Māori Boy*, dipping in and out, holding the book in both hands and seeing where it lands. It's what Helen does with the Bible, or did. I've only seen her touch it once.

—So badly written, was all she said. And went back to the I Ching.

I come to a page about Kaitī Hill, really Titirangi Hill. The marae we saw today, Poho-o-Rāwiri, wasn't always there. The Public Works Act stole an earlier site to hollow out the harbour.

+

Last March, eight months after my break-up with Nick, Cam invited me to his thirtieth. I bumped into him on campus, waiting to buy the five-dollar vegan lunch with Ashi from the stall by the Barracks Wall, which was built in the nineteenth century to block Māori from nine hectares of their own land. I got the feeling he was asking me out of concern that I would hear about it later, through someone else. There was probably an event on Facebook I knew nothing of.

I spent three whole days deciding whether to go. That's what I told people. It made me sound sensitive and anxious, and meant they offered me a drink. I scabbed two ciders, two wines, three beers and a bourbon. The truth was, I knew straight away that I would go. I wanted to see Nick. I felt as though things might be different if I could just see him.

I hear the gin bottle gulping into glasses. Ilana's talking about the TPPA.

—Fucked, eh, that a trade agreement could override Te Tiriti.

The signing is in a few weeks' time. February the fourth, right before Waitangi.

—It's deliberate, she says, her voice getting louder, —It's trying to divide activist attention.

Ashi's not a real activist: she left Elam too early for that. Ilana tells her to come to the protests. She says the march down Queen Street isn't worth it, that all the direct action will take place outside the SkyCity Convention Centre. Then I hear her jump. She's seen a cockroach.

I am so used to Gisborne cockroaches that I didn't know the American type could fly. When I found one in my bed at Auckland I spent hours cooing and coaxing what I thought was a beetle. Only when I Googled *can cockroaches fly*, did I get the Raid. I had dreams about flying cockroaches for days.

Tonight, I watch them scuttle, fat and wingless, across the carpet. The spray's out in the kitchen, so for now, I let them live.

Grandma can remember a time when there were none here. Then, in the sixties, a big load of wood came from Perth, and the cockroaches came with it, shipped straight to the Gisborne Port.

+

Nausea hits me in waves. It's not just in my stomach, it's taken over my chest and throat, it's in my face. Ilana and Ashi have opened a bag of Doritos. Their crunching is so loud I can hear it from my room. I poke my head outside and the rain pelts the back of my neck. My vomit is orange. It mixes with the sewage below. The smell is still thick in my nostrils, long after I shut the window.

+

At Cam's party, I didn't see Nick until I was about to leave. Most of his friends just knew me as the ex now, no matter how much time I'd spent with them. But then there he was, on the couch. Head in his hands as if it was about to fall off. And there was Rhiannon beside him. I felt as if my lungs had been pierced and all the oxygen was escaping, as if the discs of my spine were slipping one by one and I would never be able to stand straight again, as if I was vomiting my own heart up, vomiting in the middle of the kitchen floor. Which I was. Chunks of kūmara and strings of leeks netted between the tiles. Someone threw a wet sponge at me. Others laughed. Nick didn't come out of the next room. Cam offered me his bed, but a friend of his called a taxi and told me they'd clean it up later. I don't recall who.

+

Every time you remember something you're only remembering the last time you thought of it.

+

I brush my teeth next to Ilana in silence. My mouth still tastes like spew. The toothpaste tubes from my house grow pink-and-blue tumours around their necks. You can still use them fine, you just can't close the lid. Nick used to bring his own, and make a point of wiping the cap. And wetting his toothbrush twice, before he put the paste on and after. And brushing for a *full two minutes*. It always felt like four.

+

When I'm stiff, I sleep any way my body will let me. I sandwich a pillow between my palms and straighten my legs. Ilana doesn't get offended, like Nick would, when I say, —I need to sleep this way.

Turned away.

But I don't tell her why. It feels too hard to explain something that's not visible, on the surface: a pain that doesn't scar.

+

I dream that Bo is missing again, and we're building a tall fence everywhere there's just bush. So much of this garden is just bush.

—What point is a fence if he's already gone? I say, but no one answers.

I dream I've been flushing tampons, that's why the drain's blocked. That's why there's shit on the grass.

—It's beautiful, Ilana says, —from here.

But she's talking about something else, I'm sure of it.

And she's fucking me with Nick's cock. I wish it was mine, on my body. The wet between us is pounding in my ears. Did she hear me?

Crash into my body. Break it. Don't stop me from drowning. Where has all the water gone? I'm saying, or at least, thinking. Most of my dreams are nonverbal these days. Other people talk. And I think things. I just hardly ever say them.

89

Sex with Nick wasn't good once we were in a relationship. Something had gone from it for me, some flood of feeling: a sting, then warmth. I hated kissing him. His mouth was always too wet. I would wipe my lips with the back of my wrist afterwards.

He used to say, —You're dry. And spit on his hand.

It always hurt.

+

I remember the first time Ashi described a dehydration headache to me. Your brain is eighty per cent water. When you're dehydrated, it shrinks, and the tissue pulls back, away from the bone.

I imagine my brain, curling up inside my skull. And I imagine the membranes stretching out.

Ilana comes in with a glass. The bottles are running low, but she's filled this right to the brim. Sometimes I think she really is trying.

—Do you remember how we used to kiss? I say.

Then she stands over me and bends down and makes me feel as if we're back in her room in Westmere, a film playing on her desktop, one we haven't seen a minute of. Or we're in the bathroom at a flat party, and there's knocking on the door as she's pushing me against a wall, knuckle-deep inside me.

Sex is like a religion for her: best practised daily.

It's different for me. I can't stay inside a fantasy for long. I'm either too present, too aware of an uncomfortable shoulder or an out-of-place foot, or too far away, in another room, with someone else. But certain skins you will always fall into. Her skin, that temporary tan she keeps permanent. A pink nipple escaping her

90

wife-beater. She puts her finger in my arse—that's when I start moaning.

But, if I have to be honest, I am thinking of the time I walked over fire as a child, I know it. And it didn't hurt one bit.

+

Four years ago I convinced Nick to try anal. He thought it was too unclean. Even though he came, he never wanted to do it again, and he was angry whenever I mentioned it.

+

He used to hold my cutlery up to the light, or rewash plates before I served dinner. He couldn't dry them because my tea towels collected dog hairs.

I wanted to say, now you've just made them wet. I wanted to say that sometimes, at his house, I had to pinch my nose to stop from smelling the unrinsed detergent on the pan I fried our eggs in. Chicken period, I wanted to say, just to put him off.

+

I linger outside the bathroom. The toilet paper in my hand had been white, the water clear.

—Still nothing? Ilana asks.

I shake my head.

—Are you alright?

Her voice is softer than usual.

—Yes, I say, from practice, —I'm fine.

viii

The best time to go swimming is when dusk starts to curl in, to settle. At this hour, the sea is a womb. You'll only realise if you float in it on your back. The sea is a womb, and its pulse needs no bloodline. It can go straight to your heart in an instant. The sea is a womb, and if you let it, it'll hold you.

 —Maybe it's a good thing your period hasn't come, Ilana says, —you don't want to be dinner.

 —What? I say, no longer buoyant.

 —For sharks. They could smell your blood from a mile away.

 —That's a myth.

She just flashes a pink grin and dives under the next wave.

Sharks can smell blood from a quarter of a mile at most. It doesn't have to be much, one drop to a million of seawater.

+

Helen doesn't know where my dad lives anymore. I was a secret from his family. Except his mum, who he must have told, because she rang us one night when I was eight to say that he'd moved down south and my paternal grandad was dead.

—When?

I remember the word twisting out of Helen and into the greyed receiver.

—Last year, was the only response. Then the muffled click of my grandma hanging up.

Chris put her hand on Helen's shoulder. They avoided looking in my direction and whispered, as if I couldn't hear them, as if I hadn't heard the whole thing.

I used to think Helen was asking when my grandad had died, now I'm not so sure: about the question, or the answer.

Neither is she. She remembers it differently. She always says, —That phone call about your dad joining a cult.

And I always reply, —Not everyone religious is in a cult.

Or, —Do you think that's what the South Island is?

+

I bought Nick a ring with a cross on it. I felt too embarrassed so I told him, —I found this ring with a cross on it.

He wore it every day. I wished I had told him the truth.

+

The bach was broken into, not long after I last came here with him. Nothing was taken. The beds were slept in, that was all, and by the time Francine and Jon stopped by, a crust of bread left in the fridge had turned from white to blue. Nick was shocked that I didn't mention it sooner. It had slipped my mind for a week or two.

—I left my car unlocked while we were there, he kept repeating.

Ilana's is unlocked now. It's parked haphazardly, bonnet nosing bush. Only one tip makes it under the corrugated iron carport. Bo is growling at the tyres. I sit against it and lean backwards, and the rain gets in my eyes.

Light can take years to travel. When you look at the stars, you're really looking at the past.

+

Alfred, my great-great-great-grandad, came from Britain on the *Aurora*, the New Zealand Company's first settler ship. It landed in Petone in 1840, that much I know. The rest comes from Helen, stories bent like gold.

She says he was the ship's vet, but really that meant the butcher. He put down pets who couldn't last the trip.

His wife followed on a boat called the *Duke of Roxburgh*. In some of Helen's stories, she died during childbirth. In others, she jumped off the stern of the ship, baby in arms. But Leighton, their two-year-old son, my great-great granddad, survived.

Alfred didn't like Wellington—he thought it was too hilly to be a city. He traded his spaying needles for a horse and a Bible. When they arrived at the flat expanse of the Tūranganui River, where Gisborne is today, he hung a wooden cross around the boy's neck, claimed to be a missionary and renounced all women. Until, that is, he met a pretty whaler's daughter.

It's hard to tell what they were like. People grow indistinct over the years, their children make things up.

+

Ilana wants to find Helen's ouija board.

—She says it's here?

—I don't know, I say. —Last time I asked about it, she said it was probably at the bach.

Helen loves the future. She used to trace lines at lunchbreak, palm flat against finger. Kids at Kaitī Primary queued up over the courts.

When I was nine she gave me a mini tarot set. I sat it proudly on my desk. The book was the size of a post-it note, but the cards weren't much larger than a thumbnail. Their box was always millimetres too small. Helen would pull one at random each morning and ask me what it was.

—Nine of cups, I'd say, or, —Queen of swords.

And go back to sleep.

Ilana doesn't talk about the past: *it's over*, she says, *why do a post-mortem?* She wanted a tarot reading once, on a whim, but she told me not to bother with the first card.

—I'm not interested in my history, she said. —I know what already happened.

One day I'll be relegated to that: the not-to-be-mentioned, the *already happened*.

Right now she's hauling drawers out from dressers and dumping them, scattering hand towels and expired sunblock bottles everywhere. She's asking about the locked garage. She's riffling through all the board games rotting away under our bed, even though I tell her there'll be cockroaches. Which there are, three of them. Cluedo instructions go soggy with Raid.

I want to play Monopoly, but she says no, on the grounds of

being a good communist.

—We can make one, I suggest.

—A ouija board?

—Yeah, we can write the letters on paper. We can use a salt shaker as the stopper.

It gets very dark in Whāngārā, no city near to dilute it. The light bulbs look like yolks suspended in their pale glow. The breeze keeps lifting and shuffling our letters. It blows our *YES* right off the table, twice. We shut the doors and windows. You can hardly hear the rain.

I light the candles. There aren't enough, so I keep a bulb on, above the oven. That soft electrical purr remains. The filament inside it is aging: it flickers every so often, never manages anything more than dim. The room's full of shadows.

—Helen taught me to recite this next part holding hands, I say, —You say, *Peaceful spirits, come to us, are you there?* until the salt shaker moves.

But holding hands across the table is awkward: all of us leant together like nuns, praying. Ashi keeps forgetting the word *peaceful* and Ilana only chimes in on *come to us*. Our timing is off. Ilana lets go of my hand, but not Ashi's. I focus on the shaker to keep from looking at their fingers, interlocked. It's big and plastic and mustard, one thing that hasn't been updated.

—Then, Ilana says. —Did you see that just then?

She swears she saw it move, I swear it didn't, and Ashi agrees with us both.

We place a finger on each side. Ashi has her eyes closed, concentrating. I try to catch Ilana's gaze, but can't. The shaker is still for a long time. But then it stutters, small jolts like a body waking. For a while, I simply watch it, transfixed. Then I remember to record the letters. It's gibberish.

96

—It could be Latin? Ilana says. But Ashi says, —That's not Latin.

Some of the letters make Māori words, mutu, pokanoa, but never whole phrases. I don't point these out. Then, I feel it begin to really move. It's like an undertow, pulling. My hand is tugged from me, as the shaker swerves round the table, round a full English sentence.

Go away.

Ashi looks bloodless. —We should stop, she says.

—Let's ask who's speaking first, Ilana says. —Who are you? What are you doing here?

Watching from his eyes.

—I want to stop! Ashi is yelling. She's taken her finger off the shaker and keeps stealing glances at the photo wall.

—Let's ask it whose eyes, Ilana says.

—You might not want to call them *it*, I say. —Whose eyes?

Under the house, we spell, slowly this time.

Ashi crosses her wrists, hands clutching the neck of her T-shirt, stretching it lower. She seems queasy.

—Where's Bo? I say. —I think Bo's gone.

But he's been in the room the whole time. Ilana and I get up, and Ashi doesn't want to be left alone, even inside. She leans against me in the doorway. —I feel exhausted, she says. —Instantly, instantly exhausted.

The moon is murky, just a toothpaste stain on the sky. It could come out in the wash. Sewage advances beyond the grate and onto the lawn, stench sour in the air. We shine our phones under the deck. The blue light catches our chins and feels around like fingers in the dirt. Glossy plates of eyes stare back then dart away. It was a dog, a small dog, but Ilana thinks it was a cat. Bo doesn't chase after it.

—I know it was you, I tell her, —spelling those things out.

She ignores me.

It's only later, when Ashi's in bed and I am throwing away the scraps of paper, that I realise we didn't use our *HELLO* or *GOODBYE*. Helen taught me that you ask the spirit if they're done talking. Then you blow out the candles, to sever the connection between the two worlds, to shut the door. She never said what happens if you forget.

+

I have my first nightmare about Whāngārā. Stuart is driving me here, taking a shortcut on the beach itself.

—The quickest way, he says, —you always have to take the quickest way.

As he bulldozes across sand dunes and children's feet.

I find Nick's ring in the shallows. I throw it back in before retrieving it again.

All the beds are taken. People have emerged out of the walls and the cracks in between.

—Sleep in the add-on.

It isn't an add-on, but a two-storey house towering over our bach. In the upstairs bedroom a man cries while blowing air into the mouth of a doll. Its plastic chest heaves up and down. I thought he was kissing a real baby.

Digging relentlessly in the dark. —A present, he says. A new pōhutukawa has sprung up overnight, the first of its red fronds peeking out to the sun.

Digging relentlessly in the day. —A plastic bag, she says. Throwing up.

I don't know where the man has gone, but it isn't him I'm

scared of. It's the ghost of his wife and newborn.

Then Stuart is Ilana and we are in such a rush to leave she takes the wrong way at the end of the drive. Turn around turn around turn around.

—Not until I've found the space to.

The road continues on past where it usually stops at the marae. It curves behind the hill. Stop the car stop the car stop the car.

Heat rises, so do flames, but smoke gets everywhere.

+

I need to ask Helen where the tapu land is next time I ring.

She has a story about accidentally walking onto it, she and her brothers. Lloyd threw a stone at a gull, but it went the other way and hit Helen on the back of the head.

+

I wake with locked limbs, to the sound of rain nicking the roof, heavier now, and bruises I don't remember.

—Did you do these? I ask Ilana.

She grunts and rolls. There's a cockroach nestled in her hair, its dark ceraceous body a near camouflage. I want to get up, pretend I never saw it. But I don't. I cup my fingers and slip them into her curls. Ilana doesn't wake, not fully, but mumbles something. The cockroach scurries deeper. I part her hair, pluck it from her scalp, and gas it to death outside. She wants to fuck after that and doesn't make me clean my hands first.

Nick used to wait outside the bathroom door to ask me if I had washed them. I got in the habit of putting the tap on, just for a bit.

I didn't like to get my hands wet.

By the end of third year, my favourite thing to collect was soaps. They were cheap and easy to steal. I stole a lot from public bathrooms. And from his house, where there always seemed to be about eight bars. I collected used ones and ones still in packets. I liked hotel soaps the best. I imagined rinsing with them must have felt like clutching at the foetus of a mouse, small and slippery.

+

Chris and Helen argued endlessly about the best way to stack a dishwasher (Helen didn't believe there was one), and whether it was worth keeping spider webs to avoid flies in summer (Helen thought it was), and the *unholy* state of the fridge.

—Open cat food next to the baby spinach, Chris would yell, —again!

When she moved to Wellington, her bungalow in Petone was as kept as a showroom. She bought a couch from Domo in Parnell and paid for it to be couriered cross-country. I wasn't allowed to eat or drink anything on it, even water. That was until she got with Liz, and started scoffing Chinese in plastic takeout containers, right there, on the white leather. But sometimes I'd see her afterwards, bending over it, checking for stains or spills.

+

All morning there's been the sound of a car driving up and down the road, engine humming. A big steamer's out on the horizon. The clouds in the sky have dropped to claustrophobic levels. You can't see the tops of hills, or anything beyond. It's bucketing now

100

but Ilana suggests a dip. She says the water's warmer when the day is colder. And it's true.

+

That kind of drowning feeling. The air is all around your face, if you could only breathe it. Ilana said, —The first breath you take again always hurts.

She is an experienced drowner and I am just starting out.

—This wave, she says. Yelling, —Come, no, here by me.

She gets it right. Knows exactly where to stand for the wave to pick her up and throw her. Carry her. She can surf some right back to the shallows. I keep getting hurled below. See the Gisborne sun rippling through all that green. And I'm not sure whether I've opened my eyes underwater, or if I never had a chance to shut them.

Ilana grabs my arm but I duck when the wave comes.

Then she tells me about the first time, when she was seven. Her mum's dinghy capsized and whenever she came up for breath she hit the hull instead. She says the sea was holding her down, not ready to let her go. And then it turned and it pushed her up, shot her face first, full of air. She's the one who keeps pulling me up today.

When I look at her, I think: the ocean will never again be so in place. It shudders and slurps and turns—no two molecules will be together for long. No two molecules will find each other again. Or at least, it's unlikely.

Then Ashi joins us.

Ashi doesn't catch as many waves as Ilana, but she catches some. I keep surfacing to see them tumbling into the spray together. Sometimes, Ilana puts her hand on Ashi's arm as they wade back out deep.

—What is it? Ilana says to me.

Water is furling itself on the horizon, creeping forward.

—Stay here, she says. —It's a big one.

I'm sucked in before it's even broken. This time I can hardly see. The ocean floor has been tossed into the wave—I blend with the sand and the seaweed and the dappled sun. Then I feel the break, and know I'm being pushed deeper.

For me it isn't slowed down, like Ilana said, but sped up. A flash of light, greeny brown, something above the surface. The whir. The spin. The sea gasping, in and out, one giant lung that expands and compresses. When you're beneath it, the ocean is the only thing that breathes.

My cries are tiny silent bubbles. Even they refuse to rise. I don't know which way is up. When my arm finds air, it's a fluke. The wave has lost its clutch on me. I am no closer to the shore, but way off to the right. Ashi and Ilana are in the distance, adjusting their bikinis and lining up for the next one. The water here is over my head. I keep sinking hopeful toes towards the bottom, but I don't touch anything. That's when I realise I'm not still, but drifting, being pulled. And I hear it, the sound of NOS, a ringing that suffocates even the waves. My vision tunnels away from me. I scream at Ilana, but my voice comes out weak and guttural. I try to paddle in their direction. My legs are like tree trunks, water-logged, heavy, moving independent to me, or not at all. This is a rip, I tell myself. This is a rip. The one thing I remember about rips is that you're not supposed to fight them. I go limp in the hands of the current.

The next wave is the one that saves me. It hurls me to where I can touch sand. Exhaustion has made me a stranger in my own body. Everything I touch feels distant, as if someone else is touching it, and I am just watching them. I can hardly see. I can hardly stand. But I don't want to collapse in front of the others.

—Going in? Ilana calls after me.

This would be the perfect time to cry. The rain would hide it. It could hide it all.

When I get inside, I shot gin to get the taste of salt out of my mouth.

+

A third of our genes aren't fixed. They get coded—in the womb, in life. You can pass them on, those genes. You can pass on your fuck-ups, your hang-ups, your heartbreaks. You can pass on trauma. You can pass on guilt.

I made that up. I don't know if it was a third, or a quarter. I can't remember where I read it. But I imagine it like the sea and its salt, infinite. Floating, mixing, rearranging. Churning up bits of the past, bringing them to the surface. Or pushing them deeper. But unlike the sea, this isn't erosion. Taking from the shells and the stones and the glass bottles, breaking them down. Making sand. It's the opposite. Our DNA pieces itself together, into some-thing hard, into another layer, a more solid ocean floor.

ix

The summer I was ten Chris took me for drives up the coast, all the way to Tolaga Bay, Ūawa. I didn't know how to be around my cousins. On the first day, I joined in to make a sandcastle. But I took over when Lewis, Lloyd's boy, thought it would be a good idea to make a twig fence to replace my careful pebble one. I explained how my pebbles were the same size, and flat, whereas his twigs were different lengths, and wonky. They all went inside, but I stayed, smoothing the turrets and hollowing out the windows, until dinnertime. I saw them playing cricket on the beach and taking boogie boards into the waves. Not me—I read my book, and screeched at Jane over who could be the dog in Monopoly. I always had to be the dog. She gave in, but I threw the paper money and plastic houses everywhere when she landed on Mayfair—and bought it. I remember going down to the beach and seeing, to my left, another sandcastle, one I hadn't been a part of, slipping by degrees into the sea. And I remember finding them, later, Jane and Lewis, Eden and Pearl, all of them, in Eden's tent. Playing Monopoly, Jane advancing the tiny silver dog across Go.

So Chris and I drove. Looking back now, I realise it wasn't just me who needed the break. It wasn't just me who was avoiding something, someone, too.

+

—We're here as friends, Ilana says. —What did you think this was, some sort of romantic getaway? Ashi as third wheel?

—No, I know that, I get that. That's not what I said. I just wanted to know, what are we?

—Why do you always need a label?

It's the first time I've asked.

+

Something comes to me, something Pita said, on one of those days when he only got out of bed to answer the door.

—I don't have teaching in me today, he'd say.

And I'd say, —That's alright, I just want to talk.

A stack of books was growing beside his TV, library stickers glaring, plastic skins buckling the light. He made coffee the colour of tea and curled up in his chair, its arms swollen with lumpy padding. Cup balanced on one knee, he said, —In naming things, the English owned them, but all the stories got lost. We have to search for those stories. Sometimes, we have to make our own.

When Pita talked like this, I didn't always understand. But now, I think I know what he meant. I've been making stories up my whole life.

+

105

Ashi crouches, hand on the back of my leg. I'm face down in pillows.

—You okay? she says. It's so condescending.

—I'm fine.

—Is this about Ilana?

—No, why would you say that?

I roll over to look at her. She has a gentle, loving expression, but that's simply her face.

—She only said—

—She said what?

—Nothing, nothing really. She only said you seemed upset.

She sits on the corner of the bed and takes off her silver hoop earrings, as if she's about to lie down next to me. Yes, I think. Lie down. We don't need to do this, we don't need to say a thing. We can just lie together for a while.

But then she puts them back on again, metal through flesh.

—You know you do, she says, and when I don't reply, —seem upset.

—Well it's not about her.

—What is it then?

I keep imagining it over and over. The waves, going under. In some versions, one of them notices, points, yells. It's usually Ilana. Then they charge through the water as though through air. Dive to me. In a film, this scene would be slowed down, hair billowing round my face, my limbs flung like a ballerina's. We make eye contact underwater. I know I am saved.

But mostly, I imagine drowning. It burns when I swallow. Then my windpipe relaxes, my lungs fill with the ocean. I wash up on the beach like a dead fish, bones picked bare in patches, stomach on display, the skeleton I so desperately want to be. Only then do they see me. I imagine it again and again.

106

When I don't answer, Ashi nudges me. —You can tell me anything, she says.

—It's nothing, I say. —I'm just tired. Really.

For a moment I see her weighing this up. She looks at the door. She's thinking, it would be so easy to leave. To leave this here. She doesn't.

—You know I like Ilana, she says.

—Yeah, it's pretty clear.

—I just don't know if I like you guys together.

—What's that supposed to mean?

Too loud, I was too loud. Now she's backtracking.

—Look, I get it, I do. She's so funny. And she's confident, and smart. Not like you, not your kind of smart, but she is still, she is. And so onto it with that political stuff.

—What did she say to you?

—What? Nothing? I said that.

—Then what is this?

She looks up at the ceiling as if the words she wants might just fall from it.

—I don't think either of you see each other, really see each other.

I sit up, the duvet scrunched in my fists.

—I don't know what you're saying.

But I do know. And she's wrong. If anything, we've seen too much. We don't know how to unsee.

—I'm not sure either, Ashi says. —I'm probably reading into nothing. Like I said, I like her. She's a good person. All that time she spends organising actions and going to hui. And the money she sends her mum. And how she'll drive you anywhere, right? You've always said that. She's a good person, ignore me.

—She doesn't send money to her mum, what are you on about?

—Yeah, you know? Since her mum lost the sickness benefit last year and was put on Jobseekers. Ilana's been making up the difference.

—Her mum lives in Kohi and drives an Audi.

—That's her stepmum.

—No it's not.

I lean forwards, Ashi pulls away.

—Look, she says, —I don't want to argue this.

She's scared of me.

—Yeah, I say, —cause you're talking shit. You think you can be mates with her for, what, two months and suddenly you know her better than I do?

—That's not what I'm saying!

Fuck off, Ashi. The words sit in my mouth like a hard round lolly, delicious, tempting, just ready to slide off my tongue.

—Has your vitiligo spread? I say instead.

—No?

Her hand draws instantly, instinctively, to her shoulder. I laugh.

—I don't know how we ever thought that was Canada.

The rain's still whacking itself against the window, fat globules running down the glass. For a minute, I think I hear her crying in the other bedroom. But that's impossible. You couldn't hear anything over this weather.

+

For weeks after Nick and I broke up, the one thing I could stomach was grapefruit. I sprinkled it with brown sugar. Some segments tasted sickly sweet and others sour. My tongue prickled in anticipation.

It was the only food that didn't hold any memories of him. I thought I'd never eat mandarins or scavenge feijoas again. Thinking how he peeled mandarins, all in one so the skin held its shape. Next to his peel, mine, shreds of orange confetti. Or how he was the first person I had seen eat feijoas with a knife and spoon. I used to just pierce the skin with my thumbnail and squeeze the insides out.

+

I don't leave the room. I can't see Bo in the garden, and for a moment it yanks me out of myself. But there he is, finishing off the bread thrown on the neighbour's lawn. His coat is wet when I call him in, and I lock the door behind him.

I keep falling asleep and waking up again, though it's never any darker. The afternoon draws on, a road that won't end. I'm looking for the bend, for the point it'll turn, but it doesn't come. And the rain doesn't stop.

+

The times that I was alone, the times when I wasn't sleeping with Ilana or having lessons from Pita or working pointless shifts at Dida's serving rich people richer cheese, were times I spent in bed, rarely moving. Wasted time. Most of it on my laptop, scrolling. I trawled the depths of Ilana's Facebook to find her high-school girlfriend, the one who gave her that rose. Her name was Julia. In her current profile picture she holds a cat in front of her face, hands gripped under its front legs, small feline nipples where her eyes should be. The cat looks surprisingly relaxed. Hundreds of people wrote on her wall for her twenty-fifth birthday, saying what a kind person she was.

I reread a *Vice* article where the author had emailed a survey to everyone she'd ever slept with, asking them to rate anything from foreplay to fantasies to whether they would fuck her again:

Not memorable. Sorry.

You never change position. Ever.

If you're more mentally stable, sure, why not?

I convinced myself, for a few months, that I'd developed lupus. Then I realised I didn't have a butterfly rash, or sensitivity to sunlight, or a fever.

I spent an entire day hungover, searching the recesses of the internet for videos of orcas killing their Sea World trainers. But all I ever found was granular footage from phones, missing the main event, or clips where the trainer didn't actually die, just broke an arm or a leg.

So I watched recordings of them hunting instead. A pod cornered narwhals against a rocky coast, herding them out of the depths. They bit down on a great white off California, a tiger shark off Costa Rica. They beached themselves on the Patagonian shore for sea lion pups, learning to swim in the shallows. In Antarctica, they synchronised their swimming, creating waves to upturn the shelves of ice where crabeater seals cowered. And there was a video from a boat in the Hauraki Gulf. A slowed-down repeat of the shot where an orca surfaced with a dolphin in its mouth.

+

Down on the beach, I hold my parka above my head, above my phone, its radio waves searching. Eleven missed calls from Helen. I'm scared she knows, scared she's sensed I almost drowned. We've always been wired to the same frequency.

—You need to get to Levin.

—What?

—You need to get to Levin. Mum's sick.

Grandma's been sick for over a decade, but Helen's voice is stretched thin, calico taut over frames, fraying at the edges.

—I can't leave Mila and Jayden, she says. —But I've made next week my last, I'm coming down that Saturday.

—Why? Are you going to pay the money back?

—Mum's in Madison.

I know of it as a rest home, the place Lloyd has wanted to send my grandma for years, but Helen says it's a hospital, too. Grandma was taken in for a medical examination after she crashed her car into a tree. She had barely a bruise on her, but x-rays revealed her cancer has spread. Helen uses the phrase *last legs* a lot. Everything becomes a repetition. Then silence. Dead line out to sea.

And the tide is still coming in. It swung around this morning and never looked back. The water is rising.

+

I see Ashi boiling something, but I don't see what. Ilana is opening beers with a lighter. They clink the necks together. Looking through that window feels like watching a film. I don't know how to enter, how to break down the wall and jump into the shot. I want to stay out here longer, remain a witness. But I'll get drenched.

The sewage on the lawn has slid and pooled—a kind of Rorschach test, soaking into the soil, into the roots of the nearest plum tree. But when I look at it, when I really stare, I only see shit and paper and rain, pockmarking its surface.

+

I take my damp clothes off and sink down into the mattress.

Ilana is in the doorway, hands holding either side, braced. It takes a while for the image to wrap itself around my cornea, refract, turn the right way up. For a split second, I brim with the sight of her. Then I remember.

She says she'll sleep on the couch tonight. She's come in to tell me that, hair still dripping, saying, —You take it. You need that right? Room to lie in whatever fucked-up way you want.

How to say: no, I don't need that. I need you to sleep beside me. I need you here tonight. My jacket and jeans are in a pile on the floor. They look almost human if I squint, someone in a foetal position.

+

Nick was taught that you keep a house tidy in case someone turns up. He said that we couldn't live together until I'd flatted myself, learnt a thing or two about cleaning. He stopped saying that towards the end. We stopped talking much at all. Nick, who used to nitpick what I wore and what I did, sulked quietly instead. And when I spoke, it was only of artists and people he didn't know.

—What? he would say.

—Never mind, I'd reply. —You wouldn't get it anyway.

The words dried up on our tongues.

+

At the brink of my vision, something moves. Ilana, turning.

—Wait, I call, but when I don't say anything else she simply shakes her head and leaves. I clamber from the sheets and follow, trying to salvage something, a sentence. The front door is open, as if she's about to stand out in the rain. This'll be it, where we kiss. Where everything's better, at least for a moment. Where I know what to say.

But then I see him. A man, stocky, in blue overalls. A parked truck narrowly missing a kauri. Ilana, still angry, head swung around to call for me, until she sees I'm behind her, in my discoloured, saggy undies and holey singlet and bra that gapes.

—Smells pungent, he says, talking about the sewage, meaning the weed, looking at my underwear.

This must be Barry.

—You can deal with this, Ilana says, and heads for Ashi's room.

He doesn't move, the wet still pummelling him. I'm plastered to my spot, metres from the door. I don't know how best to cover myself with my arms.

—Thanks, thanks for coming out, I say, —in this weather and everything.

—It only just started, he says.

—What?

—It only just started on my drive over.

—Oh, I say. —It's been raining here for days.

He doesn't say anything so I keep talking, —It's never done this, the septic tank. Do you think it could've been tampered with?

—Huh?

—Do you think it could've been tampered with? I say, raising my voice so he can hear me. He shakes his head.

—No, he shouts back. —I've been here before. I checked my records. Last time this tank was emptied was over ten years ago. You really shouldn't be leaving it longer than three.

His eyes are steady. Not assessing me, that took only seconds. My body, to him, is something quantifiable. Translated to a

113

number, or a few short words in his mind. *Tiny tits* or *scrawny legs* or *bit of a beer gut, for a skinny girl.*

—I'll tell my grandma, I say.

—Huh?

—I'll tell my grandma.

The mention of her tightens my throat like a cord wrapped around my windpipe and I'm not sure if I'll get the next question out.

—Can you bill it to her? I say.

—Same address? he asks. —In Levin?

—Same one, I say. Then I realise I'm wrong. Neither of us moves straight away. I want to shut the door, but I don't know if I can reach it.

+

It's been a few weeks since I last saw my grandma, at Christmas. I try to remember if she slept late, or had a limp, or swelling joints. If her breathing was rougher, sandpaper stuck in her throat. But I can't. It was the same as always. A table covered in Bakewell tarts and gingernuts and raisin scones when we arrived, all from a packet. White-bread tarragon chicken sandwiches, pre-cut into triangles. She was shocked, or pretended to be, each time I told her no, chicken was actually meat, and no, vegetarians didn't eat it. She never touched the food herself, just sat there and watched us, slipping something else onto our plates where she could. She couldn't see the grease and leftover food when she washed dishes anymore. It was a roulette, whether crockery was clean or not.

And so we sat there and drank tea from unwashed cups and dunked our gingernuts.

—You're getting taller, she said, like every time I came.

114

I stopped growing at thirteen.

+

I read once, in the *Sunday Star Times*, that paracetamol numbs your feelings as well as your pain. So I take them, four at a time.

+

Early on, during winter, it seemed as if Ilana and I might go somewhere. We would meet when she finished work and stay up until dawn was there, at the window. Or I would go around after a shift at Dida's and we'd nap together. The afternoons were bright, but her room was dim with the blinds drawn.

+

I don't get to sleep tonight. I stay up listening to the cockroaches. If you slow yourself right down, you can hear the scrape of their legs, like fingernails on wood.

And you can see in the dark, too. There are many kinds of dark, not all of them thick. The darkest darks are in the corners and on the floor. The other darks just hover, fracturing into colour the longer you stare.

The colour I see most is red. I want to pull it together, but it's spreading, like gloss on lips, rolling, like the ocean floor, like this bedroom floor.

I can picture them. Asleep, or maybe falling that way, lids beginning to flicker. Finding each other beneath the sheets. Finding each other's softness. Ilana's downy legs, friction against Ashi's smooth ones. A head near a neck. A hand near a stomach.

Something still awake, or waking.

I turn onto my front, palm against my clit, and come, silently. Nothing like how I fake it.

+

By the time spring came, things weren't the same. I saw Ilana less and less. On weekends especially, as though I wasn't worth them anymore. I'd get a Tuesday, often, and a Thursday if I was lucky. But when I'd message her on the weekend, she'd say, *I'm tired*, or, *I'm working tonight*. No invite.

I knew she was sleeping with other people. I joined Tinder just to see if I could find her. It wasn't hard. The queer scene in Auckland is pretty small. Five minutes of swiping and the rose-coloured circles form around your face, throb outwards on the screen. *Finding people near you*. Then, *There is no one new in your area*.

Ilana's profile said, *Let's get fish and chips and talk shit about colonial capitalism*.

She only had three photos. One of her in Glen Innes, protesting the removal of a state home. She was smoking on the road in front of a line of cops, the street lamps burning holes into the night. Another, at a party, black mesh top cupping naked breasts, a since-removed nipple ring winking through. The last one was taken in the lounge of her Westmere flat, her hair curling like smoke into her eyes. Sat on their mouldy corduroy couch, drinking a VB, turning away from the person next to her. That person, that half-cropped sullen mess, was me.

+

I think being at the bottom of the ocean was a kind of test: in getting out, in wanting to get out. Like when I'm in bed, and it's morning, and nowhere else offers so much comfort, and so much darkness.

+

That time before people wake, when their consciousness has not yet dropped back into their bodies and all that's there is a shadow of themselves, a placeholder, that's when I get up. I never fell asleep, and in a way, it feels like I never woke either.

My vision is fuzzy around the edges, I can't make out the details. They're in bed together, lying close, but clothed. I sit on the edge and rock Ilana's shoulder till she comes to.

—I need you, I say, —I need you to drive me to Levin. Soon, tomorrow. My grandma's sick, she's always been sick, but she might be dying this time.

She doesn't say anything, but nods, groggy. And then she reaches out and squeezes my hand.

X

The waves come in and they stay there. I've never seen the water this high. It's starting to touch the rock wall by the graveyard, licking about the crevices. This beach, usually such a flat expanse, is squeezed to a strip of sand a metre wide. The wood hut the kids made has fallen down. A few branches are still standing, not ready to surrender. Logs, once sun-bleached, are now damp grey with sleet and rogue waves. Occasionally, one laps right up and swallows my feet. I trip over a branch when the water swallows it, too. A whole leg of my jeans wet. The rain will even that up.

I know I should feel cold, but I feel numb instead. The wind chime is whistling in urgent, staccato beats. The storm's own Morse code. Most of the sewage has slunk back down the grate, but where it spread, it's hardened, turned the grass blades black. Period blood a metallic coating on the smell of shit.

Ashi's blood. Mine still hasn't come.

+

—I made pancakes, Ashi says, when I enter the room. Then, a second later, —Jesus, you're drenched.

She drapes a towel around my shoulders and keeps one hand there.

—Have a shower then go back to bed, I can bring breakfast in.

—I'm not hungry, I say.

Food is the only way some people know how to fix things.

—I'm sorry, she says, —about your grandma. Ilana told me.

—What'd you get up to last night? I say.

—Watched that documentary until we basically carked it. What about you?

—Read.

She looks across at *Māori Boy*, left out on the bench overnight, the position of the bookmark unchanged.

—I'm not coming to Levin, she says.

—Oh.

Don't desert me, please don't.

—Ilana's definitely going to take you, so don't worry. It's probably best if you two get some time alone anyway.

I feel sick, imagining the talk they shared, facing each other on the pillow: *I can tell her. No, no, I will, I should.*

—How are you getting home?

—Lachlan, one of the guys I've been seeing. I told you about him? The one from my placement up north.

I vaguely recall hearing about a Ben studying law, but that's it.

—Yeah, I say, —I remember. He's coming to pick you up?

—Yup, she says, taking her hair tie out, unwinding a thick mass of strands.

—All the way from Auckland?

—Yeah.

—He must really like you.

She laughs. —He does.

Coiling her hair back up, a mere reflex, she says, —Are you sure it's a no to the pancakes?

+

I keep thinking about the last words I said to Grandma. A week before, Lloyd had announced he would fly her to the Gold Coast for Christmas. They never spend Christmas with her. Grandma spends Christmas with us, or Francine's family, or, occasionally, both.

She didn't go, of course. We were already at her house. But she pretended she was really considering it. On the phone to him, she said, —Oh Lloyd, if only the timing was right.

And, —If only they worked as hard as you, Lloyd, if only they could afford to come over, too.

Helen told me to ignore it. She said, —You know she's like this. You have to remember, he's her son. Her one living son.

Then, on Christmas Eve, Grandma came home from the supermarket. Scotch eggs and pork pies and corned beef and Sara Lee sticky date puddings. We do the cooking on Christmas. She knows that. We'd been planning it for weeks, even drove to Wellington for the ingredients you can't get in Levin (labneh, pickled walnuts, real balsamic vinegar, figs). There's always too much food as it is, each of us competing to take the smallest plate. Now it was overwhelming.

At breakfast, Grandma microwaved her Scotch eggs in place of Helen's freshly fried blinis. She kept trying to force the soggy grey balls on her. —Oh go on, Helen, she said, —I bought them especially for you.

At lunch, she ate a pork pie instead of my chargrilled squash with walnut salsa. What angered me most was the thought of all the leftovers, how much I would have to eat so that nothing went off, nothing was wasted. I scratched so hard with the butter knife that it left ridges on her fancy china, the stuff we always had to convince her to use, saying, *if not Christmas, then when?*

She can't see dried-on cake, or caked-on sauce, but that scratching she could see.

—Careful!

I threw the cutlery down and it bounced off my plate in her direction.

She just turned to me, calmly, and said, —If I was at Lloyd's, I wouldn't be forced into a vegetarian Christmas.

That's when they came out. Slow, open-mouthed words so she'd catch every one.

—Having bone cancer isn't an excuse to be a cunt.

I booked my bus ride home online. It didn't leave for three hours, but I took my bags and sat at the terminal, by the Farmers car park. No one walked past alone. Only raucous family groups, laughing or arguing or both as they tore along the footpath.

—Who are you going to see? an old woman asked me, her grandson beside her.

+

I can barely feel the water. That happens, when you've been soaked for too long. It's the first shower I've had in days.

Ashi comes in when I'm still in my bra and takes her T-shirt off. In the mirror, she dabs foundation over her vitiligo, carefully lifting each strap to get underneath. I watch countries sink into oceans.

121

+

I see now that the photo wall is much whiter. As if the cream paint, visible between frames, has somehow blended with skin, bleached it, as if the curtains were kept forever open. Every friend, every acquaintance in each photo chosen, is Pākehā.

+

When Grandad Wayne was alive, he went to events at the marae. He knew most people's names. He coached the boys' rugby in Gisborne, and brought the poorest back to Cambridge Terrace for dinner. Helen tells stories about Grandma seeing them come in, and just dropping her paring knife and walking out. Potatoes left boiling. He would take over.

—Nothing fancy, Helen said. —Mince he'd brought from work. Lumpy mash.

There weren't ever any leftovers. When he died, an offer was made to take his body back to Kaitī, for a service at the marae. But Grandma held him in Levin, held him in her very bed. Then she had a funeral in a church.

Helen said the person who was farewelled that day was not her father. The priest spoke of a man whose faith had kept him going.

He'd never believed in God. And he didn't keep going.

+

Helen is here at every corner with me. She's in every wall and every window of this place, like a layer of thickening skin, not always visible, but always felt.

Then again, I guess I carry her wherever I go.

I keep going back to what Ashi said. *That's her stepmum.*

The one who I met when me and Ilana went round to pick up drawers for her new flat. Her parents weren't home so we fucked on their couch until they appeared, Farro Fresh bags in hand. Shock, or maybe disgust, in their tensed jawlines. So desperate not to drop either.

That's her stepmum.

Ilana staggers out at what I imagine is midday—it's hard to tell without the sun. I feel as if a table has been moved in a room I know well, or the order of aisles swapped in my local supermarket. Something so familiar, suddenly not.

She makes mee goreng. The pancakes were going cold so Ashi ate the lot.

—Want any? she asks, as she pulls the shiny packets from the cupboard.

—You should really have something, eh, Ashi says. She's picked up Ilana's *eh*s. —When was the last time you ate?

Trapped, I say *alright*, though nothing in me wants to eat. I struggle over the bowl. The noodles are slimy in my mouth and swallowing takes effort. I wish I was like my grandma, so comfortable saying no.

+

Nick always bought the wrong two-minute noodles. The ones I couldn't eat, chicken or beef or BBQ. I kept the seasoning sachets. I thought, I can do something with these.

I was in honours at the time and it started a pattern in my practice. Things to do with our relationship. I put every Christmas and birthday card he'd given me on display in studio. I tried to make stacks of the sugar pills I never took. They all fell over, and I preferred it anyway. I brought in our mandarin and feijoa peels. I put them in two different piles, his and mine. I thought it was my masterpiece. I called the work *Us*.

+

—I'd never write about someone I was fucking, Ilana announces, —not at the time.

—You never write, I say. Full stop. But I don't say those two words. They become like all the others that couldn't be said: condensing in a cloud above our heads, hanging there, ready to pour.

—You never write. Not much.

The *not much* was my mistake. Without it, it could've been a joke.

—Oh, and who's speaking? The hotshot artist?

She turns to face me, legs apart. A fighting pose.

—No, and I don't pretend to be.

The space between us is flexing like a muscle. I know what she wants to say. That if anyone was playing a part, it'd be me.

—I pretend to be a together person, I say, —instead.

Ashi laughs and the oxygen comes back into the room. The muscles relax. Ilana's lips hold together, briefly, then part. A slow, sticky smile.

You could map these moments, like mapping lines of attraction: put three magnets in a field.

+

Nick would pick me up from Elam and we'd drive back to his without saying anything.

—What is it? I remember asking once. Outside, Karangahape Road was bubbling: small eruptions of colour from people in second-hand outfits, smells from the Indian restaurants, their doors open to the footpath. I put the window down to let the sound in.

—Aren't you cold, he said. I'm still not sure if it was a question or a statement. I didn't respond. Then, he said, —You need to stop making art about me.

I wrote that on my studio wall in black Sharpie the next day.

+

The rain just gets heavier. It feels like summer has departed, and taken with it the lazy laughs, the smell of the ocean, the beers. We have only gin left. We have only bitter jokes and a whole lot of pasta. We've lost what we were feeling, what we felt. Now we have only carbon copies of friendship, pale impressions.

+

It wasn't long after that car ride when Nick and I broke up. By then, *Us* was just two blue heaps. I got in trouble for the words on the wall. *Making changes to university property without consent.* I had to paint over it. It took eight coats, the wall paint they gave us was so watered down. Someone stole my flavour sachets. The sugar pills dissolved in the humidity and started to attract ants. Everyone was pretty mad about that.

+

It's hard to enjoy the end of something. The dishes in the sink and the sand in the mats glare, incandescent. The leftover tomato sauce I saved has spilled and run. It's turned the fridge into a crime scene. The sheets need washing, the towels need washing, the grey linen tablecloth definitely needs washing. I wonder if those stains will even come out. There are many that won't. The salt patterns on the suede, the glasses we broke, the smell of weed, the smell of smoke.

—What's on? I say. It's midday, all the lights are off, but the buzzing persists, the whispering of volts through wire. —We've left something turned on.

But no one replies.

Outside, the garden is taking a battering. The agapanthus heads swing violently, threatening to fall right off.

Rain must kill sunflowers, because there's a house in Ponsonby where they tie plastic bags around them every time it pours. Ilana laughed so hard when I told her that they looked like they were in the height of auto-erotic asphyxiation.

I turn to her now and say, —Maybe we should put plastic bags over them.

Pointing at the quaking buds.

She just stares back, blank as a screen.

+

I kept Tinder. I went on a date, actually, in December. We got a drink at Peach Pit. She looked like an uglier, goth Scarlett Johansson and was very eager to know my star sign. We bused back to her place in Beach Haven but I couldn't go through with it. She wore an amethyst around her neck. —For protection, she said. It seemed like a bad sign when she took it off. I realised she'd fucked Ilana. They had all the same moves, scratching my back, biting my areola, holding me down by the wrists.

I Ubered home. I didn't think twice about spending my last twenty-eight dollars. It was too much to even sleep beside her.

+

Lachlan, who pulls up in a Saab, is like all the guys Ashi screws. Another King's boy, good-looking in a boring way.

—You have a type, I tell her.

I'm trying to make her smile, but she looks at me with uncertainty, her lips stretching then pursing, again and again.

—You know, I say, —tall and white.

I did it. She laughs.

—Yeah, she says, —I have a problem.

Lachlan comes and stands behind her, wrapping his arms around her chest. He leans forward, as if to rest his chin on top of her head, then leans back again. I want to tell him, —She's not your girlfriend. You're only a fuckbuddy.

—It's a beautiful place, he says. —Even in the rain.

I don't reply, just look out to sea. I imagine he calls Ashi that, too: beautiful.

She wriggles away from him.

—Hungry? she asks.

—So hungry, he says, sidling right back to her. He's like a three-year-old, always seeking a mum's hand.

She boils the penne. Water keeps frothing over onto the element. I could show her what Chris taught me as a kid: she'd rip a strip of paper from around the butter, scooping up yellow, and rub a ring around the top of the pot. Every time the water grew to it, it'd hiss back down again. An invisible barrier. But I don't bother. Lachlan keeps pivoting his shoulders to watch Ashi, as though if he doesn't she'll evaporate, become part of the steam and soak into the ceiling.

That was the way Ashi's flings worked: they loved her, and she liked them for it. She seemed to fall into most of them without meaning to. She'd ring me up one day and say, *He bought me a necklace*, or, *He sent a hundred Belinda roses to my front door*. She never had the heart to tell them she didn't like pink.

—I bought wine, he says. —I put it in the freezer.

He doesn't actually ask if we want any, just pours four glasses, making his and Ashi's the largest. She gives him a kiss, Ilana says cheers but doesn't clink his glass. I don't say a thing then drink it anyway.

We are reflections on the laptop screen. I can see each of us, silhouetted. To all fit on one couch, Ashi sits on Lachlan's lap. His arms are looped low around her waist. It's difficult to look and it's difficult to not.

I am sandwiched between them and Ilana. Ashi's shins knock into mine every time Lachlan adjusts his position. They murmur things but I miss them. Too fast, too low. I hear Ashi whisper stop, but in a giggly way.

Ilana offers her pack to them. They both say no. I realise Ashi hasn't lit up since he's arrived. And Ilana keeps tapping her cigarette out in only the direction of the ashtray. The powdery remains crumple, flatten, start to sink into the carpet.

If I was going to paint her, I'd collect this ash. I'd mix it in with the undercoats, with the highlights. I'd mix it in to make the colour of the bruises on her legs and the shadow below her eyes, I'd mix it into the dead part of her smile.

+

In the last few months before my honours hand-in, I returned to painting: Nick's face, again and again. A thick layer first, which I let ooze down the canvas. Then I hacked away with my palette knives until I had the bones of him. I tried to use the mould from *Us* (the mould which was *Us*) to give his skin a blue tone. It just crumbled and clotted the paint. It was like flesh rotting away. Cadaverous. Some parts did fall off. In the places where I used too much linseed oil, his skin stayed waxy as a teenager's.

Cracks appeared as they dried. I completely forgot about the fat-over-lean rule. I decided to leave the series untitled.

+

I study the way Lachlan looks at Ashi, as if she's the only light source in this room, as if everything radiates from her and reflects back in, as if there'd be no point ever looking away. No one's looked at me like that.

When Nick said he preferred me to Ashi, his exact words were, —You're skinnier.

+

Every time you remember something you're only remembering the last time you thought of it.

+

My honours-year paintings were always a little off, dispropor-tioned. Like a bad attempt at taxidermy, they preserved something, but not the right thing. My versions of Nick were part him, part someone else entirely. Laurie said they were a great way to get revenge on an ex, but that was never my intention.

Over time, I came to recognise the faces in my paintings more and more. They were replacing the real thing.

Every time I conjured him, it was a bit twisted, a bit contorted. A hybrid of paint and person—I preferred not to picture it.

I got a B- for my paintings. Second Class Honours, Second Division. My internal marker wrote in my report: *Maybe you should try to make art about something more than a man. You used to be a feminist.*

I still don't know which tutor that was.

+

It's impossible to look away from him. Lachlan. That smug face, those smug hands, rubbing their mediocrity all over Ashi. It's as if he wants to mash it right into her, and take a little something back at the same time. They always want to take something away. She shouldn't let him. She should hold onto it all.

+

Everyone's had that time at high school when they thought they were in love with their best friend. Everyone's skipped the Year Thirteen afterball because it hurt too much. She might have dragged you onto the floor and danced with you, like she did in Year Twelve. Friendly, at first, then sexy. Pulling back, laughing.

—I think James enjoyed that.

Everyone knew James was her date.

I can hear them in the other room. Lachlan had trouble with the condom, then the angle was wrong, but now he's breathless and Ashi's moaning. Each minute he lets out another *fuck*. They're ascending in pitch. At one point they knock something over. It sounds like a vase from the bedside table, but there's no vase there. They only stop for a few seconds. Lachlan's *fuck*s are getting closer together and Ashi's moans, growing in response, keeping up with him. Faking it in straight sex is all about the timing.

+

Once I had a panic attack in the shower with Nick. We were having sex when he wanted to talk about the future. Our future. The water got hotter, the air became harder to breathe, as if all the particles had petrified into something concrete and they wouldn't fit inside my throat anymore. I knew I was about to faint. The room went black before I hit the tiles.

+

Ilana's mouth is a leech at my neck. Her lips bring everything to the surface. Tomorrow her hickeys will sit like pearls, if pearls were blue and pink.

She's undressing me. I can hardly see her, hardly feel it.

—I don't want to, I say. Push her off, roll over.

This is how it dilates. The space between us.

+

The only time Ashi and I kissed was New Year's Eve two years ago. I'd had a fight with Nick and she told me, *fuck him, come to this party instead*. It was in an apartment in Parnell. All of her med friends drank wine from bottles, not casks. None of them talked to me. She still made the rounds, doing her best with introductions. No one asked what I studied, but Ashi told them anyway.

She drank as much as I did, and I'm a nervous drinker.

Afterwards, she looked embarrassed, and called a taxi saying she had work in the morning.

I cried into my phone until Nick picked me up. I never told him what happened.

+

It seems like Ilana is asleep beside me, but she gets up and takes off without saying a thing.

—Ilana.

No response.

—Ilana.

I hear the back door shut. I still haven't managed to sleep. No sleep, in thirty hours. I don't mind it so much. I'll feel tired today, but tiredness is just your brain wanting to escape your body, or maybe your body wanting to escape your brain, and that I'm used to.

Ilana still hasn't come back, so I throw on a jumper. All your other senses heighten with the lights off. It's the same down at the beach. The static of the waves is louder, their smell more fermented. The rain is softer—it caresses my cheeks. Seaweed scratches and catches at my ankles, gets between my toes, frizzy bursts like hair. The heat has gone, as if the sky were a bath that's been drained.

It's seeped out some plughole, hidden, maybe behind the hills. The stars give off no glow.

She's almost impossible to see, a glitch in the darkness.

—Ilana!

Wading into water, headed to the island. She's on tapu land, I'm almost certain.

—Ilana!

I could leave her there, but part of me wants to see her, really see her. Touch her. To be sure it's real, this night, this woman, this strange walk out to sea.

She only stops when my hand is on her shoulder. We are up to our thighs. My eyes are adjusting. I can see her briefs are wet from the sloshing water. I can see the hairs at the back of her neck, running deep into their low V. I can see the tattoo on her ribs. The dagger glints.

—Ilana, I say, softly this time. She turns to face me. Even in the dark, I realise she's asleep. Her eyes are open, but there's nothing behind them. Just the emptiness of dreams.

Holding her arm, I dunk her under the next wave. She wakes up coughing.

+

We're in the aphotic zone, no light can reach us now. And I don't know how we're supposed to get back from here, back to the takeout we shared or her room last year, slits of sun cutting our bodies in two.

+

The showers ease off to a trickle. Sea and sky come gently into focus. The grainy blacks soften to grainy blues. I'm alone on the beach now—Ilana has gone to bed. In the distance, I see orcas, their fins slicing the horizon like butter. Bouncing up and down like rides on a carousel. But it's more sinister than that: they're in formation. They're hunting.

Here, they go mostly for stingrays. The orcas stop swimming and let themselves drop. Flip the rays over on the ocean floor, their odd mouths still smiling. But the orcas are after something different today. A whale, maybe, other dolphins. I imagine them chasing some of the last Māui dolphins, an invading force, an unwinnable battle.

+

Pita said friends don't call other friends Pākehā but it's all I identify as. Someone imaginary, someone who only resembles a person. A too-solid ghost, taking up too much room on land that will never be theirs. Or at least, shouldn't be.

I couldn't tell you exactly when he said that. The afternoons I spent with him are all blending into one, his slow litany of movements.

He would sit and stare at his cup as if considering what to do with it. Bring it to his mouth, pause, put it on the bench, pause, return to his seat and wonder where it'd gone.

—I can get it for you, I would say, already standing.

—Thanks, he would reply, still confused as to how it escaped his hands.

At other times he'd just leave the cup undrunk by his feet and stare at his palms instead, as if something was missing from them. He was like a gambler, feeling each minute loss. And like a gambler, he'd get up the next day and do it all again.

I find it hard to understand Helen when I call. It's not yet six, but I knew she wouldn't be sleeping either. Her voice is weak, as if air is too dense a thing for it to travel through, as if it keeps stopping short, just shy of the receiver. She's talking about things that happened a long time ago. She's talking about the times it rained over summer when she was in Whāngārā. She's talking about Stuart. Helen was here when he must've died. It was New Year's Day, the morning after a storm. She came to a point on the beach where the branches stood up in the sand. She says they were like kaumātua, encircling her. She made her wishes for the year. She forgot to wish that Stuart would get better. She didn't know he was already dead.

—You can't read into rain, I say.

+

The tide is finally heading back out. The land closer to the sea is marked by the water, as if the waves have fingers, clawing the sand while they retreat.

I stare at a shell before picking it up. It's light in my hand. Whatever's home it was left long ago. The sea has whittled its surface. It is smooth as a peach and the same colour. There are cracks at the base, missing flints—turned, or turning, to sand somewhere else, maybe somewhere far. I run my finger along the sharp of it, just to see if it will cut. I don't find any more shells.

+

Helen always likes to have something of this place with her. In her glove box, there's a stone, flat and pale, a perfect hole piercing one end. It was probably a weight used for fishing. She thinks it's pre-colonial, but I'm not so sure.

She remembers a time in the early eighties when a coin was found on this beach. A coin or a medal, her story changes. Sixteenth-century, a bust on one side, George III. Some said it was an artefact from Cook's first visit, but really, it could've come from any settler, at any time. A family heirloom, fallen out of a pocket. It was in the dunes, eroded by the wind.

+

Alfred, the vet who crossed the Atlantic, lost his wedding band while his wife was still alive. Maybe it was deliberate. Thrown overboard as the *Aurora* hugged the east coast. I imagine the ring settling into sand, not far from here. It might be there still, dissolving into the sea.

+

Ashi and Lachlan have left by the time I get back inside. It's not long past dawn, the first rays streaking the sky. They must have wanted to avoid me, avoid having to say anything. She's left a note on the table. *Wanted to get an early start. Wasn't sure where you'd gone.* Then, in a different pen, obviously an afterthought: *Thanks for the lovely trip xx.*

Without warning, I get a cramp that could be premenstrual, or could be hunger, or could be something else entirely.

For a moment, I see their car from above, from the treetops and the misplaced mist. I see it shooting like a torpedo, or torpedoing like a fish, a dolphin, into this country. Inland.

+

The morning Nick and I left here, I couldn't keep up on our walk. All along the beach were shells I had to pick up. Stripes of blues and greys radiating like irises. Haphazard stokes of red. Every one I found I showed him. He didn't say anything, just walked on, head facing forwards, as though he was a compass and it was north.

I felt his disapproval hot on the back of my neck when I scrambled under the seat for a plastic bag. He didn't want the sand to get on his upholstery.

—They smell, he said.

—I'll clean them when we get home. Anyway, I said, —I like the smell of salt.

Sometimes I felt as if we were two fishermen casting our nets. Often they tangled in the space between us, but they never really drew us closer.

The shells started to stink around Morrinsville. That's when I realised there were living things inside of them, drying up in the boot of the car.

—We're too far from the ocean, he said. —They're going to have to die.

Then he laughed. —You're such a bad vegetarian.

+

They've tidied her room and washed the dishes. The rest will fall on me. Maybe I could wake Ilana, ask for help, but then I wouldn't have something to be bitter about, later, strikes on an unseen scoreboard.

137

The towels and tablecloth go in the washing machine. Sheets seem like too much effort—we've been here under a week, who will know? The vacuum bag fills up with sand after a minute and I don't know where the extras are kept, so I just sweep and shake out the mats. I spray stain remover on the couches, but I don't wipe it off in time and it only makes them look worse. I put all the dishes back, even the ones we have chipped.

Ilana is terse when she rises. I know how she's feeling: like I've seen her naked. That sleepwalking, that was Ilana's naked.

I decide to be kind to her, sand down the edges.

—Hey, I say, —there's no rush. I'll make coffee and you have breakfast. I'm going for one last swim. There's no point leaving too early, the recycling drop-off won't be open.

I know full well that it is.

+

And I know full well that I shouldn't be here. I'm just another Pākehā in her holiday home, eating Vogel's and smoking over-priced indoor weed. I don't know what the hills are called. I couldn't tell you where the tapu land starts and ends.

I'm the rust on the roof of the marae, I'm the possum we didn't run over.

A ute drives past while I stand, waist deep, breakers collapsing around me out of exhaustion. It's a whole family, the kids on the trailer amongst the empty craypots, their legs dangling. They all stare at me. One waves.

Here, unlike in Auckland, unlike in Levin, my whiteness is not invisible, not invisibility. It's not the baseline, zero on the x-axis, zero on the y. Whāngārā is the first place I've ever felt it, how Pita and Ashi must feel all the time. It's like wearing another skin, one that isn't stuck on right. Or it's wearing nothing at all. This, this is my naked.

And I know it's time to go. Only decades too late.

xi

Gisborne, I am leaving you. Leaving your hills entangled, like mounds of flesh, bodies fully satiated. At their bases, branches burnt so pale they look like bones.

+

There are fewer caravans and flags and tents along the bays now. The water is fleeing these beaches, too. In places, the tide kisses the horizon.

—I saw orcas this morning, I say, smearing fingertips against my window, a vague point out to sea. —A whole pod of them.

Ilana snorts, head tipped back. —Are you sure it wasn't a wet dream?

—No, I say. —I didn't sleep at all. I was sitting under the wind chimes and I saw them.

—I don't believe you.

—Of course you don't.

—What's that supposed to mean?

She turns to look at me.

—I don't know, you're cut and dried, I guess.

—I've had a lot in my life that hasn't been so cut and dried. A lot of stories you wouldn't believe.

—Then tell me one.

—Like I said, you wouldn't believe them.

There's no point pushing her. She might give in, might tell me a story I don't quite believe. But that's because I know she lies.

Signage says this road is slippery when wet.

+

Tatapouri used to be a swamp of raupo and sedge grass. It came right up past where the car is now.

—There's pounamu buried there, I say. —From the Ngāpuhi raids.

Too tapu to reclaim.

Ilana's expression is flat, unchanged.

—Pita said, I say.

—Can you point out Mount Hikurangi? she asks.

No, I can't.

+

You're only supposed to wear pounamu if it's given to you. Nick didn't listen to that. He went into the Stone Studio on Stanley Road as we were leaving, where a Scottish couple made *New Zealand-themed gifts*: soft-toy sheep, Māori faces on place-mats, glass jandals, wall art, apparently. He bought himself a greenstone necklace carved into a matau, because he thought it was a dragon.

—It's not, I said. —It's a fish hook.

I didn't know the Māori word back then.

+

We enter Kaitī the same way we enter time, slipping back into the days of weeks, hours, minutes even. It is quarter past one on a Saturday. I want to beat the sun. It should be easy, the long days of January, its slow path across the sky. But I haven't left this late before.

+

I've never seen a photo of my great-grandad Conrad's butchery, but when we'd drive this road, Helen would point to a shop and say, —It was there.

There was always a different spot. Bernina or the Salvation Army or the bakery advertising *Chicken 'N' Chips*, enthusiastic thumbs up from a line-drawn rooster. And each time I'd been able to picture it. Glass windows, thighs dressed up on display. Behind them, headless carcasses hung like mistletoe, ribcage a perfect garland in the centre. *Order your Christmas hams now.* Out the back, strings and strings of sausages pumped from a hand-cranked meat grinder. And I can picture him, too, Conrad: white apron tied around the beginnings of a gut, maybe a bloody handprint. Discrete sips from a stainless flask. Sweeping the floors after closing.

He lost that shop. Conrad had been a generous man, especially while drunk. He paid for his neighbour's wedding on the back of a brandy promise. During the Depression he started giving away the bones, then the sinew, the trimmings, then the organs, the off-cuts and then the prime stuff itself. Wayne had to skip school to wait in the breadline.

+

The refuse centre takes us into the industrial heart of the town. There's a petrol station just for trucks. Huge tanks, the height of three-, four-storey buildings. A black Range Rover has the number plate P4IKEA. A place called Dagville Food Bar has its *Open* sign left outside, its doors closed. Scrap yards encased in chicken wire and concrete, the roadside barriers used on state highways. Ilana wants to get moving. She wants to pay to put both our rubbish bags in the tip. The man inside the booth is judging us, I can tell.

—I'll sort our recycling, I say.

There's something about throwing brown glass down on brown glass, green onto green, clear against clear: a contained, ordered kind of violence. The smash a second later. Gets right inside your eardrums.

It's why Ilana starts helping. Almost at the bottom—below the beer bottles, the shiny packaging skins from sausages, the aluminium cans, the soggy cardboard discs that slot between pizza bases, below even the empty cigarette cartons—is the fish. I must've put them in with the recycling instead of the rubbish.

—What's this?

Ilana pulls the bag out by my knot, hasty and doubled. She spins it around and around. Bathed in the translucent yellow plastic, the fish parts seem to grow together, into one monstrous ghost. The snapper head pokes forward, the way they swim through murky waters.

She unties the handles.

—What the fuck!

I could pretend I'm as confused as she is. But instead I say,
—They were on the lawn.

She looks at me as if I am rotting too, as if I have bones sticking out.

—And you didn't think to mention it?

—I thought I put it in the other bag.

—Why didn't you say?

—I don't know, I forgot about it, it didn't seem relevant.

But dead fish in a Pak'nSave bag are always relevant.

The eel will decompose, then the head of the snapper. The backbone will splinter over time, crushed under more rubbish. The tooth will remain, for a while, trapped.

The inside always decays first. Everything becomes a husk, a prison, empty plastic and pointless words, everything becomes that Pak'nSave bag.

—What are you going to do with it? she says, though it's still in her hands. I take it off her and round the back, where I pay for another landfill sticker. I hope the man doesn't notice what's inside.

Standing by the tip I can see the mounds where our bottles will end up. Three hills of glass, one brown, one green, one clear.

+

Then we're back amongst the real ones. They encircle vineyards, orchards, crispy tussock. Somewhere, a notice says: *We are cutting down trees to make room for more.* A totara lunges into the earth, having given up on the sun.

There are a thousand greens and a thousand yellows. Ones I've never seen before, never differentiated. But I know that if I take a photo, it will flatten back down to a handful, a Resene palette, the names on my tubes at home. The names of some that went in the bin.

+

I was fine with my Honours mark. What does it matter really? At least it was a pass. But I didn't tell Helen about the B- for weeks. Just pretended our grades hadn't come. It didn't make it any easier. I could have weighed the disappointment in her voice, heavy enough to shift scales.

+

Wairoa is a town of butter, bricks and animal hides. It was an early settlement—whaling station, garrison town—but there are no signs of that now, or none I can see. The houses we pass have been built in the last fifty years. They boast mown, flat expanses of lawn out front. I wonder if all the homes in Wairoa look like this, this kept, or whether it's just the main road. The ones with a view of the river.

I remember Helen saying that this land was alluvial. I was ten and didn't know what it meant, but pretended to. It's soil that's been shaped by the water it touches. Redeposited, loose, not yet turned to rock.

My great-great-great-grandfather Alfred moved here with his new wife in the mid-1860s. Members of the Pai Mārire religion had battled against kūpapa nearby. Te Kooti fought for the government, but was exiled to the Chatham Islands for supposedly firing blanks. Pai Mārire people had their land confiscated. It was sold back cheap to settlers.

145

Alfred never felt the need to build a church at Wairoa. They already had St Peter's. But he was a new Christian, a late convert from the sciences, and Helen told me, —He felt like a fraud around the Catholics.

He preferred to preach his own version of Anglicanism and Methodism, in farm houses and redoubts, at the whaling station, the dairy station, down at the pub. On the open fields where the Wairoa Rifles fired practice shots into the air. He said you didn't need to pray in a chapel when God was on your side. Maybe he believed it.

+

For the first seven years of my life, I saw my dad on Wednesdays. He told my pretty Year Three teacher that he was my uncle. I told him she was an atheist. Whenever he picked me up, he took me to a late service.

He'd shuffle me into St Patrick's Cathedral, on the corner of Federal Street and Wyndham. I found that place terrifying. The statue nailed to the wall above the altar was the only near-naked man I'd seen. I winced every time I looked at his hands and feet, phantom stabs pulsating through my own.

One Wednesday he just didn't turn up. The teachers talked in hushed tones and wouldn't look me in the eye. Secretly, I was happy. It meant I didn't have to go to church.

I don't often talk about this time – not because it's painful to me. Maybe it was, once, but whatever feeling I had has dissolved and I can't remember it. My dad is an echo that faded out years ago. No, I don't often talk about this time because people pity me. They don't get it, even when I tell them I have two mums. They don't get that two loving mums is all you really need.

Ilana tries to hold my hand outside of Raupunga—I'm not sure if it's intentional.

We cross the Mohaka River on a narrow bridge. There's a truck coming from the other direction and I'm worried we're going to scrape against it. If I was Ilana, I would wait on this side, but of course she doesn't. And of course we don't actually touch.

This must be one of the river's narrowest points. From here, it looks like just a crevice, a stream.

+

Ilana has a soft side—she keeps it well hidden. It's hard not to feel stirred, to feel somehow special, when she shows you a glimpse.

I met her in the Symonds Street Cemetery one day in October. She had work later so she was getting high. I told her how graves had been exhumed to make way for the spaghetti junction. They found more bodies than headstones.

—What did they do? she said.

—Buried them beneath memorials.

We looked for the memorials, but found wild strawberries instead, growing under the bridge. They were tiny and dark and glossy and very sweet in our mouths.

—Like you, Ilana said.

It was a little tongue-in-cheek: she was fishing for a kiss. But I liked it. I could still taste strawberry on her breath.

Everything around us was turning green: the trees were regaining their leaves and lime moss grew over the concrete. It swallowed some headstones entirely. Others shot out at odd angles, while cement barriers cracked and metal fences overturned. The earth below was moving.

And I was wondering what had nourished those strawberries, whether it could be bodies.

But Ilana was elsewhere. She'd seen, to our left, a word tagged in Sharpie: *CUNT,* on one of graves in the Catholic quarter. —Who would do that? she kept repeating. —Who would do that?

She bought Ajax and dishcloths from a dairy, and filled her bottle with water in the cemetery bathrooms. Then she sat there, scrubbing, until the letters washed away. It made her late for work.

+

There's always the point on a road trip when you think something's sparked, a wild fire. Smoke growing like mildew on the horizon. But it's always a foundry, a town centre you weren't expecting yet.

+

The Gull in Napier has a hot-food counter: wedges and crinkle-cut chips, drying out under lights and glass. Ilana buys a mince and cheese pie.

—Want some of the pastry? she asks, right hand holding out a soggy edge.

I shake my head.

—You know, she says, —there's really no way to ethically consume in this world.

Left hand on the petrol pump.

We've only seen the industrial part of the city. An airport, shipping containers next to cattle, double-headed street lamps. Factories in the distance.

I would go further in with Helen. Past the National Tobacco Company Building, now open for tours. Past the port where, in 1945, a German submarine docked long enough to milk cows. Get a coffee on Tennyson Street, drink it by the bronze statue of Pānia of the Reef. That wife, who departed for the sea each day, but returned each night. Who couldn't eat cooked food, though her husband tried to feed it to her. Who had to leave him, but not before she birthed a taniwha. Ten years ago the statue was stolen, but it was found a week later.

Then Helen and I would drive out again, past the palms and the arches, the domes and stripes and grids of windows, roses and raupo and grapevines. The Art Deco rebuild.

The 1931 earthquake killed 256 people. Buildings crumbled, flames spread. Four thousand hectares raised above sea level.

Shift that ground. Get below the surface and really shake it.

—You know your mum? I say. I look everywhere but at Ilana. An empty section, burnt grass, just beginning to grow again. There would've been a house there once. Now, all that stands is its chimney.

—Yeah, she says, slow, measured, a bit sarcastic, —I know my mum.

—The one who I met, yeah? That time we went to pick up those drawers.

—No, she says, —that's not her.

—What?

—That's not her. That's my stepmum. Gina.

Ilana isn't looking at me, either. Both hands on the steering wheel, arms stuck out straight, pushing her body right back into the polyester padding.

—Who's your mum then? I say.

—What do you mean who is she?

—What the fuck Ilana, you know what I mean. If that isn't your mum than where is she?

—Up north, Te Oneroa-a-Tōhē.

—Where?

—Ninety Mile Beach.

—Oh, I say. —Near Kaitaia?

The finger on the speedometer is twitching. Up to 120, back down to 110. Again and again.

—Yeah, just west of it. I grew up there, she says, —until I was twelve and my dad won custody.

I feel like ignoring her for the rest of the trip. Anger has taken over my entire body. The air around my face feels thick with it, as if it's leaking from my skin, sending spores that will breed, multiply.

I say, —You've never cared about me. Not even as a friend.

—God, what a line.

—So it's true then?

I wanted this to come out as a statement, a fact, but my voice breaks, inflects at the end, turns itself to a question.

—No, it's not.

Saying that is a struggle for her. She'd rather I was hurting. She's not trying to comfort me, she's trying to win the fight.

—But you lied to me, I say.

—I never lied.

—But you never tried to get close to me. You told Ashi things you didn't tell me.

—Ashi asked. You never asked. You're so goddamn self-absorbed you never ask anyone about anything. And now Ashi's gone and I'm stuck in this car with you, going to fucking Levin.

—So that's how it is.

—Yeah, that's how it is.

150

I can see one of her hands feeling for her pack, checking right pocket first, then left.

—I knew you were into her, I say. —You know she's straight, right?

—Jesus, can you try to hide your jealousy?

She slaps her thigh when she can't find her ciggies. —No, I don't want to fuck Ashi.

—Could've fooled me. What, is this the one time you've had a friendship with a girl? Not simply bedded her and moved on to the next?

—What's your problem? Seriously, tell me, what's your fucking problem?

Then she laughs. —Actually, don't. We'd be here for hours.

I wish we could leave the resentment, back there, on the road. But it's lodged in me, sitting in my chest like a dumbbell, squashing all my organs. It's going to solidify, become another knot in my back or lump in my breast, become the small pebble you feel rattling around inside your heart, but can never shake. You'd have to drill a hole, just below my collarbone, to get it out.

In heavy silence, we pass through Hastings, a city founded by men who called themselves the Twelve Apostles, harassing Māori into selling land. We pass through Bridge Pā and Pakipaki. Branches and chairs and rakes and toys lie in piles, bonfires not yet set. We pass Lake Poukawa, where all the bones were found. Palaeontologists trawled its waters from 1956, looking for remnants of things now extinct.

+

A bend in the road can hold a conversation.

I remember Chris and Helen fighting about the price of hiring a cleaner all the way along Tamaki Drive.

—I can't keep living in this filth.

Chris.

—You don't know what I do for you.

Helen. —You don't know the half of it. And you don't know the value of money. Go back to your Remuera parents. Go on, if you don't like my house so much. Go on.

I remember Chris telling me, months later, as she took me to my art lesson in Newmarket, that just because she didn't love Helen anymore, didn't mean she would ever stop loving me.

—I'm still your mum, she said, as we drove under the brand new perspex canopies of Grafton Bridge. A preventative measure, designed to keep the suicidal in, move them along.

I remember Helen, on the stretch that spirals up from Taihape, saying that this would be the year, this would be the year she'd lose the weight and find a different school and meet someone new. This would be the year. It was 2008. That year still hasn't come.

I remember Nick saying *I love you* right outside Mangatawhiri. I don't remember what I said back.

When Ilana speaks next, I feel her words etch themselves into the tarmac, a fault line laid bare.

—You can really talk, you know, about hiding things.

She could be speaking about anything. But she's not. She's speaking about one thing in particular.

—It wasn't me, she says, —who fucked someone else first, was it? You think I didn't notice? That night you just didn't reply? We were supposed to hang out. I waited for you for ages. I must've called you ten times. Because that morning, that same morning, you said I meant something to you. Do you remember that? It was all too much for you, eh, being honest with another person.

Every so often her hands make a dash for her jeans again, muscle memory, slower to learn than the brain.

—You didn't say a thing afterwards, either. Just acted like that talk never happened, like you never ignored me that whole night. You didn't even make up an excuse.

The needle is really flickering now, up to 130 at times.

—But that's when he started ringing you. Isn't it? You like to pretend that he fucked you up, made you so complex, so troubled.

Those last words are in a higher pitch, mocking.

—You probably did more damage to him than he ever did to you.

And she's right.

I broke up with Nick.

—Come in. Sit down. This is hard to say.

He cried right in front of me. He kept repeating, —Four years, four years now this.

He spent a very long time in the bathroom. By that point I was over it, wanted him gone. Or at least, I wanted him to revert to the guy I once knew, the one I couldn't have broken. I wanted to stop him coming apart in front of me, sew his seams back together, double stitch the ends. No, that's not true: I wanted him to do that himself. When he finally returned to my bedroom, I said, —Who should be the first to change their relationship status? You can do it, if you like.

My parting gift. He left soon after.

When I next went to the toilet, I saw the ring that I gave him, the ring with the cross, resting on its porcelain floor. A kind of coin, a kind of wishing well. He must have been trying to flush it.

I picked it out, rinsed it off. There's no point wasting a ring. I gave it to Ilana, actually, but she never wears it.

She's right about me fucking him, too.

It was nearly five months ago. Ilana had work until eleven. I still planned on seeing her after, but I couldn't bring myself to.

That's another lie. I just lost track of time.

I think I was curious. Curious to see how much he was still hurting. Curious to see if he still wore that jacket I gave him, the navy one with the clips (he did), to see if he still had the photo of us at Levin as his iPhone background (he didn't). Curious to know if he was seeing Rhiannon again (he wasn't, but he had, briefly). That's what the whole night felt like. Bystanding, spectating—I wasn't really there. I was watching it play out, from a distance, from behind a glass screen.

He picked me up at seven and kept checking where my hands were, if one was close enough to hold. I had to keep my arms folded to stop him from trying. He took me to dinner at Satya, even ordered the butter tofu so we could share. I let him pay for the both of us. He wanted to get ice cream in Mission Bay, but the line at Mövenpick was out the door and I said, —Let's not bother.

We parked up beside Kelly Tarlton's Sea Life Aquarium and had sex on the backseat of his Lexus. He let me put my finger in his arse and he let himself enjoy it. I didn't bother to fake an orgasm. I didn't really make a sound. He kept brushing his hand against the hickeys on my neck and chest and breasts, as if that would make them go away.

+

Ilana winds down the windows, back and front, all at once.

—We need to stop breathing the same air, over and over again.

I always liked the wind in her voice.

+

Helen first saw Ilana through the window, standing at our gate, texting me to come outside. All she said was, —Her eyebrows are drawn on too strong.

—Yeah, I said.

The next day she asked, —Are you going to tell her?

—About what? I said.

She picked at the dirt under her fingernails, but it didn't make a difference.

—Her eyebrows.

—Oh, I said, —no. No, I won't tell her about that.

+

I lost my mutual friends with Nick. They all said they didn't want to take sides. They all chose him anyway. No one called because I was the one who didn't feel enough, who didn't feel with every bit of herself, who didn't know how to put aside her own feelings. No one called because I was the reminder that things fall apart and they stay that way.

+

After ten years of heated words and small crescendos, of the occasional keyed car and flying plate, Helen and Chris broke up quietly. It was summer and all the windows were open. I remember the buzzing of the flies. Helen steadied her voice as she said, —This isn't working for either of us.

I sat straight and stiff on the hallway floor, trying to be silent. Chris left that night. She moved back in with her parents for a time. I don't know if she was surprised to be single again, or just surprised that Helen was the one to do it.

+

There's a cross at the side of the road, fresh and white like a picket fence in Ponsonby. A teddy bear lies at its base. I avert my eyes. It's like seeing something you shouldn't, a drug deal in an alley, people fucking in a car park.

—I knew a farmer who lived around here, Ilana says. —About twenty minutes that way.

She doesn't point but swings her head a little to the right. Her neck cracks and I flinch. —I stayed with him for a few weeks. When mum was fucking him.

—How old were you?

—About eight. He had this pregnant cow. It was his favourite. The birth was a difficult one so he helped her out. Reached up and grabbed the calf's back legs. They broke off in his hands.

—What?

—Maggots, she said, —they were everywhere. The calf must've been dead for a while. They had eaten right through it and were probably starting on her womb. So he took her round back and he shot his favourite cow.

And then it returns, the sound, a ringing so insistent, so deep inside my head, that I swear it could make me deaf.

—Stop the car.

—What?

—Pull over.

I throw up and it tastes like this morning's coffee. Grass floats on the river I've created, dark and narrow, running down into a ditch. My whole spine aches from bending over.

156

—Maybe you *are* pregnant, she says.

+

When I would tell Nick I was sore, he would always ask why. He forgot about my arthritis. I forget too, sometimes. The pain fades into the background, a white noise. And then it'll hit me, like now, a jab, a stab, a reminder my body is not my own, not entirely.

+

My phone rings four times but I pick up once. It's Helen calling to say she remembers the fire, the one we walked over. It was Chris' brother's birthday, up north. Ashi came too. —And you're right, she says, —it didn't hurt at all.

XII

There are fences everywhere, but no houses. Hay is packaged like shiny green marshmallows. The land is flat here. In places the grass looks ripped, soft yellow clay like flesh poking through. Arrows on the *Fire Danger Today* signs have been rising. The latest was at *Very High*.

Both our phones are dead. The radio dial is old and sticky. We keep searching, but we only find static. Around the eighty-nine FM mark, Ilana lucks out.

—This is shit, I say. —We'd be better with silence.

—This is the Doobie Brothers, she says, turning it up.

—You know this?

I wasn't aware Ilana listened to anything recorded before the nineties.

She sings a line. The car shudders.

—What was that?

She doesn't respond.

—I think you hit a dog.

—I didn't hit a dog.

—Then what was that?

—Look behind us, I didn't hit a dog.

I don't turn around in case I'm correct, or maybe, in case I'm not. The one-way bridges keep coming and Ilana keeps hurtling towards them. *We have right of way*, she'd say, if I complained.

—It's overheating.

She's pointing at the gauge on her dashboard.

—Turn the heater on, I say, —it takes the hot air from the engine.

Summer days with Nick, heat blown out of fans like heavy breath on sweaty necks, quickened pulses, raised voices.

There's a rattling sound seeping through the gospel-style vocals. It gets in between the notes of the keyboard and shakes the very bassline.

—Bad reception, Ilana says.

—Your car, I say, turning the music off.

—Fuck!

There's a smell now, too. Something burning.

—Fuck!

—You can't pull over here, I say. —It's not safe.

It's a straight stretch, open road, but it's slim, just two cars wide.

—We have to, she says and eases halfway off. We're at a strange point, between gravel and ditch. I imagine the middle of the car balancing, swaying with our respective weights.

Ilana puts her hazards on. The oil light is glowing red and the battery light will be too, soon. She pops the bonnet and stares into the engine.

—Oil's fine, she says, checking the dipstick.

We sit for half an hour, watching cars pass from both directions.

—Fuck this, she says.

She gets out and stands on the road. A Chrysler slows.

—Know anything about cars? Ilana asks.

The woman says no but they park up anyway, then both approach. A husband and wife, older. Ilana has hopped back into the driver' seat to try, in desperation, to turn on her phone. The man leans through her window, naming all the lights on the dashboard.

—Oil, petrol, that there, that one's always on on ours, no idea what that one means.

—Have you girls got someone you can call?

That's his wife. She has dyed-blonde hair and eyeliner drawn on like worms that refuse to get too close to her eyes.

—No, I say.

—No one in Waipak', no one in Hastings?

—No, I say.

—No one in Dannevirke?

—No, no one. The closest is my grandma, but she's in hospital in Levin.

—Where are you from?

—Up north.

—Where up north?

—Auckland.

An exchange of glances. I can tell Ilana's annoyed I gave it up so easily.

—Where's the nearest petrol station? I ask.

—You'd need to go all the way to the Mobil in Waipak', I reckon. Or else back to Hastings.

She stands over the engine a second before saying, —You can really smell it.

—You can, he agrees.

—And it's getting darker, she says.

—It is, I say, but I don't see it yet.

—Can I use your phone to ring AA? Ilana asks. —My dad has a membership.

—AA wouldn't come out at this time, the woman replies, but passes her cell anyway. I make the call. Ilana's swearing too much.

—They won't answer, not on a Saturday, she continues, as a man picks up. I babble without breath and he asks me for the name or number of the cardholder. Ilana whispers *Simon Hall*, and I pass it on.

—But I thought you said your friend, your girl friend?

He puts a pause there, a pause I hadn't quite managed.

—It's her dad, I say. —It's his car, I lie.

—We cover the member, not the car.

Hang up.

—Who do we know? the woman asks her husband. —Who do we know?

—I don't know.

—There's Sally and Roger, but they're up past the 'kino pub.

—Stan.

—Oh yes, Stan, Stan in Waipawa! You girls can pull in there and at least it's a place to park. He might give it a look, too.

We plan to tail the couple to their friend's garage, but the Nissan doesn't start. We have to flash our lights and honk until they stop, a reluctant U-turn.

—I know, the woman says, —I know who we can ring.

She tells us this guy has a tow truck. Would we like to be towed? she asks. I want to check my bank account, but Ilana simply says yes. Then to me, —I'll cover it.

The woman laughs hard into her phone.

—He's just getting out of the shower.

161

We wait a very long time for the truck. The couple sit in their car and we sit in ours. After ten minutes I hear them arguing in hushed tones. The only phrase I catch is *an eternity*, then she thinks to close her door.

When the man arrives, smelling of soap, he's with his daughter. I'm staring up into the truck and he's saying, —No, I'm registered with the police, you see? Levin's outside my jurisdiction. I can't tow you there. I just can't.

—We have nowhere to sleep, I say. —I have a dog.

—I'm not allowed outside of the zone. That's out of the zone, you see?

—We'll be sleeping in a car, I say.

I drag myself back to the Nissan. He follows.

—I can take you to a campsite at Waipawa. I can take your car to Stan's shop, he'll look at it tomorrow I reckon. Too late today, you see? Nearly four. I don't think a shop would stay open after four.

—It's a relief, the wife says, —it's dangerous around here, a lot of Islanders. They come for the fruit picking. Seasonal workers. Funny types, she says. —Not good to be young girls in a car around here.

The tow man's daughter is Pasifika. I hope her window isn't down. Ilana puts hers up out of disgust, then has to lower it again so he can reach in and steer, as we're hoisted onto his truck. Planks of wood and yanked chains, the windscreen pulled towards flashing lights. Gravity tugging at my gut.

The breeze is colder, swifter, up here. We fling our arms out, hands like dolphins in the wind. Everything you feel in a car, you feel tenfold on the back of a tow truck. We wobble over all the stones and vibrate across the cracks. On a train track, Ilana grabs my palm.

The tow man, his hair still wet and straggly, has a shocked look when we arrive and he sees us holding hands. But he kills it fast, and besides, I don't mind. It's something to tell Ilana about later. It's something to laugh about, later.

His daughter has called ahead and a groundskeeper is standing outside to greet us. He gives us a pet-friendly self-contained unit for a discount.

It only occurs to me afterwards that we never got their names, any of them.

+

Laurie had an exhibition opening in October. She'd made a video work that kept playing on a loop, this blurry recording of a Kim Kardashian fan crying after getting her autograph. Laurie edited it to start and end mid-sentence, with a few seconds of dead air in between. It was showing at Rockies, that hole-in-the-wall gallery where you can't actually go inside, so it was almost inaudible. — Do you get it? she asked me. —That it's about the internet glitch? That's why there's no title or abstract. I wanted to perform the loss of information. Did that all come across?

—Yes, I lied, —it's great.

Then she went and asked the next person.

Pita turned up like a hologram from his apartment. He had on the same black trackpants and crew-neck sweatshirt. I felt as if, at any minute, his armchair would materialise behind him. —I don't get it, e kare, he whispered. —You guys are too smart for me.

And we stood there together, getting cold, wondering when it would be polite to leave.

Afterwards, we got coffee at Revel. His eyes were inverted commas, opening and closing each time he talked.

163

When I asked him how he was, he lowered his head so far I thought his nose might dunk into his coffee. He hadn't touched it yet at all. —Ah, kua tatere tōku wairua, he said. —My wairua, it's been unsettled, like this.

His hand weaved rollercoasters in the air.

+

Wai means water, but I don't know what pawa means. Stan is talking about a drive belt and words that end in shaft, the cost of a new engine. *How much would that be?* It's just gone five o'clock. The car is where the tow truck left it an hour ago, he hasn't even looked inside. He's after the body. They're piled all around us: Corollas, Volvos, Rav4s. Car doors hang from rusty beams like fish in a market. There are shelves and shelves of headlamps. A caged German shepherd. In a metal barrel, something smokes.

—Hear that sound? Stan says, keys in the ignition. —Your engine won't start up. Without that belt, you've buggered it. It's burnt to smithers.

I imagine the drive belt as something soft and rubbery. Easy for a person to slice, or a possum to gnaw. *Could we have driven without it this whole way?* I want to ask. But Ilana says, —Are you even a mechanic?

—I'm the closest you'll get to one round here. Could get it towed to Waipak', but that'll cost you. And no one's going to do it tonight.

I help her roll it to the side of the road. She sits in the driver's seat with her eyes out the window and her bottom lip in her front teeth.

—I'm going to walk Bo, I say. —I'll be back.

An unclenching of knuckles, small salute across the steering wheel, her version of *fine*.

+

I pass Bowls Waipawa and Waipawa Lawn Tennis Club. *Private Courts*, they say, *Saturday Twilight Games*. Four people flash white like the bits of surf where two currents meet. Here, then there.

Fifties houses with blue roofs, tyres stacked on lawns. Dogs bark from almost every one, not separately, but in unison. A lamb bleats each time they start. I tilt my head to see, but can't. It must be round the back.

I was eight when the house behind Grandma's got a lamb. Her yard and their front lawn were separated by a small concrete barrier which I had only to sit down on, wriggle my bum across, and my feet would touch their grass. I visited her each day, tied up under the cherry blossom. It was January and the weather was clear. Her voice came out high and thin, more like a cat's at first. I could chase her round the tree until her rope was all wound up, and sometimes, I could get her to chase me back.

Helen told me off, said the neighbours had complained I was stamping on their poppies. After that I'd sit on the ledge and dangle my legs and the lamb would strain to me on her rope.

When I came back in April she still remembered me. Same in July, though that was a wet winter and I went outside less. I'd see her, through the window, cowering and sodden beneath bare branches. In October, she was herself again, just bigger, fluffier, with a louder bleat. It'd find me: in bed, in the kitchen. In December, it found me in Chris' car at the head of the driveway, arriving. The sound of gravel, a gravelly sound. Then, on the twenty-fifth, she

165

was gone. They'd kept her a year to make Christmas lunch. Fresh meat and fear: I smelt them both that day. Then I went inside and sat down to our roast.

These are memories, curling at the edges.

+

I follow an alleyway to the main road. From the top of its stairs I gain a view of a burnt-out shed, a shipping container with blue graffiti, a wood mill, planks lying processed, pink to grey. I can see where paint stops short on a fence, disused buses in an empty lot. One building, its walls corrugated, its door huge and rolling, has no windows. Skip the train tracks, yellow sign telling me to *Look Out*. Skip all of that and I can see the smoke cloud forming just above my head.

+

Conrad, my great-grandfather, was seventeen when he was shipped to Gallipoli. He lied about his age for the chance to light his first cigarette and see another country. But mostly, he lied because he'd been taught to believe in war.

+

Up a road and I'm at a clock tower, white and stark, flanked by a Canary Island palm and a Hollywood juniper. Empty flagpoles spear the space in front of a low white lectern. A World War II plaque, Roll of Honour. It carries a wreath, a benign quote, a list of Pākehā-sounding names.

The tower is for World War I. There's a mention of the sons of the Empire, a mention of sacrifice, of memory. There's a mention of God, King and Country. Below that, something peculiar.

Follow after. Follow after. For the harvest is sown.

Poppies grow in a concrete circle, silverbeet in another.

+

Te Kooti led the Chatham Islands prisoners in an escape on a boat called the *Rifleman*, all the way to Poverty Bay. There, they sacrificed a pig and a fowl, and they stopped kneeling to talk to god. From then on, he told them, they would raise their hands instead. That's where the name of their faith comes from. Ringatū. Ringa, hand, tū, to rise.

+

There was a time it snowed in Auckland. I was on Queen Street, standing at the lights. Every one slowed down when they crossed, palms to the sky, as if in prayer.

I couldn't feel it at all.

+

You can sense when you are a town's only strangers. A woman smiles at me because she thinks I am a tourist.

—We have a beautiful church, she says. —Just along that way. Don't waste your Sunday best.

She must mean Saturday. She must mean my viscose shirt, stuck to my back with sweat.

—Where's it from? she asks.

—Levin SaveMart, I say.

I don't know what she's more disappointed with, my accent or my answer.

+

Our Sunday best were the clothes we wore to open homes. For Helen, this was linen skirts and heeled sandals, back straps grating pink ankles. For Chris, tailored pants, merino skivvies. For me, it was anything that wasn't too small or covered in moth holes. I get attached to something the longer I've owned it. I made Helen add panels down the sides of my favourite dresses, thick hems to keep them reaching my knees.

She would hold off checking her lotto tickets until that afternoon, and we'd tiptoe around the villas of Herne Bay, Freemans Bay, Grey Lynn—placing imaginary furniture, deciding colours. Pretending we could buy them. We moved between rooms with beige carpet and vanilla-scented candles. Real-estate agents tailing as though we were going to steal something. I did, once: one earring, because I was too scared to take both. I didn't even have my ears pierced. I just liked the little purple beads, the way they were ordered from light to dark. My hand felt hot in my pocket all day. I kept thumbing the setting, cheap metal turning moist in my fingers.

I have the earring at home in a jewellery box. I couldn't bring myself to throw it out. If you want something so much you would steal for it, you should do your best to keep it.

+

Alfred and the whaler's daughter sprouted sons like weeds across their cheap Wairoa land. They had thirteen children, a different

168

whistle for each one. She was cruel to Leighton, my great-great-granddad, or so Helen says.

+

I know Helen would think Waipawa was a lucky place for a Powerdip. The winning tickets often come from these towns. People pay to dream, they pay for their hope. In places where there's less to begin with.

I meet Ilana at the only supermarket, a Write Price. She spends $27.48 on packet pasta and shiraz and I spend $9.60 on eight lines.

—Thanks, I say, —for paying for everything.

—I work full-time, she says. —It's fair this way, eh.

I lean in and kiss her, wine bottles clinking in their plastic bags.

+

That New Year's kiss with Ashi was soft and wet. Her lips felt elastic. Every time mine moved, they did too. But I couldn't stretch them far enough to slip in a tongue.

After she left, I looked around at the apartment—at the ankle boots by the door, at the pumpkin hummus on the kitchen island. At the girls in their black silk dresses, which had seen engineering steins and medical balls, once posed between the potted plants and the aging photographer, paid by the hour. The photos would be on Facebook, still. And Ashi would be in them. This was her real life. These were her real friends. She was always at the centre of my world, but I orbited hers.

+

169

The campsite unit has a microwave from the eighties that only runs for a minute, and only after you turn it off and on at the wall. We heat the Watties tortellini and declare it inedible. The three-cheese filling looks and tastes like processed meat, and the sauce is tomato paste, unevenly mixed with water.

Mist descends on the campground by ten, thick as smoke and just as grey. It makes the grass look damp, as if it rained, but neither of us heard a thing. Bo growls at the windows. I try to take him outside to pee. The first go, I get him down the steps, no further. He stands still, paralytic, for him. The second time he won't come out the door, even when I tug his collar. He simply stares and stares at the nearby trees.

I smoke my weed and Ilana smokes her Winnie Blues. We both drink red wine. I notice a spill on the table, but when I touch it, it's completely dry, not ours. Probably bought from Write Price too, but not the cheapest bottle of shiraz, $8.90, opposite the frozen peas.

When I see marks on the wooden floor in the bathroom, I feel jealous of this last woman here, whose period came on time, or even early, taken off guard in a new place.

I fail to sleep again—the wooden beams on the ceiling go on and on forever, like a runway I can't lift off from—and it's as we're leaving the next morning, packing our bags to carry back to the car, that I notice the red splotches on the lining of the curtains. I wonder, for a second, if we stayed in the wake of something violent.

+

I end up in the Settler's Museum while Ilana is waiting for the Waipukurau mechanic. I don't know why. There were photos outside—starched white Victorian families on glue-puckered paper. Bows in hair, lace at necks, even the baby's legs crossed at the ankles.

It's empty, no one at the counter. The lighting is artificial. Rooms are cubicled by glass walls. You can look but you can't touch. Some have rows and rows of old cameras, or leather shoes, or kitchen tins: Bell Tea, Edmonds Custard Powder, something called Rinso.

The smallest room has only a totara log in it, erect. Once a post in a nearby pā, maybe. Nothing else. *Display under Construction.*

I spot a framed health warning issued after the 1931 earthquake. *No cars allowed to leave Waipawa without a permit from the Mayor.* I Snapchat it to Ilana. She opens it, but doesn't reply.

Photos line a hallway. A girl's face in an oval frame, convex glass. A family on their front porch, names handwritten onto the sepia border. A child adorned in so many flowers she looks like a florist's display. Members of the First Borough Council, white beards or brown moustaches. A man standing, jacket pulled to one side, showing off a pocket watch. His seated wife looks somewhere off camera.

There's an ad for the Family History Centre in Waipakarau. *Find Your Ancestors*, it says. A pixelated photo from Google Image Search, lone mulberry in a field.

+

I was asked to draw a family tree in Year Five. The teacher told me off for putting Chris as my other parent.

—Who's your father? she insisted. —Your father goes there. Every child has a mother and a father.

—I don't, I said.

171

But I did what I was told. My schoolbook grew a lopsided tree. If it existed, it wouldn't have been able to stand.

+

Every time you remember something you're only remembering the last time you thought of it.

+

There's a faux Victorian dining room, bedroom and child's room.

Crocheted tablecloth, spindly wooden seats, metal teapots on a metal tray.

Hanging white nighties, powder on the dresser, pictures of roses in gilt gold frames.

Then a round knitted rug, an oversized trike, black-faced doll in a high-chair.

As if the older daughter has just set the dining room table, then wandered off to check on the lamb. As if her mother has been folding washing before she heard the baby cry, leaving some hanging over the cast iron frame of the bed. As if the kids are at school, but will be home soon.

As if they might return, all of them, go back to their chair, their linen, their meal. As if they might step back in any minute now.

+

When I was younger I imagined that if I died, my drawers would be picked over by a team of archivists.

I imagined them treating each box braid bracelet, each sketch

172

on scrap paper, each aerosol can of Impulse (*Sweet Smile*, *True Love*, *Temptation*) as if it was a fossil of an unknown dinosaur, or record of a lost language. I imagined them brushing dust off my pencils and taking photos of the moisture damage on my books. Numbering every single thing, categorising them again and again.

I could picture the exhibit. Objects in clear cabinets, a little description for each. *Pink-tint glasses, given at age four, outgrown at age eight, kept for the transparent floral pattern at the sides. Maybelline Fruity Jelly Lip Gloss in #04 Framboise/Raspberry. Opened but never applied—she liked the smell so much that she was scared of it running out. Coin purse in Japanese shippo pattern, three five-cent pieces within, dated 2001, 2003 and 1996, no longer legal tender. Metallic oil pastels, unused, but maintained in a specific colour order. Note: this is not the same order she bought them in. It is a better, more perfect order, with the green next to the gold, because of its proximity to yellow.*

But in reality, if I had died, it would've been Helen going through these things, and she would've simply cried.

+

An attendant materialises behind my shoulder, a long grey pony-tail and a face too close to mine. —What are you doing here? she says.

—Just looking, I say.

In the war room, there's a wall's worth of medals. Red and green felt behind. Mannequins in uniforms from World War II, World War I, earlier. Shadow box frames hold the photos of men who fought. Some are taken after the war, grave men in suits. Most are from before they left—they're smiling. Lists of operations, refill pages, dates and signatures. Metal binoculars and sketches of the Ruahine Ranges. A placard about the New Zealand Wars. *Te Kooti's exploits over twelve years caused much trouble and anxiety, not only to Hawke's Bay, but to the whole colony.*

There's a picture I can't look away from. Something too familiar about it. It looks like my grandad Wayne, though of course it can't be: it's much too old for that. The label says he was second in command during an offensive against Te Kooti, after the rangatira went into hiding. The man's jacket has red panels down the side, a sash cutting his chest diagonally. Medals studding him like they are stars and he is the night sky. A gaunt face.

Today is the day I take methotrexate—the nausea can't be helped. I almost throw up in the museum and have to run outside for fresh air. But that image stays with me. It's not one I forget easily.

Neither is the image of Ilana sagging against her car. She looks pale, small.

—Your water cap's popped off, the Waipukurau mechanic says. He's met us in Waipawa to assess the job.

—Look here, it's missing the bit in the centre. Now, I don't know what did that, it could've been broken already, or it could've been the heat. Which would mean something else made the water drain, it's completely dry. But I can't find a leak in your pump. I need to get the head off, have a proper look. How much smoke was there? If your engine got hot enough to melt the cap, the head could be warped. That's a big job. I'd have to send it away to be sanded.

His eyebrows are missing, and I can't tell if he was born that way or if he lost them, bent over some car like this. He keeps pointing into the engine with erratic blackened fingers. Ilana gets in, shuts the door, cuts him off. I follow.

—What are we gonna do? I say.

She shrugs. —I'll get my dad to pay for the repairs. He says it should only take a few days.

—But how are we going to get to Levin? We can't stay in Waipawa forever. I need to see my grandma.

Nothing.

I ring Helen, who calls Francine. She's been in Tokomaru looking at farms that are going organic. She says she can pick us up, borrow an enclosed trailer for the Nissan. She says she likes Waipawa. I don't know how.

Waipawa.

I look it up on my phone. *Pawa (noun) smoke.* The example given is about smoke being used to resuscitate someone who's drowned. It seems fitting. Waipawa. The kind of town you might visit just to put stones in your pocket, walk around for a few days and see how they feel, whether they excite you or make you sadder.

And I realise then that I never saw the river.

XIII

Francine arrives in a cotton shirt, rolled to the elbows, and caked gumboots. Her jeans have milk stains. There's a cross around her neck, but you'd only see it if you knew to look.

Her car smells sour, like something rancid. The backseat is hard and uneven. I can't get comfortable today. My joints feel like the knots in trees, trying to grow but growing malformed. I ask Ilana if we can swap seats. She looks annoyed but doesn't comment.

We pass a marae with a field of cars parked outside. We pass a graveyard with two ten-litre bottles of water placed on a chair beside its wire gates.

—Why would that be? I ask, but no one hears.

Francine is focussed on the window, the washed-out view, as if someone left it boiling too long on a stovetop. Overcooked.

—This is dry here, she says. —Bad topsoil.

+

After escaping the Chatham Islands, Te Kooti was in exile. Colonial forces took up a scorched earth policy against the Tūhoe people for hiding him. Three contingents closed in, from the north and the west and the south. They murdered and imprisoned, burned pā sites and crops, killed stock or ran it off. But Te Kooti got away.

+

—Look at that, Francine says, —the number of animals to that paddock. That's overgrazing for you.

—Look at the state of that fence.

Then, —This is prime farming land right here. For sheep, not dairy. Where we are is dairy country, much damper. But they can do what they want here now. With those big irrigators. Look, cattle there. Would've been unheard of a few years back.

I watch the prongs of sprinklers turning and turning on the Takapau plains.

+

All water has salt in it. Too much irrigation makes the salt build up in the soil. Salinity rising. Defeats the purpose: roots find it harder to absorb moisture when it's salty. So they apply more water, the leaching fraction. Eventually, the earth erodes. In New Zealand, up to three hundred million tonnes of dirt are carried out to sea each year. We live and farm on unstable lands.

+

Nick got a speeding ticket, three years ago, along this stretch. We were headed to Wellington after four days in Whāngārā and I'd made him bring my easel. I thought I might paint while we were away. I didn't. To get it back in the car, we had to put the base in the boot, then lean the legs over the back seats, axle hovering, precarious, next to our heads. A pendulum, like the one swinging between us: cold words, angry glances, back and forth, back and forth. The faster he drove, the more it swung. So he drove fast.

+

Francine drives at a steady one hundred. No straying.

—Want to take a scenic route? She asks.

The Pukeora Sanatorium sits, yellowing, on a chunk of limestone. It was built in 1918 to treat tuberculosis in returning veterans. Fresh air was considered the only cure. It's a winery now, a winery with a view.

The walls need a clean and some of the concrete paths are cracked. Drainpipes run the height of the stone facade, but they're old, no longer straight, like a toothpick bent between two fingers. Signs advertise an artist working here: *Studio and Gallery*. There's a washing line round the back, T-shirts and socks floating on a breeze, right to the edge. As if they mean to fly off.

+

I throw up on the side of the road, translating Pukeora: hills of health. Francine's talking about everything but her mum.

—You can't buy Roundup in Europe, she says.

—Yeah?

My voice is still weak and acidic.

—Poison. People don't know, but you can't buy it there. That's why we all get so bloody sick in New Zealand. Do you know they spray it on the potatoes? They spray it to take the tops off. They say the potatoes don't absorb it. But if it's dry enough, roots will soak up anything.

+

Alfred and his family were poor in the early years. *You'll eat what you're given.* That's what he said to his kids, and what Leighton said to Conrad, what Conrad said to Wayne, and Wayne said to Helen. *You'll eat what you're given, that's what my dad always said.*

The inheritance of words. I have a few of Helen's. I keep them in my pocket, but sometimes they slip out: *arcana, cuppa, choc-a-bloc. This diet that I'm on.*

+

Ilana's bought a packet of Kettle chips, chicken flavour. And she's smoking out her window. She didn't ask, and Francine keeps staring in the rear-view mirror, but not saying anything. The Ruahine Ranges crest and fall like the notches in a spine. Like a voice about to break. They hold up the sky.

+

Norsewood was once part of Seventy Mile Bush. It extended from Hawke's Bay, to the Wairarapa, to the coast. There's just a patch left, less than a thousand hectares. Settlers felled the whole thing, turned it to pastures.

Baling wire rusts in bundles, like angel hair pasta left out to dry. An old bridge sprouts from the ground, only grass below. Vestiges of a river diverted, or a river parched. A bright yellow digger straddles it, scooping stone, pulling up concrete as if it was weeds.

+

I wake up and we're in Woodville. Francine's getting something from the boot. Ilana's in the driver's seat.

—We're stopping for dinner, she says.

—Here?

—Apparently there's good fish and chips.

—We're half an hour from Palmerston North.

—I'm hungry.

—They won't have anything vegetarian.

—There'll be chips.

Māori travellers used Woodville as a rest spot. Then hunters, walking from one side of the Manawatū Gorge to the other.

Now, Woodville's where the railways meet and the wind is caught in metal arms. Seventy Mile Bush is just the name of a sock brand.

—Look, Ilana says as we enter, —tossed lettuce salad, your favourite.

She orders the $6.40 crumbed fish filet, $2.80 hotdog, one serve of chips, $2.50, and six battered oysters for $4.50. Plus a can of Coke. Francine gets one of the meals, the kind that come on a plate, grilled fish, salad, chips. I buy a bread bun and some tartare, two dollars together. Francine gives me her salad.

—Are you sure you don't want more? I can get you your own chips, she offers.

Outside, there's a couple arguing on the footpath.

—You're an alcoholic, I hear the man say.

—Then what are you, fryhead?

He tries to come inside, but she grabs his T-shirt.

—Stop involving other people! he yells. —Stop making a scene!

—I've already called the cops, Troy. I'm just waiting on them.

The shop walls are blue and the tables are made of cheap fake wood. Everything here is pseudo, synthetic. The smells of fish and hot oil battle in my nostrils. Nausea sits in my stomach and chest like something solid. I hate eating in these joints. Transitory places, places you should only sit down in to wait.

—Good suggestion Francine, Ilana says, her newspaper empty, greasy shadows all that's left.

We pass by antique stores on the walk back to the car. I see adzes playing tetris with a wall, a whole stand's worth of Mills and Boons, deckchairs for four dollars, nails and bolts and screws for ten cents each. A very old box of soap powder called Taniwha. *Extra Whiteness, Extra Brightness.*

+

The windows in Pita's living room look down over Queen Street, that road carved out by water, thousands of years ago. The Waihorotiu Stream used to run freely, before it was set to concrete.

—She's roretia, he said. —Trapped beneath that road.

He was talking about the taniwha. We were both staring at the glass.

—I hope she breaks out, I said.

—Me too, he said, —I hope she breaks out and knocks the Sky Tower over on her way.

From there, the city looked like an overcrowded mouth.

Buildings chewed their way right down to the waterfront, wet with the air's saliva. It sunk that one sharp tooth into the sky.

+

Ilana heads the wrong way out of town, racing the rabbits in the adjacent fields. It takes the Tui brewery for me to notice. Women in underwear on its sign. A meat processing plant across the river, a graveyard across the road.

—You can connect up this way, Francine assures. —Cuts out Palmy. Cuts out the Manawatū Gorge. Not a bad thing.

There was a slip back in 2011. I remember watching it on the news. Boulders two metres wide. Soil disrupted, argillite fractured.

The gorge is beautiful, though, even with the wire netting holding the rocks in. Train lines tunnelling in and out of view.

When I told Pita about my old route, he told me the name, Manawatū, came from the story of a chief. When the chief saw the mouth of the Manawatū River, ka tū tana manawa, his heart stood still.

+

This way takes us past the Fonterra processing plant instead, a $240 million expansion completed only a year ago.

—Dairy prices fell straight after, Francine says. —It's been empty ever since.

+

Leighton, my great-great-grandad, followed his father Alfred into the clergy. Unlike his father, he was devout. He mortified his flesh: starving himself for five days at a time, abstaining from sex for months.

—His kneecaps flattened, Helen once told me, —from kneeling so long on the wooden floors of churches.

That was the Christmas the oven broke. Helen made cake in a pot on the stove and ate none.

—He used to flog himself, you know, with one of those whips.

Francine scoffed, and shut the door to the bedroom where her daughters slept. —I wouldn't listen to that, she told me.

Leighton made a point of living frugally. He married late, to a shy woman from a small coastal town in north-west Poland, and had his first son at fifty-three. Conrad and his older brother slept in dresser drawers as babies. It was only when their father died that they discovered his savings: four thousand pounds. A small fortune, a secret one. He'd left it to his grandchildren, none to his sons. He had *given them enough*.

Helen says Grandad Wayne had never seen so much money in his life. He didn't know what to do with it for years, just left it in an account. She said he thought it was a mistake, a forgery. He thought if he tried to use it, it would bounce, set off an alarm, an alert, somewhere, maybe underground. It had to be either real or fake, and as long as it was in the account it was Schrödinger's cat. It was neither.

+

We're circling on unsealed roads. Stones fly like sparks. A hawthorn blooms late and isolated in an unused field.

—In Ireland that's called a fairy tree, I say.

—What? Ilana asks. She drives with one hand on the wheel

and the other outside the car completely, a lazy reach for the roof. Her elbow balances on the rim of the open window.

—A single hawthorn in the middle of the field. It's bad luck to cut them down. People in Ireland won't do it, they build their houses and roads around them instead.

—Hawthorns?

—Yeah, when they're alone like that, I say. —You see a lot of them if you drive around the Irish countryside.

—Oh, have you been? she says. She knows I haven't.

—There was one growing over the supposed grave of the original Dracula and a film crew wanted to exhume him.

She inspects her forearm as though it isn't her own.

—They did it, cut it down, but they started having all these strange things happening on set. Batteries going from full to dead, people getting sick.

—Pretty normal things, then.

—Just wait, wait for it. When they developed their footage, this must've been the nineties or something, it was black. All of it. They'd got nothing.

She looks over her shoulder, to check if Francine's asleep. She is.

—My grandad asked Mum on his deathbed to cremate him, Ilana says.

In patches, the road is slick with oil. It's straight now, smooth. She speeds up.

—But first he wanted her to eat his heart.

—Was he losing it?

The sun has slid down to the horizon. It catches the windscreen, and for a moment, the whole things burns white. I shield my eyes with my hand.

—Not really, he was just a bit strange.

—Just a bit?

Ilana flips down her visor.

—My uncle wouldn't hear it. He buried him in Paihia Cemetery.

—He could've at least agreed to the cremation part.

—That's what I thought.

Through the window, you can see the shooting upwards of trees in their adolescence. The loosening outwards of those in old age.

—Mum didn't get over it. She saw him each night in her dreams, sitting in his spot by the TV. But she could never get him to look away from it, to see her back. She'd call his name, but it was like he couldn't hear her.

—That's really sad.

I want to put my hand on her leg, but I don't know how to spread myself wide enough.

—So she dug him up.

—What?

—In the middle of the night.

—I don't believe you.

Ilana's foot presses down harder on the pedal. The trailer rattles. Rows of pines bleed into one continuous green stretch.

—Of course you don't, she says. —You're cut and dried. But I can still remember Mum, she goes on, —shoulder deep in that cemetery. I remember the sound of the shovel and the smell of his coffin when we reached it. And I remember the smell of his heart, too, braising in red wine and rosemary. By the time the police arrived, he was almost tender.

—Why wasn't it in the news?

—He died in October 2001. Other stuff was in the news, I guess.

185

The sky bruises, blood sucked to its clouded surface. Pink, then purple.

—Lucky, I say. —That the police arrived, that you didn't have to eat it, I mean.

—Not really. I think that's what fucked Mum up. That she'd desecrated the grave for nothing, that his body would end up in evidence bags in some police morgue.

—You don't think she was maybe a bit fucked before? I say.

—She was a good mum, all right. Better than Gina and Dad put together.

When she speaks in that way, that voice, it's like a little electric shock, the kind they use to train dogs. *Don't do that, don't say it.*

+

The Mangahao Power Station is the earliest of its kind in this country. It is fed by nearly five kilometres of pipelines, threaded like a needle in and out of the Tararua, catching all the little streams. Damming two rivers. Killing seven. Construction workers, that is.

We drive the rest of the journey with eyes fastened to the road.

xiv

Levin is a place with too much sky. It is a bulging blue belly that presses down on you, holding you to the spot. Maybe that's why no one ever gets out.

This is a town where people come to die. The retirement villages have names like Somerset and promises like *Your Ticket to Freedom at an Affordable Price.* The cry of ambulances sounds all through the night.

It has a Salvation Army store and a SaveMart, a Paper Plus and a Postie Plus, a rebranded Hoyts cinema that plays movies two weeks after they finish their run in Auckland. It has boy racers and a whole lot of meth. It doesn't have much else.

+

Helen says Grandad Wayne became an artist when he moved here. The basement, separated from the garage by a door, from the hallway by a staircase, was his. No one else could enter. He was working on something down there, or at least he would say, —I've got work to do, before descending into concrete, each night after dinner. He wouldn't say anything else.

When he died, all they found was junk. He'd been to a lot of auctions, always looking for a bargain, looking to rescue some perfectly usable piece of gardening equipment or kitchenware or roll of carpet or three-legged table.

—It just needs a length of wood nailed in, he'd say. Or, it just needs a lick of paint. Or, it just needs an engine replacement.

—Probably destroyed it all, Helen said, meaning the art. —It's probably where you get it from, your painting.

I thought that was hopeful. But how would I know? I was too young to remember any of it. Grandad died when I was four, only three weeks after Stuart.

+

We pull up to number thirty-one. Francine helps us unlock, unload. Bo jumps from the back and runs straight into the garden.

—He's a good dog, she says, —just underworked. Ask Mike from next door to tow your car to the mechanics, he'll help you out. Whatever you do, don't use Grandma's guy.

—You're not staying? I say.

It's one of those granite questions. It looks light until you try to pick it up.

—No, she says. —No, I'm going to keep making my day trips, once a fortnight. Like I always have.

She touches the place where her cross is, beneath her shirt.

—Last time I came, she says, —Mum didn't recognise me. She thought she was talking to Helen. I had to keep reminding her, showing her the photo of me on the bedside table.

When someone can recognise your photo but not your face.

The Tinder match who stares in the supermarket, trying to place you over the agria potatoes and Chinese garlic. The person you added on Facebook, years ago, after meeting one time at a party. Your own mother.

She picks at a skin of paint, scaling on the garage door. —Of course I want to be there for her. But why make it so uneven? Why is it that we're more there for people in death than in life? I don't want to be. I want my memories to be balanced.

The sensor light catches in her eyes.

—But I pray for her, I pray for her every minute of every day.

+

When we get inside, it all seems the same. The tide lines on my grandma's cups, the cupboards full of gingernuts and cockroaches. A faint smell of piss that hangs around longer than the cat himself. There's a calendar from 1994, still pinned open to September and a particularly yellow painting of Stratford-upon-Avon. Doilies on every surface.

—You're taller, my grandma says, like every time I come.

But that's a lie, because she's not here. She's in Madison. One of those assisted-care units. They call it a suite, because it has a bathroom attached.

+

I used to find it hardest to get to sleep in Levin. It's where I had my worst nightmares. I can't explain how a place can feel so light during the day, then so heavy at night. The morning sun in the living room will defrost your bones, but the dark returns the ice to their hollows.

I found out about the basement when I was twelve. My grandad didn't only live down there: he died down there, too. Hung himself from a hook in the ceiling.

I've always believed that places hold onto these things longer than people.

+

—Francine's not one to talk about it, Helen says. I have to turn down the volume on Grandma's landline to stop her voice cracking up. —She's a doer instead. She'll file your tax return, or fix your fence, but she won't sit and talk about it with you. It's just how she is.

I know what it's like to be a vessel that never spills. But someone's turned Francine on her side, and she's draining. You can't put back what's lost.

+

I remember her in Gisborne, when I was ten, showing me how to kill a cray on the gutting table. All I remember is that it shat itself when it died.

+

There is no such thing as a beautiful death. Wayne came home early from a trip to the bach and was found, four days later, by my grandma. He hadn't died instantly. It could've been an hour before he choked, or the circulation was finally cut off from his brain. His face had lost its colour. The blood had pooled in his feet, turning them black. There were scratches all over his neck. But his body was already decomposing in the summer heat, so nothing exact could be said.

+

Sometimes, in this house at night, I swear I hear the sound of footsteps going up and down the staircase or the sliding of the garage door.

Tonight, I hear only a strange scratching of twigs against tin.

I try to close my eyes, shut so tight I won't see faces in the windows with the lights out, though I can see that anywhere. The face beside me on the pillow—that's the one that's temporary.

+

I can't remember much of my dream except that Grandad was in it, complaining about the soil.

—Too much blood, he kept saying. —Too much blood to grow anything decent.

+

I check for my period, but my undies are clean, white. I've almost given up.

+

Retirement homes are dead-ends. They are places tired of living, places sick with it. That's why they're so easy to die in.

Laceleaf grows in a blue pot in the Madison foyer. I wonder if they know it's toxic. There's a poster that says, *We come from all around the world to help you.* It's a daisy chain of arms, pink, pink, pink, tan, pink, pink, soft brown.

The respite rooms are split into two wings, Manhattan and Brooklyn. The woman at the reception tells me my grandma's in Brooklyn, then, —No, wait, she's been taken to the general hospital.

—Just for x-rays, she adds, seeing my face. —And a few tests.

+

It is one of those days when you see the moon at two in the afternoon. The sky as pale as fish flesh. There's a faulty streetlamp, daytime shining. We have been walking in our own shadows—but for a second, as we pass under it, we have none.

It's a decent stretch to the Horowhenua Health Centre. Queen Street to Oxford Street to Liverpool. Almost every house has an add-on sunroom, facing north. On one side of the road, they have taken over the territory of porches. On the other, you see them poking out the back. Across the train tracks, someone is trying to sell pine cones for five dollars each. Arrows point this way for the Latter Day Saints and Seventh Day Adventists, that way for the War Veteran's Home and the hospital.

It looks like a church, from the outside, one of those modern types. Painted bricks, single storey, wide overhang—peaked, but only slightly. Double-height windows at the entrance, wall of glass. A lack of right angles.

Inside, the exposed steel skeleton reveals the tilt of the ceiling. Halfway up, the weight-bearing posts multiply like spider legs towards the roof. Circular lamps are hanging suns. It's all designed to help you forget where you are.

Ilana takes a seat and I approach the front desk.

192

It must've been more than tests, because they've put Grandma in a bed behind one of their blue curtains.

—She'll be transferred back this afternoon, I am assured by a nurse who smells solely of cigarettes.

I don't know what to say to my grandma, so I wait until she wakes up.

—You're skinnier, she says. I could say the same thing about her.

Then, she reaches over and pats my hand. It's not something she's ever done before. I worry that touch might be enough to tear her skin.

+

People clot in the waiting rooms and all down the halls. A young woman walks between the inpatient and maternity wards, hands on her lower back, so you know she's either pregnant, or just given birth. Her stomach hasn't deflated at all. It pushes aside her unzipped hoodie, convex bellybutton making a pimple on the hospital gown.

—Congratulations, I say.

—Thanks, my boy's sleeping.

Her hair is blond below the forehead, dark roots clawing their way down her face. Her skin, her cheeks, the tips of her nose, are red, as though she's the one who's newly born.

—Want to see a photo?

She pulls a phone from her pocket. On the screen is a mirror image. Two babies, same chubby knees and full eyebrows, same curl towards the centre. One's pink, one's slightly blue.

—That's Cole, who's sleeping. That there is his brother. I haven't thought of a name for him yet. I was sure I'd be having a boy and a girl. I'd picked out Carlie for a girl. Carlie and Cole, don't you think that goes well?

—Yes, I say.

The phone in her hand is like an eclipse. You can't look directly at it.

—But I can't think of a boy's name to go with Cole. Dan and Cole, Luke and Cole, Sam and Cole. What do you think?

If I unfocus my eyes, I can make the specks on the lino disappear. Blink and they're back.

—I don't know.

—Neither. I want to get them both registered today. On the day they were born. But it's so hard to decide.

She looks down at the photo again before closing it.

—I was going out for a smoke, do you want one?

—No thanks, I say. —I'm just finding my friend.

+

Ilana says lots of people want a photo of their baby when it's died. Lots of people like to hold it, too, kiss it, register it.

—I would've been a twin, she says. —In the womb. All left-handed people, we ate our twins. Absorbed them completely.

—That must be a myth.

—Look it up.

But I can't stop thinking about that woman, her twinless twin boy, her stillborn still living on in present tense.

+

Every time you remember something you're only remembering the last time you thought of it.

194

Helen wanted a second child. She was too old to have one—and Chris said getting pregnant, giving birth, those were things she didn't want to do.

When I was fifteen, Chris told me she was trying to get pregnant with Liz. They'd even found a donor: a chemistry teacher and alto in the local choir. She showed me a photo of him once and all I remember saying was, —You better hope your kid doesn't inherit his nose.

But she didn't need to worry about that. Chris was infertile.

+

They say you might not ovulate for six months after stopping the pill.

It wasn't true for me. When I broke up with Nick, my period returned after only two weeks. It felt as though my insides were emptying out. For three days, I had to change my tampon hourly. Last time I visited Grandma in hospital, when she was in for a transfusion, I bled all over the seat. The nurse told me it was okay, they were used to cleaning up *spills*. The chair, like everything else here, was plastic. I could hear the crinkling of a mattress protector when my grandma rolled over. There were hand sanitisers by every doorway with signs reminding you that *99% of infectious diseases are spread by poor hygiene*. I wondered how she slept in a place that smelt of Spray n' Wipe. It reminded me of Nick's house.

—He was such a nice boy. Such a nice boy, she said intermittently the whole time I was there. I left angry.

+

There are still a lot of photos of him at her house. In the most recent ones, taken in Levin, he has his arm around me. I'm never looking right at the camera. They should be light, the way I remember them on the screen of his phone or Helen's point-and-shoot, but they're not.

It's something that happens to all the photos from here. They turn out darker than you expect. It's as if shadows inch their way into the frame after the fact, into pools of developing liquids and SIM cards.

+

Ilana laughs. —Did you get the snap from Ashi?

—You tell me, she says when I don't reply, —what's there to do in Levin?

The SaveMart is in the old Horowhenua Electric Power Board building, erected in the 1920s, now run-down and cracking. There's an unused section beside it, barbed wire. A cut-out policeman by the door holds a sign warning about video surveillance. Someone's scratched off the pupil of his right eye.

The smell of dust and old age permeates. I riffle through the Designer Ladies section, comprised of Glassons and Veronika Maine. You have to go further for the special pieces. It's always at the end of a rail, or sorted into the men's section, that you'll come across a princess coat from the fifties, or women's wide-leg trousers from the war. And you know what it means. Someone's just died. Their wardrobe: bagged up, donated.

It used to be opposite the park instead. Helen and I would spend whole afternoons there, peeling our way through rows of hangers. Everything I showed her, she would dismiss, —Too big for you, or —Too small for me. Then she'd re-find it, ten minutes later, —This is my colour, or —Wouldn't this look good with your leather skirt?

Whenever I'd wear it, later, she'd say, —Oh look, it's the top I found you.

After circling the men's shirts a few times Ilana says, —It's all junk here. Someone should burn this place down.

+

A shop selling dairy pumps is next to a discount store, baked beans for ninety-nine cents. Outside the Horowhenua Council buildings two poupou weave the Tararua with feather quills, Te Rauparaha's broadsword with the settler bayonet, a huia and a milk tanker. There's a Christian bookshop called the Beacon which sells *I Heart Levin* ashtrays.

We have walked far today. My feet swell over the tops of my shoes. I know that when I sit down, and lift them up, and try to spread each toe, sensation will flood back in.

Harvey Bowler Funeral Services boasts a reception room and chapel. Chinese restaurants sell chips and burgers and bacon and eggs. Piercing parlours refuse to do gang-related tattoos. *Please Do Not Ask.*

+

A TV architect once said Levin was the ugliest town in the world. He said the Liquor King was the only redeeming building. Helen told me this, but she couldn't remember the architect's name.

I said, —Kevin McCloud?

—Who?

—*Grand Designs.*

—No, not that one.

—Restoration man? The shed guy?

—No, not them.

I didn't know any more TV architects.

Like everything else that happens here, this man's words had fallen into some parochial hole, too deep for memory, too small for Google.

+

The only bar I know of in town is called the Boardroom. It serves drip coffee in a big pot to keep people awake at the pokies. There's a Tui sign on the roof, and paper in the window. *Monday: 11am till late.*

—Do they think five-thirty is late? Ilana says.

I say we should go home but she wants to try the RSA, a twenty-five pounder field gun and a real-estate sign outside, *Call John Pope.* A printout by the bar reads, *Hearing Aid Batteries Available Here.* Pixelated photos show the little silver discs. Poppies in each corner. Another says, *The bar staff are also the fire wardens.*

The walls are lined with medals and tacky watercolours, battle scenes mainly, donated by members of the public. The ceilings are perforated, the type you find in classrooms.

There's an unused pokie and thickset words on the wall, *Ca$hcade Jackpot.* Below that, *Gaming machine for sale, see office.*

A man announces twelve raffle tickets are left. Hampers of Favourites and orange juice and ready salted chips cover a table. A band plays the *Country Calendar* theme song.

Ilana challenges me to pool. She's good and I'm terrible. A

couple of men, late sixties, ask to match us.

Every time Ilana sinks a ball she puts her arms around me: neck or waist or hips. The shorter of the men can't stop staring. He nudges his friend each time we touch, but his friend always misses it, eyes on the green felt. When we win, Ilana kisses me, open-mouthed.

—Fucking lessies, the tall one says.

—Do you have a problem with that? she's quick to fire back.

—Which of you is a member here? his friend asks.

I go to lie: me.

—We're not, she says. She's smirking. She wants this, an argument. She's set it up, aligned all the balls, hit them straight and strong.

—Let's leave, I say.

—I want another drink.

—Can we please go?

I feel stares on my back the whole way to the door. I wish I could pull myself in to a pinprick, so small no one would ever notice me, no one could ever see. I'd be invisible, white against a white wall.

+

My grandma has these old seventies scales, pink with yellow specks. The moment before stepping on is always tense. My legs never want to: they stiffen at the knee. The lines whizz and blur. The scales make a clack, and then, are still. It measures in stones so I convert it to kilos in my head. It's hard to read exactly where the needle falls, the marks are so far apart.

The number at the end is what matters. Not as lumps of fat, or dress size, but a numerical value, diminishing.

XV

This is a true story.

One night in Levin, the living-room window kept opening. It overlooks the driveway and you can only open it from outside with a ladder. I closed it, I'm sure I closed it: it must've been three times. But I woke up in the morning to wind blowing through the hallway and onto my face. Something wanted to get in, or had.

—I don't know about that, Ilana says.

—But I'm supposed to buy your mum single-handedly exhuming your grandad and cooking his heart?

Ilana laughs and scrunches her fingers through her hair. —I can't get over you falling for that.

She tells me the cremation part's true: her grandad did want it. Though her mum never touched the grave.

—I was just pulling your leg, she says.

I can't look at her. My eyes feel sore and wet, as if I've opened them underwater. But she has her back to me already, picking at her thigh, an ingrown hair.

+

Horowhenua means rippling ground, or shaking earth. Our fights have a seismology. You could plot them on the Richter scale. Whāngārā, 5.4. Gisborne, 2.8. Right outside of Napier, 7.0. I can still feel them, our aftershocks, as far away as Levin.

+

I dream we're back in Waipawa, but the unit is decorated like the inside of the settler's museum. It's not a unit anymore, it's a caravan, parked in the same camping grounds. But the caravan has no wheels.

How will we ever get out of here? I say, or at least, think, as I rub my growing belly.

I wake up throughout the night and wait for my eyes to adjust each time, to be sure it's not real.

+

In the morning, I relearn how to bend each joint. Movement comes slowly back to me. It's like a language I knew years ago, but haven't spoken since.

I hear the lock turn on the front door, the sucking of the frame, the pop when it opens.

—Who's there?

Grandma has been paying a woman to feed her cat since she's been in Madison. Cleome was Miss Horowhenua back in 1979. Now, she singles out the people on her street over eighty and befriends them. She's standing in the kitchen holding the spare key, still dirty from its spot by the lemon tree. She holds it up as if there's another lock, one I can't see, right in front of her.

—What are you doing here? I say.

—Where's Basil?

—The bowl and food are outside.

—I was only checking to see if your grandma is home yet.

—She's not, I say. —And we'll be here for the next few days. I can leave food out for him.

—I'll see you tomorrow then.

Cleome has always unsettled me. She can enter a room quieter than anyone else, and she talks as though she misheard what you just said. Helen found her once, looking through the receipts in Grandma's purse, pocketing them as though they were cash.

+

Levin was settled by Pākehā later than most places, 1880, when the Wellington–Manawatū railway cut through. The Muaūpoko chief, Keepa Te Rangihiwinui, agreed to sell land for a township—under conditions. Every tenth section was to be granted back to Muaūpoko people. That never happened. The town was to be named after his father, Taitoko, but they named it after the director of the train line instead. Levin means lightning, I think.

+

We pass a church built in ombre bricks, red to brown, brown to red, creating zigzags up its walls. *God cares for you*, comes the message from the shrubbery.

+

Leighton, like his father Alfred, was never on an official mission, not a Christian one. But he saw beyond the small town of Wairoa, with its flat plains and hard men. He went north, silencing Māori, preaching his story of God and King and Country. He made a point of taking no horse, leaving on foot, as a sign of his humility before the Lord. Yet when he returned, years later, it was on the back of a Scottish Clydesdale. A tall man, thin as a silver birch, blue felt kepi on his head.

—That's, Helen said, —when the flogging started.

+

Bo pulls on his lead the whole way. Lazy houses shuffle past us. Lean-to carports shade un-driven cars, held for children who've gone overseas. Swing sets and trampolines collect leaves and rust, bought for grandkids who no longer visit. Walls are weatherboard, white, maybe yellow—or two-tone and concrete, the mottled finish of the sixties. Fake stone strips down the sides. There are big lawns at the front, none at the back. Windows wear decorative shutters, the kind that don't shut, or pale pleated awnings. There are garden gnomes and garden angels. There are hanging pot plants and punga stumps, freshly pruned rose gardens and bright blue hydrangeas, sweet gums or sometimes, even, a date palm dwarfing it all. A sickly yellow moss grows in the cavities. Everywhere, daytime TV can be seen through pulled lace curtains.

+

The receptionist gives me the wrong room number. I walk in on a woman, even older than my grandma, watching *Jeremy Kyle* in bed. She's one of those people who wears their life on their faces.

It's as if you could lower a needle into each line, each crevice, and that life would pour out into chord progressions, pour right into the air.

Not like my grandma at all. She's stony as ever. *Emmerdale* playing so loud it almost crackles. But she pretends she wasn't watching when I come in.

—Can I turn that off? I say.

She just raises her eyebrows. I think she's sitting on the remote. The TV's held by brackets high in the corner so I have to stand on a chair to reach the power button.

—This is Ilana, I say, who holds out her hand, from habit, then pulls it back in. Grandma's hands stay under the blankets.

—I know, is all she says.

—You brought your picture, I say, pointing at a watercolour of sand dunes on the wall. It strikes me as odd. She's refused to move for years and now she's packing pictures when she comes to respite.

—That's not mine. Everyone has that.

But it's exactly the same: same bleeding skies, same blunt black in the bushes, same flicks of birds flying off in the distance, same frame, undulating and white.

—I'll get the nurse to bring you girls some biscuits.

The nurse has a forehead that takes up almost half his face. He leaves us with a plate of Anzacs and gram crackers and shows us the station for making coffee. We don't.

—The Anzacs here, they're terrible. Don't bother. But gram crackers, gram crackers were your grandad's favourite. He would eat a whole packet for tea.

—I wish I'd known him better, I say.

—He wouldn't have put up with your vegetarian carry-on.

She sucks on her false teeth. They slip against her gums and make a sloshing sound.

—That man was always in his basement.

Ilana is stuffing gram crackers in her mouth, two at a time.

—What do you think he did down there? I ask.

—Oh, he read and he pottered and he felt awfully sorry for it all. He spent a lot of time feeling sorry.

—Sorry about what?

—You know, the bach and that whole palaver. Sorry about where the money came from. Sorry to inherit the medals.

Ilana's interested now. Her chewing has slowed.

—Oh no, he didn't want those medals. They went straight in the bin.

—Grandad's?

—Wayne never saw war, you know that, no no no, Leighton's medals, the major.

—He was too old to go to war.

—Not that war. The one right here.

She fixes on the watercolour for a few seconds.

—Here in Gisborne. Do you know it snowed once in Gisborne? All the way to sea level. It was on the lawn the next morning.

It did snow once in Gisborne, but that was 1939.

They say either your body goes, or your mind. With Grandma it had been her body. Her teeth were first. She hated her dentures—the dentist said she'd get used to them, but she never did. She would take them out at random if she thought no one was looking, dunk them in the nearest glass or cup. You had to be careful if you left a coffee unattended. Sometimes, swimming just below the surface, was a whole set of teeth.

Her eyesight was next. Dishes, once impeccable, now a palimpsest of dinners past. And she made the same sound whenever you gave her a card. A kind of pleasant *hmmpf*. You could catch her later, magnifying glass to the mantelpiece, reading what she'd missed.

Her hearing's been getting more selective for years. She couldn't hear me say the mug was stained, or that her power bill had come, even when we were in the same room. But she could hear Helen whispering in the kitchen about her mechanic, all the way from the lounge.

Now her mind is going too. Maybe the cancer has spread to her brain.

+

Nothing in Levin ever really changes, just ages.

An empty for-sale plot has signage for the dog park, from the days when it stretched this far. By the new entrance, there's another real-estate placard, *Unique Native Bush Setting*, leaning against an acorn tree. Both sections have been on the market for years, as long as I can remember.

Kōwhai Park has green plastic bins everywhere in the shape of upright dogs. They look like playing pieces from a knock-off Monopoly set, magnified and full of shit.

Cabbage trees, macrocarpas, rimu, big bursts of harakeke. The bush is dense but the paths are clear. A fence separates the park from farmland—unused, as far as I can tell, only seagulls standing in it. Bo barks at them.

A couple of kanuka have been felled and wood-chipped on the spot. Their flowers and shavings lie in mounds, the softest rubble. A ditch has opened up by the side of the road, encased in bright orange netting. It is filled with mud and rubbish, Coke bottles, McDonald's wrappers, mainly. You can smell Lake Horowhenua when the wind blows. You can smell how much it stinks.

Another of Keepa Te Rangihiwinui's conditions was a town square and reserve by the lake. That didn't happen either. This park is the closest thing.

A woman in cargo shorts, no dog in sight, tell us, —You're going to need your coats today. If you stand in this field and look to the mountains, I said to Jim, that's snow that is. I'm staying in these bloody things. Once you're in long pants, you're buggered for the whole year.

The Tararua Ranges poke their naked tops into the clouds.

+

I'm unpacking the groceries when Ilana comes in holding Basil, Grandma's cat.

—Where did you find him? I say. —How did you pick him up? He hates people.

—He was down in the garage.

Basil is an overweight British Shorthair. Not purebred, but you can tell he thinks he is.

—He's purring, I say.

—Do you know, she says, —cats purr when they die? When they die and when they give birth.

Then she puts him down and she takes the Vogel's from my hands and puts that down too. She doesn't kiss me, just lifts up my T-shirt and latches onto my nipples, hard. I whimper. She thinks it's out of pleasure. Turns me round, bends me over the bench. The cold of the metal is the only sensation I like. She's rough, her nails are long, she hasn't used any spit. The way she crooks her index finger makes me feel as though I'm going to cry. *Softer*, I want to say, *go softer*, but I think she'll laugh at me. I fake to get it over with.

—Aren't you going to return the favour? she says.

—I'm not in the mood.

+

The mechanic rings to say he found water in the oil. Not much, but some, and it's not a good sign. Might need a new gasket, or something.

Water and oil don't mix. Everyone knows that. You only have to look after it's rained, see the slimy colours patterning the gutter. You only have to try to make perfume. Picking the camellias from your grandma's neighbours' garden, crushing them in tap water, until you realise they don't have a scent. That's when you sneak her essential oils from the cabinet, mix in myrrh and rosehip, watching them float to the surface like scum. You still tried to sell it, in a stall, outside. You were seven. You could get away with that sort of thing.

Ilana says *fuck* after she hangs up. I ask, —What is it?

Even though I heard. I don't know what else to say.

+

My grandma met her mechanic that same summer. She hired Archie because he was British. But he wore Swanndris and smelled of sausage rolls and liked Paul Holmes, thought he was a good mechanic's son, a good bloke. He offered to give Grandma driving lessons, though her driving didn't improve. We think he was teaching her all the road rules wrong, and confusing her indicator stalk with her windscreen wipers, just to keep a customer. She was still paying for them last year.

Her cars never passed their warrants, either. Last time we were here, Helen paid for a real mechanic.

—Who would do this? he kept repeating to himself. Bleach had been added to the petrol: the inside of the tank was rusting, the fuel lines, too. Bird feed was found in the air-conditioning tubes, baby mice in tow. Tinfoil had been put between the filament and the lights, which explained why the battery never lasted.

Grandma said it couldn't have been Archie.

And I understood. He was one of the only people who still came to visit regularly, even if he charged.

+

Pita had a way of suggesting I come round without ever asking. —I'm doing nothing this Sunday, he'd say. I knew he was lonely and I knew I was one of the few who still saw him regularly. Until I became uncomfortable. I wasn't sure what he wanted anymore. I wasn't sure what it meant when he'd hug me or when he'd look up from his coffee cup and say, *How've you been e kare?* or, *I read something that reminded me of you.*

I think that's why it's been hard to stay in contact with him. Or maybe that's just an excuse.

+

I don't know how long the home phone has been ringing before I pick it up. The voice on the other end is modulated and crisp, one I don't recognise. It takes me a while to work out it's Jules.

—How was the bach?

—It was wet.

—We heard about the toilet. You do realise we're getting forwarded your grandma's bills? It certainly was hefty. You girls know not to flush tampons right?

—It wasn't tampons, it was the tank.

—We heard about your car, too. Why didn't you ring, what's his name, your grandma's lovely guy? Archie?

I twist the cord around my finger, tight.

—Look, this is to say Jane and I will be in Levin on Friday.

—We should be out of here by then, I say, —if the car's fixed. We have to get back.

—Oh, that's not a problem. We won't be staying at number thirty-one. Remember not to flush any tampons there either.

+

My period is now two weeks late. There's an egg locked away in my uterus, like a teenager in a small town, like Wayne during the war, like Grandma in Madison.

+

I have one recollection of Grandad Wayne, but it could've been planted there by Helen's stories. Prefab memories, like houses: you can walk right into them.

He hated people who picked flowers, especially his flowers. When I was four, only a month before he died, he found me decapitating his alisons and placing them on my head. He didn't stop me, just joined in. Helen says when I came inside it looked as if I'd been standing out in December snow.

It is always summer when I think of him. His hair so curled it looked scorched.

The shower has two taps, red and blue. You have to be careful never to finish turning the blue off before the red. I almost burnt myself as a kid.

Birds on the shower curtain and snails in the birdfeeder. One daffodil pin and one poppy, in the jewellery box by Grandma's bed, trotted out each year: she doesn't believe in paying for them more than once. Painted flowers, plastic flowers, fabric flowers—roses, orange at their tips, dust in their folds. Cross-stitch fields of them. Everything but the real thing. The garden's gone to ruin in my lifetime, without Grandad. Some of the trees still fruit, the feijoa, the oversized lemon (a kite-eating tree), and there's an ash in the corner, now more moss than bark. But the rest is just weeds.

+

I watch episodes of *Obsessive Compulsive Cleaners* on YouTube. One man's hoarding is so bad his daughter has to sleep in a motorhome outside. He still calls it collecting. A woman goes through two bottles of bleach and three pairs of gloves, every day, on her own house. She's terrified of cats. Cats put their bums on things. Women who hate germs so much must hate their own vaginas.

+

I have memories of being made to tidy the kitchen cupboards here as a kid, and finding flour and sugar loose in all the drawers, flour and sugar that Grandma still scooped up, surreptitiously, to put into her shortbread—the only thing she ever baked. I have memories of getting mixing bowls from under the sink and finding them caked in cookie batter, ants dashing madly away.

It's filthy, even by my standards. I have to force myself to start dinner, roast tomatoes with garlic and thyme.

Heat distorts things. Like air rising off the road, rippling mountains. When I open the oven door, the window becomes water.

+

Grandma would hang around the kitchen when Helen was cooking, dropping comments about the amount of oil in the pan, or the ratio of carbs to protein. Then she'd go to bed before we served up.

She always claimed to be a Catholic. She called the cracker and the wine, the body and the blood, her little Sunday treat.

But Grandma wasn't Catholic in England. Helen says she was poor and Presbyterian. She tries to use the upper-class words, but she often slips. Serviette instead of napkin, lounge instead of drawing room, tea instead of supper. For some reason, I'd thought Grandma was rich, before she moved here.

+

All Ilana says is, —Soup during summer? Then, —It's nice.

—I can't eat anymore, I say.

Memories of how I found the pan, brown, of the slick down the side of the balsamic vinegar, something oily. A feeling growing in my stomach, trying to force its way out.

I take Bo for another walk. I just need to escape.

The streets here are the only ones that aren't flat. A slight upwards inflection, like a question at the end of town. I stare into windows as I go by. I see a man filleting a snapper. I see the back of a woman's head, too still, even for sleep. One house has a sign, *Clairvoyant and Card Reader, Call Val for an Appointment.* A wooden smiling sun and concrete frogs by her door. I stare into Val's window and see nothing.

In Levin, death creeps right past you. Don't look and you won't have to witness, you won't even notice it.

Four young guys speed along the road in a lowered Skyline. They slow as they pass me. One says something, and the rest laugh.

The horizon darkens. Less sun in the atmosphere, refracting, making blue. It's the clouds' fault. They've moved in and sucked it all up.

Sometimes I think the same thing about Ilana. When I'm with her, I'm almost cold. She absorbs all the light.

+

I cooked so she should've done the dishes, but they're still there when I come home. She's in the cushioned rocking chair, TV turned up, but she's not watching. I drop a cup into the sink. I can't tell if she's heard. It's something stupid on, like *Who Wants to Be a Millionaire.* The audience cheers as the pink mug clangs in the belly of a pot.

—Can you turn that shit down?

She doesn't say anything, but twenty seconds later reaches for the remote.

I don't know what to say then. The dishes are almost done.

—My aunty and cousin are coming to Levin, I try.

—Francine?

—No, another. Jules. It's not until Friday.

—So we need to be gone by then.

—Not really, they won't be staying here.

—But they'll drop by. I didn't agree to this meet-the-family tour.

She rubs her temples and says, —This is all becoming too much.

Fucking someone is like buying a canvas. For a while you can keep it blank, in that corner of your room, on your desk, by your bed. For a while, because it can become anything, it is anything, too. But it doesn't stay that way. It turns into just another reminder of everything you can't bring yourself to do, everything you're scared of. Eventually, you have to paint it, or you have to chuck it out.

+

I didn't actually get rid of all my paints. On that Tuesday night, the eve of rubbish collection, I fished most of them from the bin. They might need a wash when I get home, before I use them again.

+

I throw away the soup dregs. That's when I notice it, cramped beside the bookshelf in the hallway: Grandma's watercolour of sand dunes, same skies, same bushes, same birds, same frame. She was right. Everyone has it.

XVI

You can't drink the water in Levin. You have to boil it, and even then, it doesn't taste right.

The *Listener* published an article on Lake Horowhenua and titled it *Lake of Shame*. Up until 1987, all the town's sewage was dumped directly into it. It still gets contaminated today every time a nearby pumping station overflows. Farmers still release their run-off, fertiliser and manure. And Levin's biggest storm drain, stretching all down Queen Street, still mainlines straight into its waters.

Once, there were kakahi and whitebait and eels and koura. They're all buried beneath layers of hypertrophic mud. Now it's home only to introduced species: goldfish, perch, the Levin Sailing and Rowing Clubs.

There's a plaque, proclaiming Lake Horowhenua to be a *visible symbol of the co-operation and brotherhood between the races* and *for the use and enjoyment of all*.

Translation: Lake Horowhenua was stolen from Muaūpoko, an iwi already accustomed to great raupatu. It happened in 1905, the then-government citing *the reasonable rights of the public.*

The reasonable rights of the public to yacht and to plunder, to fish and to soil, to row and to dump.

+

Ilana got her car back today, and spent the last three hours down by the lake. That's what she says, anyway, when she calls.

I slept in and dreamt about teeth. They were rotten and throbbing but I wanted them to stay put in my gums. Then Ilana came along with her pliers and pulled them, one by one. Out of my mouth, they were gleaming and white again, white against white, on my grandma's best china.

Look what you've done, I thought. I couldn't speak at all, without my teeth.

+

I visited Pita at the start of December. He apologised for not having any sour snakes.

—I've started looking after my taitai. But I'll get some for you, e kare.

That was the last time I saw him. I agreed to go around again that Saturday, but Ilana called to say she was free, and I texted Pita and told him I felt sick. He said it was fine, it didn't matter. *Hope you feel better.* I couldn't stop imagining the bag of sour snakes, opened and waiting on his counter. I didn't feel better at all.

Over and over, I draft the same email. *Kei te pehea koe Pita?* as if that's something you can just ask.

I stalk Ashi's Instagram instead. It is perfect selfies and vases of

216

flowers, screenshots of Snapchat filters gone wrong. Candid photos of her in bikinis on couches, slipping further into Lachlan's arms.

Remember he's replaceable. She probably has a dozen other Lachlans waiting on the sidelines. *I love them all differently*, she would say, as though love was something you bought at the supermarket, and you could just choose a different brand, another flavour. *I love them all differently*, she would say, meaning: not at all.

+

Ilana picks me up. I ask how much it cost, but she doesn't want to talk about it. I ask her if she saw Cleome as we went out the front door, peering into the living room window from the footpath, but she says no. She drives to Madison without looking at me once. The air grows stagnant in my lungs.

+

My first and only driving lesson was in the car park by the lake. Archie snorted at the photo on my learner's licence, and at his own jokes about Aucklanders. When he laughed behind the wheel, his stomach squished against it. I was grilled on a mix of road-and-kiwi code, while I bunny hopped and stalled.

—Do you know how many metres away from an intersection you have to park?

—No.

—Or the maximum speed for towing a trailer?

—No.

—Do you like rugby?

—No.

—Ever killed a chicken?

My grandad planted the foliage that lines that car park back when he was in Levin's Rotary Club. It's mostly cabbage trees and lancewood and toetoe, which my grandma still calls rabbit ears.

+

Grandma asks where Ilana is and I say at the garage. I don't want to tell her she's waiting in the car.

The longer I spend in Madison, the filthier it seems. It's all microscopic, the dirt, but I know it's there, bodily fluids precipitating on every surface. No amount of bleach could get rid of them. These floors have seen piss and shit. Phlegm-covered tissues have littered that table. My grandma is lying on sheets people have died in.

The nurse from yesterday walks past with a white bin bag, not fully tied at the top. I can smell the adult diapers, acrid and synthetic. When I look at him, he pulls the drawstrings. Another, a Māori woman, comes in to ask if we need anything.

Grandma raises her voice a few notches just to say, —Biscuits.

The way you might when speaking to someone who doesn't know English.

I tell her Jules and Jane are coming to see her, Lloyd must be close behind.

—They haven't told me, she says. —Your brother has only called me once since they locked me in here. Do you know what it was about? My damn will.

She thinks I'm Helen right now, Helen or Francine. I don't correct her.

—It never comes to any good, inheritance. Look what it did

to your father's family. Conrad stopped talking to them all. Blood money that was. Couldn't get it clean in the wash. At least Wayne got the bach from it.

—The bach was from Leighton's money?

—You know that. Remember the Christmas Conrad showed up? Smelling of brandy and swinging his father's gun. It was the same year as the tsunami warning. Remember that sound? We had to drive to higher ground.

Now I just let her speak. When your mind softens, memories can grow in it like soil, sprout from nothing.

—You were so upset because you forgot your Ginny doll. We almost turned around, but I put my foot down.

—Ginny dolls were before my time, Grandma, I say.

She looks at me, really looks at me then, eyes cut in half like fruit.

—Oh yes, is all she says.

+

Strips of mounted lights stretch from the front of the Unichem to the back, slicing the ceiling into lanes. Grey carpets, grey walls, a retail assistant who paces like a polar bear in a tropical zoo.

I scurry around the aisles. I find the pregnancy tests near the back.

There are two to choose from, LifeTell In-Stream Home Pregnancy Test and Clearblue. Clearblue is more expensive by four dollars, but claims to be ninety-nine per cent accurate. The woman at the checkout asks me if I'm sure I don't want the double pack. — It's the more popular option, she says. —Cheaper per stick and it's good to have a spare. They're better at detecting the hormones the longer you wait, but we all want to get home and find out, don't we?

She's beaming.

I keep my purchase in its brown paper bag and stuff it away in a drawer as soon as I can.

+

I remember the drive back with Nick after having sex outside Kelly Tarlton's. The streetlights shivered on the surface of the sea. He said something about disturbed water, but all I remember now is liking the phrase. And imagining throwing myself into the ocean, washing myself clean.

+

The kitchen looks even dirtier today. It's as if layers of grime have settled, like sediment, like silt, over all the countertops in the night.

—I don't want to cook, I say.

—Then let's go out, my shout.

Sometimes I think Ilana only offers so she can choose where we eat. I tell her the Indian place is good, but we end up in Cobb and Co, Grandma's favourite.

The interior is dark with wood. We sit in the courtyard so Ilana can smoke, next to a mural of the Tararua Ranges, with its thick outlines of ridges, as if painted by a child.

Once we're given menus, she takes no time at all. She calls the waiter over and orders the Cobb Carnivore: 200g Premium Angus Rump Steak with five Cobb's Country Ribs.

I'm put on the spot. There are more vegetarian options than I anticipated: nachos with salsa, mushroom fettuccine, pumpkin and ricotta lasagne, a burger. I do silent sums, and choose the lasagne.

—You realise this place is settler pride, I say. —With the saloon doors and everything.

—Can we just have a nice meal? Or is that not possible with you?

I sink into my chair.

Ilana calls the waiter back and orders a pint. —Want anything?

I shake *no*.

There's a palm in a pot that keeps nodding, even though there isn't any wind.

When the food comes, my pasta is overcooked, and my pumpkin, under.

—You should've heard some of the things my grandma said today, I tell her, as I shift the skin of the cheese around with my fork. —Talking about dolls and guns. She even called the deposit on the bach *blood money*.

—I think you should listen to her, Ilana says.

—She's gone batshit.

—She's muddled, but she's not crazy.

—Are you saying you know my family history better than me?

—No, I'm saying she does.

I can never win with Ilana. She's done with her meal first and watches me eat. I've finished all the hard chunks of pumpkin. I was saving the cheddar and béchamel for last, but having got this far, I'm full. I push my plate over to her.

When we get up to the counter, the waiter asks, —Split bill?

—Yeah, cheers, she says.

Quick, desperate subtraction in my head. It's Wednesday, the day before my benefit payment. I don't have enough.

—Jesus, Ilana says. Then, —Fine, put it on mine.

I try to say *sorry* or *thank you* but the words will not dislodge from my throat.

On the way back, she sees the bar, open.

—I'm going in, she says. —You're fine to walk home.

It's not a question.

+

Nick would always say, —Dinner and drinks came to forty-three.

Even though I was standing next to him as he paid. He liked to remind me how expensive I was, get half back later.

+

Crossing Exeter Street, I see Archie. He's taking a teenage boy for a night-time driving lesson, or else he has a son too young, a grandson too old. Whoever he is, Archie tells him to speed up. I have to run right off the road. They pull close to the curb, laughing.

Then they take off, backlights like fake jewels set in the greying air.

+

Number thirty-one is a thing of stitches, part Wayne, part my grandma. A war raged between the photos of London and the paintings of Gisborne, the portrait of Diana and the portrait of Te Whiti, the Royal Worcester porcelain figures and the carved model of a marae. Nowhere was this truer than the bookshelves. I skim my hands along spines. Alan Bennett's *Writing Home* next to Leo Fowler's record of the wharenui, *Te Mana o Turanga*, and a book of Māori proverbs. *The Queen's English* by Arnold Wall next to Friedrich Engels' *The Origin of the Family, Private Property and the State.* E. M. Forster's *A Passage to India* beside *Polynesian Mythology*, no author on the cover.

But lately she's been winning the battle. His paintings were taken down to have the glass repaired, or fix a hook, then not put back up. His model marae collected so many dead flies it was moved from the lounge to the spare bedroom. His books keep falling behind the cases and not being retrieved.

Nothing of his gets chucked, just shuffled to the back, as if in a pack of cards.

Whereas Grandma's stuff is rising to the top. Last year she found a Turner print of *Rain, Steam and Speed*. It's hanging in the dining room, the one she never uses, because the Victoria rug's too expensive to walk on. Her cabinets with the sliding glass doors gather patterned saucers and cups with pink roses and dust.

It's what I will think of, when I think of her. Rooms soaked in this yellow light. The ash tree breaking out in blossom. Gin and tonics, complete with a lemon slice, fresh from the garden.

But it feels different without her here. I find Bombay gin under the bench, but no tonic. I don't even bother with a lemon. I use one of her best glasses, cut crystal. I have to remove a post-it note from the bottom. *Lloyd and Jules.* It's not Grandma's handwriting. I start to find them all over, behind every original painting, every art deco vase or lampshade, every mirror with a scalloped edge. *Lloyd and Jules. Lloyd and Jules. Lloyd and Jules.* The only things of any value, monetarily, at least. So I move them. I put them on the lids of burnt pots and bundle them into old jumpers. *Lloyd and Jules* on the shower curtain, *Lloyd and Jules* on the underside of tea-stained doilies.

I find the title to the bach in the bottom of a cabinet next to Grandma's computer, beneath Ian Bostridge CDs and Westpac statements and floppy discs. I put it in the bin. It won't do anything:

223

property these days isn't held in pieces of paper. But the corners soak red with cold tomato soup.

I find the envelope amongst her stockings, *Cooper Campbell Law* stamped across its seal. Below, in Grandma's hand, *My Will.* I can't bring myself to read it. But I slip it inside flesh-coloured stockings, and I jam the drawer with a sock.

+

Two weeks after we broke up, Nick rang me, drunk, telling me how much money I owed him. Seventeen hundred dollars, he'd calculated.

+

This is a house full of ghosts. That's what happens when you hoard.

A suitcase of Stuart's things sleeps in the spare room—no one ever opens it. I got a shirt from there as a teenager and Helen told me to put it back.

The Christmas cards go up on the mantelpiece and don't come down. *Season's Greetings* and not much else. Same with the mass letters the elderly send each other, boasting disguised as keeping-in-touch, *Jason bought his second home, our granddaughter Lucy got married in Saint Paul's, the kōwhai tree is flowering.*

I see she's kept one from Nick. *Thanks for the time, you were generous.* That's a lot, coming from him.

But then again, I cherrypick the worst memories, trundle them to the front. I think about them over and over again, as if they're my Hail Marys and they're going to save me. If I don't, I end up thinking about the good times. Like the time he brought me dinner from Satya when I stayed late in the studio. Or the time he picked me up from a party in Manakau, when I was too poor to Uber home. Or when I woke up once, here in Levin, and he had washed every single cup, scrubbing their insides until they were bone white.

+

Sometimes I think I can hear his breathing. Sometimes I think I'm just imagining it.

I hang up first. I always do.

+

On the packet of the pregnancy test it says you can get your result in a minute. I wish it wasn't so fast. I want to delay it for as long as possible.

The stick is wrapped like a muesli bar, blue shiny plastic, ribbed at each end. I rip it open. Not so much a stick—it's curved and arched. It looks as if it would make a good tongue depressor. Say *ah*. It smells like surgical gloves. That weird plastic off-ness of the nurses' room in a GP clinic. Lift up your sleeve.

I worry most about who I would have to tell. Could I keep a pregnancy from Ilana? Could I keep it from Helen?

Concentrate on the actions. Each one is simple in itself. You walk to the bathroom. You take the cap off, you pee, you stare.

Watching the white window. Waiting for its lines to turn visible.

Keep the ringing at bay keep the ringing at bay.

+

Of course, I know I'm not five months pregnant. But I didn't just see Nick that once in August. I saw him again and again. I could say I don't know why I did it, but I do. When I thought he was fucking Rhiannon, I was jealous, and I was turned on. It'd been years since I'd been sexually attracted to him and it was only because he wasn't available anymore, wasn't supposed to be. But he was. He was too available. He would drop anything if I said I felt like seeing him, even for an hour. He would be waiting outside mine in fifteen minutes with a semi and sweaty palms and some sort of cliché. *I missed you*, maybe, *I still love you*, a red rose.

Helen saw him one night.

—Do you have to keep breaking his heart? she said.

But that was what I revelled in.

Then I stopped answering most of his calls. The game had lost its excitement. The sex had lost its appeal. When I did pick up, I refused to say anything.

—Speak to me, he'd say. —Tell me what I did?

—Speak to me, he'd say. —I just need to hear your voice.

I didn't even give him that.

+

One straight blue line. Negative. My ribcage expands. The air hits my lungs so hard that it could be water itself.

I try to stand but my jeans are still huddled about my ankles. For a second, I loll on the spot, like a drunk at a crossing, then I hit my head on a white sconce and fall, stomach first, onto the bathmat. I twist onto my back and scrunch fingers into my belly. It puckers in my hands, easy as moulding clay. The damp seeps through my T-shirt. The mat's still wet from this morning's showers. Ilana's shower. She could be home any minute. I pull my jeans up first, then myself. I shunt the test and its packaging into the bin by the counter.

+

My grandma used to call me a changeable beauty, but that's not exactly true. My looks do change, from one moment to the next. My features are always wriggling around in my face. It's the beauty part that's not quite right. Sometimes I am, beautiful I mean, from a certain angle, in a certain light. But sometimes, unfathomably, I am very, very ugly.

+

I hear her before I see her, Ilana, struggling to find the front door key under the mat. Stubbed toes and swearwords making dents in the silence. I could get up, I could turn on the outside light for her, but I won't.

—I hope you didn't drive home in this state, I say, even though I know she hasn't. The sound of the car would've been the first thing to wake me.

—I'm sorry, she says, slurring. —I'm sorry I left you back there. I can be a bitch sometimes.

—You're always a bitch.

—That's not true, is it?

—Maybe not when you're this drunk.

—I'm just, she says, —I'm just wary, you know, of getting too close. I feel like I don't really know you.

—You know me, I lie, —you know me as well as anyone.

227

XVII

Sometimes when Ilana moves I feel it beside me: a whole ocean rocking backwards and forwards beneath the sheets. It keeps me awake. Tonight, she turns to spoon me in the dark. —I'm sorry, she whispers occasionally. I can't be sure whether she's conscious, or merely saying it in her sleep.

And I want to fold her back, flatten her like a postcard, someone I've been to once but never really lived in.

+

I dream I am in Whāngārā, but it looks more like Waipawa. A man knocks on the door, irate.

—You've left your window open.

+

We don't wake in a good mood. *On the wrong side of the bed,* as Grandma would say, but maybe we're just in the wrong bed altogether, sharing it with the wrong person.

—You were wasted last night, I tease, which Ilana doesn't like. She pretends that she doesn't get drunk.

—You were rude, she says.

—So were you.

And that's how it starts. Or maybe it was earlier, when she spilt her coffee on my jeans and I got angry and she said they were too big for me anyway. Or maybe it was later, maybe it really started with what she said about my grandma.

—I think she's telling the truth.

Because she is, isn't she?

The men on my grandad's side, they weren't missionaries. Alfred was, originally, but they both became soldiers: him a lieutenant, his son, Leighton, a major. The New Zealand Wars. That's where the money came from, my grandad's inheritance. I knew it already. For Pākehā, the task is always to forget.

There's something of them in me. There's flesh to exorcise.

But I say, —What the fuck would you know? You don't know anything.

—I know you're in denial. I know you're full of guilt. You know your white guilt doesn't help anyone? she yells after me, because I'm already out of the room.

Into the hallway. Shut the door. Into the bathroom. Shut the door. Into the toilet. Shut the door. Ilana's there, pushing on it, forcing it open.

—Leave me alone.

—Stop running away.

So I emerge, stand there in the bathroom with her. Pink paint, pink tiles, pink scales on the floor. China ducks on the wall. Two of three, the other must've broken. I consider throwing one of them, not at her, near her, just to hear it smash.

—I'm not running anywhere.

That's when I see it. The pregnancy test in the bin, white handle on display.

She follows my gaze.

I can hear the dripping of a loose tap.

—So you are pregnant?

Drip, drip. Drip.

—It was negative.

—Why did you think you were?

—I didn't. I…

The words stick in my throat like a piece of gum. Spit it out before it loses its flavour. But I never do. I always chew mine till there's none left.

—I thought I might be.

She straightens up so that she's almost my height. Ilana has big bones which seem to swell on command, calcify like a mollusc. Tensing all over.

—You couldn't have thought you were five months along.

She knows I slept with Nick in August, nothing more.

—I slept with another guy, alright.

—Who?

Her front lip curls upwards.

—It was him, wasn't it?

—What's it to you? Why do you care who I fuck?

—I care that you're a liar. I just don't get it. Why would you go back to bad sex? But you know, I had a feeling.

She thinks she's smarter than me. I can tell.

—Oh really? Did you have a feeling when I faked it with you, too? Or did I get that past you?

The drips are irregular now, clipped and infrequent. Drip. Drip, drip.

Like the way rain starts, or the way it ends.

—What are you saying?

Her hands fall to the backs of her thighs. Cups them. How you'd cup someone else's, not your own.

—You've never made me come either.

Ilana could take most things, but not that. She bolts. I follow, though I have nothing to say. I'm about to tap her shoulder, touch her arm, something, when I notice Cleome. She's standing in the dining room with her hands over her ears. When she spots us, she jumps, as if she's the one who should be surprised. She's pissing herself. It makes no sound as pee runs in rills down her legs, steeps into the Victoria rug.

Cleome says nothing, only darts to the front door.

And Ilana's gone. Ripping round the house, screaming *fuck* and *where are they*, looking for her cigarettes, forgetting that she smoked them all at dinner.

+

Grandma used to smoke when she ate. When she ate, and when she cleaned.

She quit two years before she was diagnosed. She always blamed the stress of quitting, not the smoking itself.

+

The paper of a twelve-year-old cigarette is parched and crunchy between your fingers. You have to be gentle to keep it intact. The tobacco is dry and thinned. It falls out like bits of curly hair from a razor. The inhale is harsh.

It doesn't taste like anything, really, except smoke, except heat.

I'm not heartless. I showed Ilana where my grandma kept her just-in-case-pack, in the kitchen drawer, the one spilled with flour, unused themed napkins, loose rubber bands. Under all of that. You had to know where to look.

Now we're sitting on the back porch, smoking them till they're gone.

Almost gone. I pocket one for later.

—How far away is your car?

Breathe in.

—A couple of blocks.

And out.

—If you leave now you could be in Auckland by five.

In again.

—It won't take that long.

Out.

There's a lag, between my breath, and hers.

+

You can only look away from something for so long. Face the other direction, give it no name, but ignore it long enough and it takes its own shape, its own name. It's like alluvial soil. It may start out loose, small, separate pebbles, eroded by water. But eventually, it lithifies, the parts become one. Turn to stone. Eventually, you have to look at it.

If Ilana hadn't left we would've become something. Not something good, but something all the same. So she had to leave. It had to become nothing, nothing at all.

+

When Chris and Helen got together they thought it would last. Ten years later and Chris was flying me down to Wellington every term for a weekend. To Helen, she had always chosen *the worst weekend, the worst possible one*. There was always a reason why I shouldn't go. At the time I thought Helen was paranoid, but maybe there was an element of truth to it. Three years in a row I spent Mother's Day in Petone.

+

Every time you remember something you're only remembering the last time you thought of it.

+

Nick marked out the shows in newspapers and clicked attending on Facebook events. They were painting exhibitions, every one. I thought he was trying to make a point. Now I see it for what it was: just his way of trying.

+

I don't pause before answering my phone. I pick up, because I think it's him.

But it's Helen and there's an edge to her voice. Something you could come up against, fall over, if you're not careful.

Lloyd got a call as he was driving to the bach with a real-estate agent for an evaluation. He arrived to see a dozen people carrying water from the sea in buckets. And Nellie, standing on our lawn, directing the whole thing.

Only the kitchen was lost, and half the photo wall.

The fire department doesn't know how it started yet.

I imagine it was one of Ilana's cigarettes, burning quietly like a secret under the floorboards. Maybe it was burning the whole time we were there, its smoke mingling with ours. The slowest of fires.

+

How can fire be painless when you walk across it? If it can burn wood. If it can melt plastic.

+

I'm starving, even though I ate dinner last night. That kind of hollowed-out feeling, as if someone's been scraping at my insides with a chisel. But I can't bring myself to cook. I put Vogel's in the toaster. Ilana had the settings wrong: my toast pops up charred. So I put on more. Not one this time, but two.

Then butter and Marmite.

And another two.

I eat them in the dining room, no plate. The piss has already dried. Crumbs fall as I chew.

Lots of feelings will give you the sensation of hunger, if you let them.

+

I remember when Ashi first told me she was trying to lose weight. She asked if I wanted the chips in her lunchbox. We were eleven, sitting on the stone fence of Ponsonby Intermediate. I thought it was absurd. But I ate them anyway, crinkle cut and delicious.

234

It's top of my Facebook feed. *Ashi Prasad is in a relationship with Lachlan O'Connor.*

I feel ill. My vision is blurry and I need to lie down. I swing in and out of sleep—big, sickening transitions every time I wake. Because every time I wake I remember all over again. I remember everything.

From my bed in Auckland, I tell Helen what's happened. There are flies buzzing round my face that keep bursting into flames. I kill one in my hair.

—Have some soup, she says.

I tell her, no, it's summer. Then I say, —I don't feel here. Actually here.

Ashi is in the kitchen cutting garlic. Her bun silhouetted against the window, huge and round, a cartoon halo. Light spilling across the floor like milk. —You should really eat something, she says.

This bedroom is an abattoir. I'm slicing Lachlan head to toe, skinning him with the precision of a butcher. Pink flesh below.

Not just Lachlan, Ilana too, Nick, Lloyd. I cut them into little pieces, so small you could fit them in your palm. Bite-sized bits, so small they couldn't possibly hurt you.

Then I wash my hands.

See, I can be a butcher, too.

+

I bunch myself up, unable to move, thinking of something Ilana said today. We were talking about Kohimarama and the darkness that surrounds it. Land in the wrong hands.

—The girl who died at Bastion Point, the one in the fire, you know she's still there, Ilana said. —She'll leave when the wrongs are righted.

Until I realise that was a dream, too.

+

The sound didn't rush into my ears this time. It's only when I hear it—that helicopter, that warning, that endless siren—when I consciously hear it, muting everything else, that I understand I've been hearing it all day. It was there when I got up, when I smoked those cigarettes, ate the toast, checked Facebook. It was there through the phone call with Helen, so quiet at first I didn't discern it. So quiet, it blended right into my panic.

+

Eating is the way I can distract myself. Constant sums in my head. Like a hundred and ten for the glass of gin. Like eighty-five for the half bowl of tomato soup. Like nine hundred for the lasagne. Like one-forty for every piece of Very Thin Vogel's. Always overestimate, just to be sure. Get it down to zero get it down to zero get it down to zero. A daily total which carries over if I fail. Sometimes, it's hard to concentrate when I'm busy counting.

Today the numbers go too high. Nearly three thousand calories. I finish the whole loaf and still feel empty.

I'm dead weight, locked in my seat at the kitchen table with the garish floral print. If I look closely, I can distinguish stain from petal, red wine from stamen, dried mayonnaise from the leaves. I know if I turn the toaster upside down, black crusts and crumbs, months old, years even, will fall like shrapnel. A cockroach might scuttle out, too.

I go to the bathroom and I vomit and I vomit and I vomit.

I need to shit, but I can only manage nuggets, dark and shiny.

There's a discharge now: not period red, but brown, the sort I get when I've skipped menstruating for months in a row. This hasn't even been six weeks yet. It's my body that's discoloured it, like milk left in the fridge after its best-before date. I never read those. Maybe I should start. I want to be like that woman on *Obsessive Compulsive Cleaners*. I want to bleach everything. I want to enjoy the feeling when it hits the back of my throat. I want to feel the fumes on my face, under my skin. To bathe in it.

I take a shower instead. But the water comes from Lake Horowhenua. How can you wash yourself clean when the water isn't? I turn the tap up higher and higher.

I know I should feel hot, but I feel numb instead.

When I get out, my skin has turned bright pink. I can't put my clothes back on, it's too painful.

Then I grasp where I am: number thirty-one. By Helen's rules, that's a four. I try to remember if it used to be different, twenty-nine, say, until local planning or a bored small-town council shifted everyone a little to the right. But no, as far back as I can remember my grandma has had the same letterbox, white and tin and scroll-top, numbers nailed to its face. A three, and a one.

+

My thoughts are stuck on a loop. They go round and round and round and, strangely, the thing I think of most is fucking Nick in the Kelly Tarlton's car park. Right below Bastion Point, overlooking Ōkahu Bay. Where I fingered his ass, fingered until he came. The emptiest of sex, the emptiest of feelings, on land saturated with the past. On tapu land, I'm sure of it.

+

I get the text. *Pita's been hospitalised.*

George says she stopped by, knocked and knocked till a neighbour came out, told her the news.

+

I almost ring Ashi to ask her if she remembers walking through fire with me. But I'm scared she will have forgotten. Or I'm scared she'll remember it differently. I'm scared she'll weaken the memory: it'll become drawn, a used tea bag in the sink. I'm scared she'll think it hurt.

+

And I wonder what I will remember today as, later. The day the bach burned down and Pita went into a psych ward. Or the day Ilana left and I ate the whole loaf of Vogel's. The day I didn't know what to say to Ashi anymore. The day I called Chris, crying, saying I just really need one of my mums.

Because I'm either feeling everything right now, or I'm feeling nothing.

xviii

The receptionist at Madison wears barbell earrings and a stern expression. She sees the blisters ascending like bubbles on my forehead and tells me this isn't a general hospital.

—My grandma, I correct her, —I'm here to see my grandma.

She says visiting hours are almost over, but I'm already through the Brooklyn doors. There's someone vacuuming in the room of the Jeremy Kyle fan. The sheets are off her bed.

Grandma's eyesight is too far gone for her to notice anything different about me.

—Do you want the rest of my lunch?

On her bedside table are two chicken sandwiches, one triangle gnawed at, as though by a rat. Small, wet bites.

I tell her about the post-its: *Lloyd and Jules, Lloyd and Jules*.

—You get in there, she says. —You take what you want love.

I could count on one hand the number of times she's called me that.

+

Her original prognosis was two months. She said goodbye each year at Christmas, until she gave up on dying. It was taking too long.

+

Ghosting is when you leave without saying a thing. But that's not always how it happens, is it? Becoming a ghost, an actual ghost, isn't always so quiet.

+

Grandma says someone died last night. Three thirty-two, she saw it on her clock. She was woken up by the death rattle.

I picture the woman with the grooved face. The music must have fallen from it. I picture the way they would have carried her out, blank, covered in a sheet, gripped by two pairs of hands.

We say death's clutches because death is willing to hold us, willing to never let go.

+

Wayne left a suicide note. *Don't sell my stuff.*

Lloyd always said, —But he didn't say not to chuck it.

Ringing Grandma saying, *it's time to get rid of it all.* Lead anchor at the bottom of the house.

+

—I brought something for you, I say, taking out the cigarette. Grandma doesn't realise what it is until it's in her hands. Wordless, she heaves herself up from the pillows and I rearrange them behind her, shut the door, and light it.

I ask her why Conrad turned up at the bach that one Christmas.

—You know he inherited nothing himself, she says. —Your grandad tried to help him out. He sent cheques for years. But in the end I said, *that's enough*. It was our money, and Conrad wanted it all. He came to say that land was rightfully his.

I think about that word, *rightfully*.

—Well he did more than just say it, as you know. He was dying to get his hands on it. Took Wayne and three of the locals to restrain him. Then I went next door and called the cops.

We say people are dying for something: for love, for money, for their quarter-acre dream. But what we really mean is they would kill for it. Some have.

I say, —Why was Conrad so angry? I thought his brother didn't inherit anything either.

—Oh no, he did. Everyone did but him. Conrad and Leighton had fallen out. But why should we be made to pay?

—Fallen out over what?

—Conrad said World War I was a more honourable war.

—Than Leighton's? I ask.

—Yes.

—The New Zealand Wars?

—Yes.

—And you know, she continues, —Wayne thought neither were honourable. *They were both a waste of lives*, he'd say. But he was smart enough not to say that to the men in his family.

Smart, or possibly scared. Smart, or simply folded into this family's silence.

—Did Grandad see his dad again? I ask. —After what happened at the bach?

—No, but his mother still visited, right up until we moved to Levin.

Grandma has finished her cigarette. Ash speckles her clean white sheets. I help her to lie down again, brush the duvet twice. The studded receptionist gives me a dirty look when I leave. I wonder if she's smelt the smoke.

+

I remember Helen telling me about her nanna. A frail woman who used to bake the best Anzac biscuits in the world. We found the recipe once. She'd given it to Grandma, but she never made them. They called for a lot of butter, sugar, and two eggs. They would've spoiled, shipped to distant battlefields. It's lucky her son never saw one.

And I remember something else Helen told me about her, as we drove across Gladstone Bridge in Gisborne. *Nanna always came round alone.*

Then again, I could be inventing that. It seems too perfect, too timely a recollection. Pulled from the recesses like a fish already on a hook.

+

As a kid, I used to walk on these roads. I don't know if there are more cars now or if I was braver then. The streets would heat up and stick to my feet like glucose syrup.

Today I stay on the footpath. Shoes on. I have the sudden urge to get a Brazilian wax, to lie on a mattress and feel a woman dressed in all white press and prod and smooth me—to feel it hurt, but only just.

242

Chris can't get me till Saturday. She says I need to be up early. She says she'll drive me home.

+

I wake in the night, again and again. I can hear it all, even the things that aren't there. Footsteps, breathing, someone beside me. The sheets feel like sandpaper on my skin.

Dreams come in discordant snatches. My hands are red as I dig in the sand. My hands are red as I touch Ilana.

—Don't mind me, she says, —I'm only bleeding.

—We have to put out the fire at the bach, Francine replies, —before the open home.

A small crowd lines up for the viewing. We're standing on Cheltenham beach in Auckland.

+

I've never stayed here alone. The house feels empty and too quiet. I can't seem to grow myself big enough to take up all this space. I put the TV on in the morning, for the white noise, and hole up in the bedroom. It's the one place I can fill.

I finish *Māori Boy*. Ihimaera says tangata whenua travel in their dreams. They can talk to their tūpuna, heal familial wounds, find taonga. It's a comfort to read.

Then Jules and Jane pour in. I am in odd socks and a T-shirt that smells. They are in clothing that looks cheap, though you know it's not: jeans with faded thighs, racer singlets. They shriek when they see my face. —What's wrong with it?

The blisters have popped overnight and are now sore and weeping. I lie and say sunburn. They stare as if I'm contagious.

243

And I sense it, the drop in oxygen. Having to share it with them.

—Gosh, girl, why are all the windows shut? Jules asks.

—The flies, I say, weakly.

She opens the bay doors before she even takes off her sunglasses, huge and dark and disconcerting. Jane just stands there, flapping her hands in her face and looking distressed. Then she excuses herself, leans against the porch with her palms on her knees, head bent forward. When she comes in again, she says, —How could you stand that stench?

I hadn't noticed it. There was a faint smell of cat piss at first, but that's gone now.

—Basil? I say.

—What?

—Grandma's cat, her shorthair.

—No, the house itself. How long since she's cleaned?

She and Jules walk through the rooms, touching things as though their arms are snakes approaching prey. Slow, then very fast. Snap back. They open cupboard doors and squeal, lift up the corners of rugs, point at the dust and the stains, muttering, —We knew she wasn't coping by herself.

It makes the place look cleaner to me. It makes all the dirt and dust inconsequential.

+

I ring Helen to ask her if there's anything she really wants, before they grab it. She just cries and says, —What a question.

But she rings back five minutes later saying, —A few things, actually.

She directs me to a line drawing of a chair by a window in the spare room, Grandma's fake emerald earrings, the good type of fake, Grandad's gardening shirt, and their early copy of *Peter Pan*.

—Can you keep an eye out for my Ginny doll? She had a polka-dot dress and red barrel curls. I'm not sure she's still around.

—Grandma said you almost made them turn back during a tsunami warning because you left it at the bach.

She laughs. —I'd forgotten about that. God, what an awful holiday.

+

Last summer, after Elam finished, I slept in till two most days. I didn't have my job at Dida's yet. Helen went to the doctor to ask if suicide could be genetic. Then she called me to say that our GP had said no, but depression can be. At that point she lowered her voice, a deliberate opening, a tilted head.

—Good to know, I said, and hung up.

+

Stuart was a suspected suicide, of course. The toxicology reports were inconclusive. There were his SSRIs, and low levels of Unisom. They couldn't say the exact date of death, so it's possible the drugs may have continued to metabolise, fade away. There was some suggestion of contamination, but that came like a footnote, crammed in small font at the end. Those tests take weeks. He had already been turned to smoke by the time the results were back.

+

It feels like the house is a corpse and we're all picking at it, picking the bones clean. I take the pile of my grandad's *National Geographics* from the seventies and eighties. Lists down their sides: *Pandas—Orange County—Blue Water. Acid Rain—Atlantic Salmon—Zimbabwe.* I bag up some of my grandma's plastic flowers. They remind me of her. I look for the doll, but I can't find it.

Stuart's suitcase cowers like an animal in the corner. As if it can see me seeing it.

It flew on the plane with his ashes, hard and boxy and not very big at all. When I unzip plastic teeth from teeth, it gives off the stale smell of a charity shop, things kept too long. Nothing is folded. Whoever packed this packed it fast, as though they just dumped the contents of his drawers until it was full. They weren't very selective. In amongst the knitted jerseys and Morrissey tapes and bundled white socks, still imprinted with his feet, are condom packets, unopened, and boxes of prescription meds. Panadeine and Prozac for pain that ended decades ago.

The strange thing about stuff is that it outlasts people.

+

I remember going to a show with Nick called *The UnNaming of the Beast.* All the figures looked like ghosts, their bodies bent to fill gaps. They were the colour of shells.

The paintings were made using only salvage materials from Christchurch. We were still trying to salvage things. Nick spent a precise minute looking at each painting, as if he was doing what he supposed was right.

I kept the price list from that exhibition. I couldn't afford anything, I just liked the titles.

+

Somewhere, floating, is an island of rubbish twice the size of Texas.

+

I take *Meat Is Murder* from the suitcase. I don't have a way to play it, but I might, one day. Then I slip down to the basement. I know that everything here will go to the tip if I don't save it.

There are corroding gardening tools: trowels and edgers and secateurs, a hoe and a saw. Gloves muddy from the last time they were used, twenty years ago. A wheelbarrow missing a wheel. A desk missing two drawers. Flax ketes, oil lamps. Cat carriers that smell of pee.

I don't know where to start. The bare high-watt bulb is completely obscured by its own brightness, a sun flare in a room with no windows. It illuminates the particles of ambling dust. I decide to tackle the bigger things first. Rolls of carpet, rolls of wallpaper, moth-eaten. Damp quilted mattress, faded print of roses. A stained fuel can, the smell of petrol. Broken fans and fan heaters. Old bikes and springs and headboards. Once all metal, now all rust.

Oxidisation is a process of letting go. The iron gives up its electrons to the air. The air takes them away.

+

I try to estimate the size of Chris' boot. It can't fit everything. I choose the iron headboards, picturing them against the white wall of a gallery, leaving ghosts of themselves in flaky red. The fan too, it's old, fingers separated from blades by only the scarcest of wires.

The deeper I go, the more I find. Tubs of house paint and bottles of fertilisers. Upholstered chairs, un-upholstered chairs. I can fit two of the fold-out deck types, threadbare fabric seats. I might remove them altogether, make them unusable. That would look more conceptual.

Records without sleeves and windows without glass. A mouldy poster for *Twelve Angry Men*.

I can see the show now. I'd write a proposal about the inheritance of objects, link it to the inheritance of trauma, or violence, or guilt, or hoarding, or something. I'd make subtle references to my family's darker figures, but leave it oblique, so everyone thinks I'm smart and deep, so Helen doesn't get too upset. It would've been perfect in Fuzzy Vibes, that underground feel. But of course, that's closed now: Karangahape's rising rents. Maybe it would work in Artspace. I'd title it *The Un-Naming of the Past.*

+

I hear Jane, or maybe Jules, screech. They've probably realised the post-it notes have been moved.

Stacked in the corner are cardboard boxes with brand names. *Krispa: they're not like other chips. Pams Cherish Nappies. Huntly and Palmers Cream Crackers, cut here to display.* A dotted line. Inside, I know there is more. Things on top of things. I can't see them, so I can pretend they're not there.

That's how I deal with the stuff at home I know I shouldn't keep. The gifts I never wanted, my high-school calculus textbooks, stowed under my bed in boxes. Chris bought that neck rest for me, I think, or I'll relearn differentiation, one day, when I have time. The problem is I've had a lot of time, and I haven't looked at a page of it.

248

But today I bring down one box, then another. Most are filled with Grandad's books. *Speeches and Documents on New Zealand History, Tuhoe: The Children of the Mist, Takitimu, Living with History Two.* I pick one up. There are sections marked with dog ears and yellowed newsprint. They're about Te Kooti. I pick up another. Te Kooti is flagged again. The scorched earth campaign, over and over. Each time it appears there is the same scribbled annotation, quiet, pencil almost faded. I could rub it out, I could brush the words off with just my thumb's sweat. Each time, in the margin, my grandad has written: *Dad's dad.*

The southern faction of that invasion left from Wairoa.

+

It's in the Pams box that I find all the photos.

There's an album coated in red leather, thick cords binding the pages together. There are no sleeves, no holders in the corners, no crepe paper between pages. The photos were simply glued on, and now lift around the sides, threatening to fall right off. They've turned sepia, or maybe they always were.

I see my great-grandad Conrad's shop. It's nothing like I'd pictured. Centred door, windows small and panelled. The white balance is off, so I can't make out the display, if there was one. The white balance is off in most of the photos. Pale clothing blends right into pale backgrounds, cutting bodies in half. Heads float like ghosts, like wall decorations.

Other photos are loose, dark and patchy, hard to decipher, as if pictures need light to stay alive too. Some are behind broken glass, skinny landscape frames that place portrait next to portrait, a lengthy line of men. Boys in school pictures. My grandad on his wedding day. Men in uniforms. I recognise one from the museum in Waipawa. The sashed man, the medalled man, the major in the New Zealand Wars.

Leighton has my eyebrows. Or, more accurately, I have his.

+

I come from a long line of butchers. Murderers and majors and fathers who threatened to kill their son, all for a slice of seaside property.

+

Jules comes downstairs carrying rubber gloves and a bottle of bleach. —You might want these, she says. She sees my pile: the headboards, the house paints, window frames, bike parts, records, the fan, now joined by two boxes, one of books, one of photos. — We should really hire a skip, shouldn't we?

—Oh no, I say, —these, these I'm taking.

xix

If God was a hot air balloon we'd all be believers.

They rise like the glass baubles in a Galileo thermometer on a cold day. Red first, then blue—the baskets, those little tags of temperatures. A balloon drifts so far over the town that it looks as if it'll never come back.

One of these days, that'll be me. It will be the last time I visit. Levin will become just another State Highway town I drive through on my way to Wellington. There'll be nothing to tie me here.

—Do you remember the accident in Caterton? I ask Chris.

She's lining her boot and backseat with sheets. She doesn't want Bo or my grandad's crap to touch the upholstery.

—What accident?

I point at the sky. The hot air balloon collided with a power line and went up in flames. They tested the pilot's corpse: he came back positive for THC. I remember the sound Nick made when that came on the news, a sort of satisfied grunt.

—Doesn't mean anything, I say. —That will stay in your system for months.

Chris looks at me.

—How much have you been smoking lately? she asks.

+

When I first slept with Ilana we would get high and do things: get high and watch a movie, get high and order takeaways, get high and have sex. At the end we just got high for the sake of it: got high and sat on benches, got high in the light of laptop screens, got high and didn't talk.

I have to remind myself to use past tense.

+

I stare at the bed we shared. Chris calls to me asking if I need any help. My bag is packed, but I have the sudden unshakable feeling that I've forgotten something. That I should be taking this pillowcase for the scent of her or checking the sheets for any stray curls. That I should grab the cup she drank from. Scoop up all the words she left behind.

And I'm not sure if I'm trying to remember her, or erase her from this house.

I make thumbprints on the photos of Nick and me. I feel like a giant, blotting out his face with just a finger. A year ago, I couldn't bear to look at these. But they're like lavender in an old love letter, flattening. They're like olives in brine: over time, they become more palatable.

Chris is in the hallway now, forcing me into one of Grandma's awful wide-brimmed hats, pastel and woven, chiffon flower on the

252

side. —You're not getting sunburn on your sunburn, she says.

Then she laughs until she cries when she sees it on.

+

Places look uglier than I remember. Foxton is dead expanses of driveways, a concrete company that calls itself Roaches. *Tanks for Sale.*

+

It was from an old cursive letter to her dad, paper disintegrating in her hands, that Helen learnt Alfred had been buried not far north of here. Sometimes, on our way home, we would drive around and around those parts, as if looking for an unmarked grave. I think Helen thought she'd know, just by the feel of a place, by the soil his body had fed, the grass he'd grown, the dust from his bones flecking the bark of a tree, making it pale. The roads were always quiet. Sheep would be grazing, then run off, not used to seeing cars.

+

Sanson is all tractors and diggers and trucks. Not out in fields, but in hard grey yards.

Bulls trades in bad puns. *Veget-a-bull* outside the grocery, *Cure-a-bull* outside the doctor's, *Full-as-a-bull* outside the pub. Opposite from Scully's, the upmarket lavender-soap store, is the police station. *Const-a-bull.* One sits outside in his car. Chris speeds past, going sixty-five in a fifty zone, but he does nothing. White woman in a white car. Not his type.

Helen and I were always stopped, though that was for being slow. She would cleave to the left side of the road and pull over often, but people still slumped on their horns.

—We've had complaints, the officer would say. —You realise you're doing eighty?

—It's my daughter, she'd say, —she's feeling sick.

Usually we got off, but sometimes there was a ticket. We learnt to take the National Park route because it was more desolate.

+

I point out the huntaway statue to Bo in Hunterville. There's a building, *Gallery One* painted on its front. Boarded-up windows. A motel which calls itself a hotel, old Coca-Cola branding still nailed to its wall, faded to the colour of strawberry ripple ice cream. A diner that you know won't sell vegetarian food.

Mangaweka had its airport cafe, a plane you could sit inside to eat. Now I think it's a museum. It looks much cruder than it used to, almost papier-mâché. I wanted to go in, as a kid, but Helen would make me wait for Taihape, where the coffee was better.

There's a fault line running underneath here. It opens up the road each year. I remember a bus driver announcing it. *This is where the concrete gives in. This is where we shovel gravel.*

Just out of town, a huddle of trees lean, as if blown by the same wind for years and years and years.

+

Ashi and I used to clamber over the trees in the Domain. The ones that grew huge, varicose veins bulging from the dirt. Roots so big they could hide you. Helen would watch as we lurched between branches. Ashi always kept to the lower ones and I always got hurt. I thought I was the better climber, but now I see that wasn't true.

I draft and redraft a message to her. *Congratulations, I saw your relationship status on Facebook* or *Hey how are you?* Nothing profound. In the end I go with, *I think I found a jumper you left behind.* I can buy one in Auckland.

+

When missionaries arrived in Waiōuru, they grazed merinos on the tussock. Te Kooti brought his warriors here and they feasted on the flock.

Now, Waiōuru is a military camp. It's a tiny strip, three unmanned diesel refuelling spots for freight trucks and the National Army Museum. It looks like a Scandinavian prison: adjoining blocks of concrete, some smooth and stained, others serrated. Strong brutalist lines. There are New Zealand flags flying and a red sign saying *Home Fires Café.*

I wander while Chris orders the coffees. In the gift shop, you can buy poppy everything. Poppy brooches, poppy wine glasses, poppy vanity bags. On the tables there are old ads from the war wedged between plastic holders. *Destroy Surplus Food Coupons: Don't give them away—every coupon destroyed means more food for Britain.* Chris comes over with serviettes wrapped around the cups.

—Be careful, it's hot. They didn't double them up.

She says the food in the bain-marie looks as if it's been there since Monday so we'll have to wait for Taupō, but then she buys two egg sandwiches ten minutes later when she fills up at Z, and puts one next to me.

We're silent for a while. It's a comfortable silence. I check my phone for a reply from Ashi, but there's none. The tallest of power lines transmit beside us. They are huge steel crinolines, dresses made for giants. If I was with Helen we would wind up all the windows—she's scared of the rays. Forget the active peaks. Rangipō Desert is flanked by three: Ruapehu, Ngauruhoe and Tongariro, the belly of Māui's fish. It's not an actual desert: there's too much rainfall for that. But the land was made barren by eruptions thousands of years ago. This place is rich in nothing but pumice and tussock and ash.

I don't touch the egg sandwich, but I like that I can, if I want to.

+

—How's Liz? I say, only hours too late.

—Actually, we broke up.

Her words are bare, no skin on them. We both stare straight ahead. The road markings flash and are eaten by the hood of the car.

—I'm so sorry.

There's one of those pauses, when you're not sure who's supposed to speak next.

—It happens to the best of us, huh kiddo.

Chris puts her hand on my shoulder and squeezes. Outside, pine trees stand in methodical rows, waiting to be felled. Tongariro-Rangipō Prison is signalled by a series of blue Department of Corrections signs. It's just one road off from the highway. I tried to look at it on Google Street View once, but it wouldn't let me. The little yellow man would pop right back into his spot on the corner of my screen.

It used to be Hautu Detention Camp. It's where Wayne was detained during the war.

+

You can pass through Tūrangi without even noticing it. Motor lodges for tourists who go trout fishing. A place to buy boats: Yamaha, Hutchwilco. Residents in damp homes struggling to pay their power bills. I guess it is like anywhere else. Land taken from hapū who didn't want to sell, wāhi tapu stolen, built on top of.

+

Not far north of here, Te Kooti was defeated at Te Ponanga. Not far south, he was defeated at Te Porere. Two fingers lost from his left hand.

+

Chris taps impatiently on the steering wheel, waiting for a Skoda to vacate its park.
    —What's he doing?
    I don't mind the wait. I don't feel like getting out at all. Taupō is in full school-holiday bloom, swarming with people, like sugar left on a bench in summer, all the ants and the flies and the cockroaches. Jet boats carve trails into the lake, kids screech from the train ride, mothers grip them to laps as their little limbs fling in each direction. Everywhere people are wearing shorts, bare

shoulders, ice creams melting down wrists. The park looks too green, as if it's been digitally enhanced, and we're just standing in front of the screen.

I walk Bo while Chris pays to use the Superloo. A boy in a flat peak and a girl in Havaianas traipse side by side. Every step she takes makes a slapping sound, plastic on foot. In the space between them, two arms are straightened, extended, expectant fingers. They brush a few times before he picks up the courage to grab her hand completely. I've never hated strangers more.

There's something about being depressed in summer, when everyone else is happy. I wish there were glasses for it, ones that block out the sun, sepia tone to take you back in time.

+

Nick's voice is a world away. There's a woman talking in the background. I hold my phone closer to my ear as if something so simple could erase the distance.

—I can't take this, he says. —You can't ignore almost all my calls and then ring me yourself.

—Aren't we friends? I say.

—No, he says, and hangs up.

There's sweat on the phone from my hand, from how tight I held it.

And there's a text back from Ashi. *I think I have everything?*

+

Chris drags me to a cafe called Replete. It's been here as long as I can remember. Her, Helen and me sitting outside on the pavement. I would always mix sugar and salt into the dregs of their coffee cups, read it like tea leaves. *Look, look what happened to your foam.*

Today I ask to sit inside. Chris starts saying something about *such a nice day*, but stops herself.

The counter is overwhelming. There is every type of sandwich: focaccia, panini, wholegrain, croissant. Stuffed kūmaras and risotto cakes. Fat slices, caramel and walnut, ginger. Overpriced samosas. Sweet chilli dipping sauce.

Chris is complaining. Words I haven't taken in. Listen. Something about a sausage and fennel frittata. —Well, why don't you do all-day breakfast?

The waitress is nervous. Her pen hovers above the pad. She keeps looking over her shoulder for someone to back her up.

—Give it a rest, I say.

Chris sighs and then laughs. —It's fine, she says. I don't know if she's excusing herself or the waitress. —What's the satay chicken slaw like?

The girl says it's one of her favourites.

—But what's the ratio, Chris pushes, —chicken to cabbage? I don't want a salad.

The waitress is flustered. Blonde strands keep falling from her ponytail and she keeps pushing them behind her ears. Chris orders the Vietnamese pork claypot. The waitress goes to the kitchen to check they have the ingredients.

—What do you want? Chris asks me.

—I'm not, I start, but end up staring into the glass, at my reflection not the food. She decides for me. —You don't want anything from the cabinet. There, look, smoked mushroom quesadilla.

It's the only vegetarian thing on the lunch menu.

When the waitress comes back, Chris apologises, no eye contact. But she pays with a fifty dollar note and tells her to keep the change.

She lifts her knife and fork before the food has even hit the table. Then she braces her elbows on either side of the pot and hangs her head over it, steam hitting her face.

—Mm, that smell.

Lemongrass.

I am slower to start. I eye my quesadilla as though it might come alive and jump off the plate. There is cheese oozing out the side. It draws me in. Once I start, I can't stop.

—I thought you looked hungry, Chris says. —Hungry or exhausted.

Tiredness is a kind of gravity: it pulls you to the ground.

There are banks on either side, a yellow sign telling us to slow down. I can't remember anything past Wairakei.

+

And this is where it always ends. On the Southern Motorway, hemmed in by street lamps and electrical towers, like Christmas trees left on the side of the road, bald as twigs. The Tāmaki Makaurau air clings to you, making you aware of every inch of skin, the whole circumference of your body. There's a truck trapped beside us, *Earthmovers Auckland*. A van advertises pest control and carpet cleaning. *Call Keith*, it says, next to a big Gisborne cockroach.

XX

One hundred yards of fabric
Fifty-six pounds sterling
Fifty wool blankets
Twenty cotton shirts
Twenty pairs of trousers
Twenty iron hatchets
Ten iron pots
Ten waistcoats
Ten caps
Four casks of tobacco
One box of pipes
One bag of flour
One bag of sugar

+

It's easy to forget that the land you live on is stolen. Ponsonby is
a place that actively forgets. It's forgotten the raids. It's forgotten

when Pride March was a protest. It's forgotten the pā sites, Te Tō and Okā, now drowned beneath swimming pools and multi-million-dollar villas. It's forgotten that College Hill was once Waikuta Stream. It's forgotten that Te Wai-o-Hua, and later, Ngāti Whātua, would have gathered flax and fish at Cox's Creek, or that Freemans Bay was a trading post. It's whitewashed all of that.

+

As soon as I got back I primed canvases—that's the easy part. Watery layers of gesso, mittens of paint on hands, strands of hair stuck together or carefully picked off wet surfaces.

This is the way a line unfolds. Tentative, at first. Hold your breath. And then let it fall out, the parts you can't keep in.

Ilana, fractions of her, never the sum, the whole thing. Fingers clenching the steering wheel. Teeth so small and sharp. Her rose, beginning to fade. You have to thin paint right down for tattoos: they're paler than you think. Orange tan like a glaze smothering everything, yanking her inwards. Razing any depth. Her face I frame by the scrape of a palette knife. Layers of pink and sienna pulled into scratchy ridges, stunted and stunting. Cut off.

Ashi, the hum of Indian yellow undercoats left visible around her head, like thick morning sun in her hair, like a saint. Sometimes I paint an oily stain of Lachlan behind her, catching on the weft of the canvas. But I always go back later and brush over him, leaving only shiny splinters.

I used to think of the time between thought and stroke as a kind of blockage. But I've realised it's a processing instead. I go to paint my grandma and it comes out like the old woman with the musical face. So I'm not ready for that yet. Give it time.

I haven't done anything with Wayne's stuff. Helen was furious I'd brought it all home, so it's been stacked in my room for the last week, what I can fit. The rest is on the porch.

But I still dream about that exhibition: paint can overturned in the centre, separated colours spreading across the gallery floor. Everyone would have to walk around it. Windows, glassless or cracked. Bike tubes making shadows that finger the wall, from their perch on a stack of books. Newspaper stubs poking out like toes. I'd pretend the assemblages were accidental.

The abstract would be in Helvetica Light. It would talk about objects as a realised curation of self, the online made tangible again. It would talk about hoarding as a kind of screen, piles of stuff to hide behind. It would talk about the Depression. It would talk about how broken something has to be before it can't be fixed. It would talk about everything but my grandad.

Now I think I'd call it *The Permanence of Things*, or, *Every Thing Is Permanent*.

I researched that island of rubbish, too. It's floating somewhere in the Pacific. Do you know that soon, in the sea, rubbish will outweigh fish?

—Yes, Helen said. —You told me that yesterday. When are you getting rid of this shit?

+

She isn't here. She's in Levin, left five days ago. Before she went I used the backseat of her Mitsubishi to dry some of the oils. She was sick of them tessellating across the kitchen table and balancing on chairs. The car was broken into (she'd left her purse on the dashboard) and a painting of Pita stolen. I was chuffed they thought it worth stealing.

+

Pita's out, but he's on a community treatment order. Forced to take Olanzapine and Fluoxitine and meet with a care coordinator each week. We joke in our texts about that word. Care coordinator. It definitely doesn't fit. We're going to start lessons again, when they lower his meds. When the words come back to him. They've been leaving me too, ngā kupu, without the practice.

+

I rehearse the expression I'd make if I saw Ilana again, the casual throwaway *hey*. Stand in front of a mirror honing the details. Enough eye contact, but not too much. Flat tone, a bit surprised, a bit amused. Cement it to memory.

+

Do you know what happens when someone blocks you on Facebook? It's not as simple as no longer being able to see their page. They don't appear tagged in photos anymore and comments they once posted come up with their name a ghostly grey.

+

I take Bo for walks. They almost always wind through Westmere. I never go down her road, just slow, and look at it. Every second house is being renovated, Portaloos checker the burns. You can smell the shit and piss. It's late January and the streets are in heat. People are drawn to them like dogs, barking along the footpaths, rabid. They wear their Nike running gear to walk to the cafe up the road. Takeaway coffee cups let everyone know they bought fair-trade. Ponsonby's there, under their fingernails. You can't see it through the Butter London—*Opaque Mint* or *Come to Bed Red*—but they planted a horopito just this morning. Supporting New Zealand natives since 1999. In a place where everything can be bought.

Everything, but bumping into someone.

+

I've been in touch with Ashi. We've agreed to get coffee on a few occasions, but each time she's forgotten, or I've pretended to forget, to get her back. She invited me for dinner two nights ago. She'd moved into her first flat, in Arch Hill, and Lachlan has water polo on Mondays.

All the light bulbs were bare, and all the walls, cluttered. Upcoming gigs and upcoming protests, Māori vocab printed onto thin paper: *Matapihi: Window, Tatau: Door.* Photos of people I'd never spoken to, but recognised through Facebook. Fairy lights, orca stickers, black mould.

—I like it, I said.

—It's great, eh? Oh shit, do you mind fish sauce?

I said nothing. I said, —Do you want to go to the TPPA protest this Thursday?

She said, —Ilana told me I should bring my camera.

So they were still in touch.

Then, it came out, an unexpected sentence, stillborn. —It feels like she's cut off my limb, like I'm walking round with no right arm.

Ashi put down her fork. —I don't want to take sides, she said. —Please don't make me.

+

I went home and breathed my own stale air and searched for signs of Ilana online. Staring at the screen where her Facebook page used to be, an exclamation mark in a yellow triangle, a hazardous kind of road sign, *Sorry, this content isn't available*. I checked my Kiwibank statement, and found she didn't use my card at all that day she and Ashi went into town.

+

In February, there's no excuse not to go out. Facebook sends reminders of each event, and it's warm at night, in Auckland. Even warmer on Karangahape Road, as if the street is a centre in the city's anatomy, the circulation a little faster here than anywhere else. The bodies and the lights give off heat.

There are two signs in the windows of shops that have closed. The first I saw in an empty sex store. *For Rent. Call Nicolas Wood*. I didn't recognise Nick's name immediately—I'd never heard him called Nicolas before. My eyes felt leaden. I couldn't lift them off the block font.

My Elam friends treat me just the same. We talk and talk about the things we don't like until we're sure why. Sometimes I want to bring up Ilana. I wonder what they think happened: whether it was me who ended it or her. It takes up a lot of my attention. I often lose track of the conversation.

Occasionally, I have to hold myself to the spot, to avoid wandering up to Symonds Street Cemetery. Every part of me wants to see that grave again, the one Ilana scrubbed, to see if the word *CUNT* has reappeared like moss, like an inescapable epitaph. To see if she really did clean it, or if I imagined the whole thing. To remind myself that people become memories all the time.

+

And it still comes—the nausea. Reaches a limp hand from my stomach and jams inside my throat. But I'm learning to eat again, despite it.

+

On Wednesday I met George and Laurie and Soph for Malaysian. The chairs were plastic-backed and new, the lighting was hard and fluorescent. The white tablecloths had scalloped edges and the mirrors, ornate frames. There were gold fans suspended above our heads. It was hot, but they weren't on.

Laurie talked the whole time about Finn. They sleep together now, when he remembers to text her back. I asked the waiter twice whether the laksa was vegetarian. Twice he said yes. But there, below my bok choy, was something hard and spindly, looming. The end of a fish bone. It must've broken off in the stock.

Soph told me to just pull it out, eat around it.

+

I go to the TPPA protests with Soph. Ilana's right, she is a mouth-breather. But it's easy to ignore.

Flags are shoved in the air and draped over shoulders. Tino Rangatiratanga, He Whakaputanga, Unite, Mana, the occasional

Green Party, Che Guevara's face. AAAP have one that takes three people to hold up. Messages are sprayed onto sheets and scrawled onto cardboard.

TPPA: Not for my moko.

People before profit.

One just reads *Death*.

My favourite placard is painted on a real-estate board.

This government is illegal, it says from the front.

Barfoot and Thompson, it says from the back.

Hitched to a white picket, the tip fresh with dirt.

+

Helen called yesterday. Grandma's still in Madison. She says she's getting worse, but Francine told me there's been no change.

And the fire department figured out what started the blaze at the bach. Faulty wiring. I'd forgotten to turn the mains electricity off.

I spent the day denying it. I composed a memory where I flicked the switch, right before we left. —It can't be, I said, —I remember doing it. I remember standing near the hot water cylinder. I remember the heat.

But part of me always knew it was my fault.

+

We outsprint the cops to the centre of the intersection. On the Hobson Street on-ramp, no cars can go west or south. We sit and link up. My arms are sweaty.

—Tell me what democracy looks like?

—This is what democracy looks like!

One cop circles us with a DSLR. Ilana's on the other side of the ring. I get the feeling we've both seen each other, but we don't acknowledge it.

—TPPA?

—No way!

—TPPA?

—No way!

The riot act is read over their megaphone, and we move to the lights at the Nelson Street off-ramp. The journalists run alongside in their leather skirts and crisp shirts and Adidas sneakers.

—They say sign it.

—We say block it.

—Sign it.

—Block it.

—Sign it.

—Block it.

—They say sign it.

—We say fuck that.

—Sign it.

—Fuck that.

—Sign it.

—Fuck that.

Ilana's leaning on the girl next to her, who wears ripped shorts and an open smile. Ashi takes a photo of them. She has a lanyard round her neck as though she's media.

The guy next to me is a historian for the Waitangi Tribunal. He writes reports on the claims of Ngāi Tahu.

—Had a hard time with my daughter last night. She would not stay in bed. A night in the cells would be a nice break.

There's a cop who keeps looking at me. His ruddy arms bulge from his gloves as if he had to really stuff them in there. He stands like all the others, hands clutched in front, elbows wide, his legs particularly spread. But he's not staring straight ahead—I'm to his left.

He could be the policeman I spoke to on Karangahape Road a week ago, my fifth day back in Auckland.

That night we watched four white boys get handcuffed, upright. And we watched one brown boy have his head smashed against concrete. We tried to film it on our phones, but the most any of us captured was the end: seven cops dragging a small and bruised body, photos of the blood it left behind. That was outside Whammy. We hadn't gone in yet. I can't remember who was playing.

Anxiety fattened in the pit of my stomach. Each day it grew a little larger, a little heavier. I couldn't stop picturing that cop, the one that had stood over us, his face morphing every time. —They stole a car, he repeated in my head. —We can arrest anyone, no matter their age, if they steal a car.

Summer is light fingertips on your back, pressing harder the longer you stay outside. A flat palm against the nape of my neck. Someone pumps sunscreen into our hands. The shifting of our formation is gradual as more protesters break through, join in. Ilana's only two metres away now. I make sure not to look in her direction.

+

At the Cook Street off-ramp, Ashi is dragged across cement and pebbles.

—Army of the rich.

—Enemy of the poor.

A cop pushes me, when I'm merely side-stepping him back over the motorway barricade. I hope Ilana doesn't notice I'm giving up. I see her later, holding Ashi's elbow, inspecting the graze. There's not a single mark on me. I know because I check.

+

I have these dreams where I find myself at the wheel without brakes. Any control I had is zooming past me, or maybe I'm the one zooming away from it. I don't know how to find the brakes, stop the car.

+

Tides of protesters wash up and down the roads, claiming different intersections. You can wander Mayoral Drive or Albert, Wellesley Street or Victoria, right down the centre line.
—Whose streets?
—Our streets.
—Whose city?
—Our city.
—Whose land?
Māori land. The chant goes cold.

+

Whenever I go drinking, I walk home, even if the night has chilled. I like to wander past the strip clubs. Mermaids, Calendar Girls, The White House. Depends where I'm walking from. I don't look inside. I prefer to pretend she's looking out, and seeing me.

+

—There she is.

Soph points at Ilana, all arms and legs and skin, touching everyone and everything. —Look, I don't really feel like sticking around.

I'm alone again. My period comes in the Wellesley Street toilets. The blood is dark and thick, moving from me like a stagnant river, tipped downhill.

I miss the arrival of the hikoi from up north, but I re-enter the crowds as they squeeze into Federal Street. Huge washes of fabric hang from bamboo poles, edges frayed, reds faded to orange. Flags that have seen more protests than I ever will. The woman in front of me pushes a pram. Her shoulders are sunburnt. The skin, where it has peeled right off, looks overexposed like a photo. She must've been walking for days.

That's when I see Pita. Outside, for the first time in months. He's bellowing the chants.

—Pita, I call, —Pita, worming between people, wrists together, extended in front of me, as though I'm about to be cuffed, as though I'm not white. —Pita, you made it.

—Look, he says, —Look how many people there are! Look how many turned up over this one thing.

We stand there, side on. I have to crane my neck to gaze up at him. And when I do, I see the revolving restaurant of the Sky Tower fanning out from his head like a halo.

+

I can't say whether I've ever been in love. I thought I was, a few times, with Nick and Ashi. Even, at points, with Ilana. On those mornings when we'd watch the sunrise together, then pretend we hadn't. On our bed at Whāngārā, when she kissed me. In the

272

cemetery. But I always look back and say, *that wasn't it.*

+

On the Saturday after the protest I walk a different way home: down the St Kevins Arcade stairs, past Myers Park, the church. Onto Hopetoun, a pause for a minute on that bridge.

I don't see any strip clubs, no neon flashing on my face.

But further along, in the gutter, I see a dog metres from a parked car.

Her back legs are contorted, bent at an angle, one too far forward. She isn't dead, not yet. I'm not sure if she can tell I'm there, feel me patting her. Her fur lifts away in chunks, only stuck on by blood. She's silent, her chest inflating with irregular beats.

A man comes out from the closest villa. He's angry with me, he keeps repeating, —She's white, she's not hard to see. She never goes on the road. She's white.

Lips stretched over adult braces. They're fluorescent green, and I can't stop thinking, he chose that green. That adult, probably Nick's age, lay on a dentist's chair and chose that specific colour. He may have even picked it for Christmas.

The man leaves, goes back into the house, and I'm not sure if he's gone for good. But he returns with a woollen blanket to wrap her in. Then he pushes me off, jerks away when I try to help. Cradles the dog. Carries her inside. Slams the front door with his foot.

It's only when I am washing the blood off my hands in the Mobil bathroom that I realise he thinks I'm the one who hit her.

+

Helen rings on Sunday. Lloyd's using the fire as leverage to inherit the bach. She and Francine can't help with the cost of repairs. He says he's the sole person who can care for it.

She tells me I need to do something with Wayne's things, or it all goes to the tip. I don't think I can put it in a gallery now. I've given up on that. Bringing it to Auckland made me understand: it's still the same stuff wherever I put it. I'm not good at throwing things out. Even when they're rubbish, even when they're damaged. I can't do it until I'm sure the thing has no use, no chance of being mended. Maybe that's why I'm so bad at ending relationships. I hold onto everything for too long.

+

In one of Wayne's books, one I brought home, there's a story of a chief who was so tapu he had to be carried on a stretcher to stop the land he walked on becoming tapu, too. I told Pita about him on the day of the blockades.

He laughed. —I wouldn't mind that myself.

—I'll give you it to read.

His chin stifled a bounce. It could've been a nod or an Olanzapine twitch. Then we hugged. Maybe it was friendly, or a second too long. He was walking me back up College Hill, sun slipping in the sky.

+

The media forgot the protest in a day or two. But I think the city, the streets themselves, will remember it for a while. There will be fewer cars using the Nelson Street on-ramp. There will be sunblock and sweat on the intersections, until the next time it rains. And the chants, trodden right into the ground, will remain, silent vibrations echoing in cement.

+

On Monday, I see him again, the dog owner, trying to stretch his hose out onto the street. He's aiming for the brown smear baked into the concrete. It could be anything, really. I want to say something like, but the memory, you can't get rid of the memory. You're just hosing it into the water, and that memory is running off down the road, to the nearest patch of soil it can soak, the nearest drainpipe. That memory won't rinse clean. It'll just get muddier and muddier.

But I cross the road so he won't see me. I don't say a thing.

The list on page 261 is a full account of the items used to 'buy' the entire Auckland CBD from Ngāti Whātua.

Other iwi with claims to this land received nothing.

Source: Sorrenson, M. P. K. 'The Maori People and the City of Auckland: An Historical Survey.' *Te Ao Hou: The New World*, no. 27 (June 1959): 8–13.

ACKNOWLEDGMENTS

Thank you to the late Michael Gifkins—I wish that I had met you. Thank you to Ann Hatherly and André Gifkins for keeping his legacy alive. Thank you to Patricia Grace and Lloyd Jones for seeing something in my manuscript. Thank you to everyone at Text Publishing, especially Michael Heyward, Alaina Gougoulis and Lara Shprem. Thank you to my mum Linley for teaching me to write, and teaching me to love reading so much. Thank you to the rest of my family, in particular Mary, Sara, Felix, Rupert and my grandma Sheila, who is nothing like the grandma in this book. Thank you to my partner, Michael, for all your support. Thank you to my MCW class at the University of Auckland: your advice and encouragements were invaluable. Thank you to Paula Morris, for turning my pipe dream of writing a novel into a reality. Without you, there would be no *Attraction*.